Volume 2

Misty Simon

Magically Suspicious Mysteries Volume 2

Published in the United States

Copyright © 2021 Misty Simon

All rights reserved

Cover copyright © 2021 Link Simon

No part of this publication may be reproduced, storied in, or introduced into a retrieval system, or transmitted in any form, or by any means (electronic, mechanical, photocopying, recording, or otherwise) without written permission of the copyright owner.

The scanning, uploading, and distributing of this book via the internet or any other means without the permission of the owner is illegal and punishable by law. Criminal copyright infringement, including infringement without monetary gain, is investigated by the FBIO and is punishable by up to 5 years in federal prison and a fine of $250,000.00. Please purchase only authorized editions and do not participate in or encourage piracy of copyrighted materials. Brief passages may be quoted for review purposes if credit is given to the copyright owner. Your support of the author's rights is appreciated.

This is a work of fiction. Any resemblance to person(s) living or dead is completely coincidental. All items contained within this work (names, characters, places, incidents, etc.) are products of the author's imagination.

This book is dedicated to everyone who loves a little mystery with your paranormal! I hope you always find the light in the darkness. And to all the readers who are having a blast romping along with my girl Verla! She sees you, she is you, she's amazing, and so are you.

Thank you to my Boot Squad and Nan for your wonderful attention to my book and for encouraging me to make this happen. Huge thanks to Natalie J. Damschroder for awesome formatting and Link Simon for awesome covers! Thanks also to Christine and Maureen for convincing me that I could do this!

By Faire Means or Fowl

Chapter One

STROLLING THROUGH THE FAIRE on a beautiful Wednesday afternoon, all was right with my world. I waved to Barnaby, the dragon blacksmith at his forge. He was making a sword and wowing the kids, who stood far enough back not to get burned but definitely close enough to bask in the warmth of the flames. These were the nieces and nephews brought by Barnaby's brothers and sisters. They were fully functioning dragons, unlike Barnaby, who could blow smoke but not fire and still hoarded like no one's business. But because he wasn't full-fledged, he'd been edged out of the dragon world. He'd found a home here at the faire, though, and as far as I knew he was content and happy to be right where he was.

As were we all. Or most of us anyway. I couldn't speak for everyone, as a few of our villagers had left last week, looking for new places with less problems than we were currently experiencing at what I lovingly referred to as our faire of misfit paranormals. I wished them well and sent them off with blessings. The faire was the kind of place that for some it was forever and for others it was a stopover until they got themselves together and then moved on. Either worked for me.

"Verla! Come see what Josiah is doing!" A small child ran up and grabbed my hand. Lucy? Lucky? Plucky? Mya! There were so many dragon children I couldn't always remember their names, but I tried. She was from the clan of dragons up north in Canada. They came down every year for our one-day paranormals-only faire.

This year we'd had to move it back two weeks due to the recent trouble we'd had. But I had been unwilling to completely cancel, and so here we were, still celebrating, just a little later.

I looked forward to seeing them every year, though I really wished they would stop growing up, since that only meant I was older than I had been last time I'd seen them.

More than it just being a family day at the faire, it was also the chance to get back to our normal, and we were celebrating here at the ren faire in Effington, Pennsylvania.

Figiggly, my dear little Chow, trotted along at my side as I was dragged over to the forge.

Josiah was Mya's brother and stood almost six feet tall already at only fifteen or sixteen. He'd keep growing, too, if his father and mother were any indication. They were both over six feet tall and were a stunning couple, while also being incredibly nice and awesome.

Barnaby was one of the ones with family who had loved and still loved him, no matter if he was a fully functioning dragon or not. But since so many other clans had shunned him, he'd chosen to remove himself from the politics and the issues that other clans had brought to their door.

This wasn't the only time of year that the family visited Barnaby, but it was the only time they all came together and had their annual family reunion.

One where Josiah was firing the forge all on his own. He'd shifted into dragon form and stood almost eight feet tall. His scales radiated the color of the sun with golds and reds and oranges rippling over his body like a rush of fire. He winked at me as he bellowed out another belch of flame to heat the metal Barnaby was working into a long sword.

There was laughter and joking and general all-around happiness. That feeling right there swelled in my heart to the point where I wanted to bask for all the days to come.

But another faire-goer pulled me away to be a part of their family time, and then another, and another. I had known it would happen like this, it always did, so I hadn't made any concrete plans to be anywhere at any precise time until later.

And it was an all-day affair. We had started at ten this morning and we'd go long into the night. Since it was midweek, there was nothing that had to be done tomorrow, and so everyone planned on being here for as long as the gates were open.

I finally extracted myself from the impromptu concert featuring the steam punk organ and a team of thirteen drum players with rawhide drums they beat on with fake bones to go check on some of the people who I knew didn't have families to invite in.

My first stop was Trice. She was entertaining a bunch of moms in a tent by putting Pix, her miniature winged lion, through a series of tricks. The little beast did flips and burped out fire. Then he threw the whole tent into shadow and started cooing to the many babies in strollers.

Within seconds the children were all asleep, and then the real fun began as the women each got henna tattoos. Everyone pushed everyone else to get something totally outrageous and to put it someplace where their partners would have to go hunting for it.

I declined to go next, as I had no partner to find any risqué tattoo, and I was fine with that.

Of course an image of Finn Taragon, my ex who had returned to the faire a few months ago, popped into my head, and then he popped up in real life at my next turn.

It was like he knew...

"Having a good time?" he asked, hooking his arm into mine. Fig nudged him from the other side, and he stopped, pulling me with him to lean down and pet the dog he'd given me as a peace offering. One that had changed my life in the best of ways.

"Is my Uncle Morty coming today?" he asked.

I shrugged. "Not that I'm aware of. He usually stays away—unless he's coming for you?" The owner of the faire tended to leave things to me, and I appreciated Morty's confidence even when mine was shaky.

"No, my mom is heading in, though, at some point."

My heart stopped. I did not want his mother here, but how could I keep her away? I gulped. I'd just have to endure the hugs I'd missed almost more than my husband when he walked away, and the feeling of belonging that had been so much bigger than just being Finn's wife—being part of the family that came right along with him.

I would not cry. Would. Not. Cry. This was going to be fine, and I'd show her around if I had to. Or maybe I'd hide in my cottage over at the village and not come out at all. I could totally feign a headache. In fact, I felt one coming on right now without faking.

"That's nice," was all I said as I clasped my hands together and looked anywhere but at him.

He blew out a breath. "Should I not have invited her?"

"No, of course not. It will be nice to see her."

"She still asks about you."

I gulped again and was never so thankful as when I saw Pheeney, Dalvon's new phoenix, soar above the trees. Our resident protein-shake-drinking vampire was letting the bird have her way around the faire, since on weekends she usually stayed nested so that normal humans wouldn't see her too much.

"I'm going to go check on how things are working out with Dalvon's new apprentice. Have a great day. I'll see you later."

Fig didn't follow me at first, preferring to stay and get his pets in with Finn. I didn't even turn around. The dog would find me eventually, and it was safe enough here at the moment that he could do whatever he wanted.

Making my way along the path to the field where Dalvon was putting on a bird show with our falcons, hawks, owls, and the infamous phoenix, I applauded with the rest of the crowd. Pheeney dipped her feathers and then spiraled straight into the sky in a whirlwind of color.

I heard the jingle of the collar I'd put on Fig this morning to keep track of him and turned to grab him up for a hug.

And found myself face to face with Finn again. Okay then, no hint taken there. He was, of course, welcome to go wherever he wanted, too.

"I need a volunteer!" Dalvon shouted to the crowd. A forest of hands shot into the air.

"Verla Faeth! Mistress of this beautiful faire! Why don't you come on over and show these people what we're capable of?"

As the only hand not raised, I groaned at Dalvon's cheer and offer. I didn't want to be put on display, but there was nothing I could do to escape him now.

Someone, perhaps Dalvon's guest, came over to lead me into the center of the field, like I didn't know where to go. Dalvon smiled at him and took my hand from his. I had no idea who he was, but they looked like they could be related, maybe around the eyes and chin. The guest definitely didn't have the bright red hair of Dalvon, yet there was something familiar about his features. If we had run the faire the way Finn wanted, I would know all the things about all the villagers. Who their family was, what talents they possessed, and what things were in their pasts. But since we didn't ask questions around here, I wasn't entirely sure of the relationship.

What I did know, though, was this place better than anyone, and I knew exactly where Dalvon wanted me to go. I just didn't really want to go there.

But for the faire I would do this. It didn't matter what my personal feelings were at the moment or that I both dreaded and yearned for a visit with Finn's mom.

I'd put on the show as I always did and then smile. That was who I was at my core.

Dalvon bowed over my hand in the courtliest of gestures and then asked me to stick my arm out.

I did, and Pheeney squawked then flapped herself down from the sky to land delicately on my forearm. It never ceased to surprise me how light she was. Her wingspan was enormous, and she looked so solid when she flew through the air, but in reality, she weighed less than Pix.

"Now, my lovely people, gather round as we tell a story of love and loss and light." Dalvon had surprised me with his storytelling abilities over the last few days. He'd been quiet and solitary when I'd first hired him. A huge help with an issue we had run into, but then he had kind of gone into hiding for a bit, just him and the birds.

Five days ago, though, he'd emerged as a showman and had delighted the normal faire-goers over the last weekend with pyrotechnics and a precision with the birds that I hadn't ever seen before.

And then there were the stories.

"There once was a man who ran through the wild —he dodged and darted and avoided anything that was mild. He decided to stand still for just one second in time and that was when he realized a pause was really quite sublime. So he stood and he stood and he stood some more—he stood so long he resembled a tale from lore."

That must have been Pheeney's cue, because she bunched herself up on my arm, rocketed up into the sky, and then burst into flames. Her ashes came down in a shower of sparks that looked a whole lot like Rip Van Winkle resting against a tree.

The crowd went wild! I stood there absolutely delighted and baffled and bemused all at the same time. My brain kicked into gear and made a wish list of things that we could show normal faire-goers, those regular humans who came to the faire Fridays through Sundays. I could just imagine their absolute awe at this display.

But there were some things that had to remain hidden, and this would have to be one of them. Though I did wonder if there was a way for us to somehow skirt around the edges of showmanship and set this up with some projectors and a light show. It was worth considering, especially with the promises of ultimate delights for the weekend of Halloween.

While that thought was still running through my mind, Pheeney landed on my forearm, fully back to her beautiful self and preening her feathers. When she was done with that, she nestled into the hollow between my throat and my cleavage and cooed.

"Such a pretty bird," I said back to her, using my free hand to pet her neck a second before something jerked her out of my arms and across the sky like yanking a chain.

An invisible chain. What the hell?

My gaze immediately darted to Dalvon, but his eyes were horror-stricken and his mouth slack.

Okay, apparently this wasn't part of the show.

Chapter Two

BEFORE I COULD FULLY panic, Pheeney appeared on my arm again, shaking her head and grumbling fiercely. Her eyes darted left and right as she grumbled some more.

Dalvon had raised his head and was speaking gutturally in what I thought might be Latin. Before he called anything otherworldly to him, or sent out a curse like no other, I tapped him on the shoulder and transferred the bird to him.

"What? Where? How?" His eyes widened with each word and then filled with tears.

I shrugged because what else could I do? "I don't know why or who either, when is not in question, though."

We both looked around at the crowd. I didn't see anyone acting strangely. Everyone was once again clapping and talking animatedly to each other like that had still been part of the show.

"Let it rest," I told him quietly. "If you didn't do that, and I didn't do that, and Pheeney didn't do it, then we might have a problem. Just bow and end the show. We'll get together afterward."

He raised bloodshot eyes, but he nodded and then put a smile on his face.

"Thank you, everyone, for being here! Pheeney is tired now, so this concludes the show, but we appreciate your applause and your hearts!" He bowed. Pheeney flared her wings to their incredible wingspan and hopped on top of his head. The crowd laughed and started to disperse to various other shows going on.

Dalvon blew out a big breath. "Verla…"

"Not right now. Let's take this somewhere else." I smiled as guests walked by me, still chattering about the awesome display and how cool this place was. I agreed with them, but it was going to be worse than hell freezing over before I let something happen to any of my villagers again.

"Can you meet me at the tavern in ten?" I asked Dalvon. "Put the other birds away in their enclosures but bring Pheeney with you. I want to see if anything else has been happening throughout the day."

We parted ways with Dalvon walking away looking like some kind of bird tree. Every hawk, owl, and falcon perched on some part of his squat body. Pheeney still held pride of place on his head.

As soon as he was well on his way to the aviary, I picked up my pace and had Figiggly trotting right along with me on his tiny legs. He hadn't grown in size like he normally did when bad things were happening, so maybe it had just been a mishap. But I had a hard time believing that, especially with our track record lately.

I wasn't quite ready to change my Days Without an Incident board back to zero, but I did want to find out what else—if anything—was happening around here.

To get the lowdown, it made sense to talk to Finn since he was in charge of maintenance and security in this little faire of ours.

And just like before, the thought of him seemed to bring him to my side.

"Forgetting someone?" he asked from right behind me.

My heart nearly jumped into my throat and my neck flushed hot. I'd forgotten to find him before I walked away because I'd been concentrating with Dalvon and Pheeney. Well, not only wasn't that very nice of me, it also sucked.

"I'm sorry." I blurted the words out before I could think better of it. He wouldn't have fallen for a lie that I knew he was there the whole time anyway.

"Eh, what else is new? I'm like the part of the scenery that no one ever notices because there's too much else going on. No skin off my nose. And it makes my job easier if I have to handle a security thing, right?"

Well, crap. I could try to talk my way around this one, or just lay it out on the table. Table-laying it was. "Look, I wasn't ignoring you, I just get nervous when I'm put in the spotlight, and then when Pheeney got snatched away and then returned obviously peeved, I had one thought."

"The faire," he said before I could.

And why did that make me feel guilty? I cleared my throat. "Yes, the faire. With everything that has gone wrong over the last two months, I just got caught up in the thought of someone trying to steal Pheeney. I was on my way to find you, actually, to see if anything else has happened, as far as you are aware. I guess you don't have anything extra, since you've been sticking with me most of the time."

"Nothing new. I can ask around and meet you at the tavern if you'd like. Ten minutes, you said?"

My forehead crinkled. I smoothed it out as soon as I felt it happen. "Yes, ten minutes would be great." I looked down at Fig, then back up at Finn. "See you then."

Finn walked off in the direction of the village, and I was left to wonder how I had lost the upper hand on that one.

I shook off the thought because there was no hand and no upper or lower.

Dammit.

Picking up Fig, I staggered back under his weight. When I checked him over he wasn't any bigger, just heavier. "Hoo boy, I think we might need to put you on a diet."

He licked my face and smiled at me with that doggy grin that got him treats every time.

I booped him on the nose. "We have a job to do. Let's go do it." I set him back down again because there was absolutely no way I was going to be able to carry him around the faire in my custom-made brocade dress and these heels.

As he trotted along beside me, I made sure to keep the smile on my face even as my brain was working a mile a second and my eyes darted everywhere so as not to miss any more trouble.

I stopped by the stables just to make sure Seawaddle, the kelpie, was okay. No one was around, so I stepped up to his stall and peeked in. But he wasn't there.

My breath caught in my throat, and then I gulped. This was bad. This was very bad. We still hadn't been able to get a full handle on what he could do and how he did it. His whole purpose in life was supposed to be luring people to their deaths in water, and we had plenty of that down at the creek. Which, of course, was all the way on the other side of the property.

Ignoring the heels and the way my calves felt like Pix, the little winged lion, was chasing me with fire, I ran. Fig couldn't keep up, but I couldn't slow down. Until I heard distinctive neighing in the jousting ring and ground to a halt, breathing heavily and nearly choking on the dust the kelpie was kicking up.

Was that a rider on his back? I squinted to get a better look, but I still couldn't see. Whistling as Trice, his owner, had taught me to do, I waited for him to answer or come to me.

A shadow darted off to the left out by the horse, but I couldn't do anything about it because the horse was coming my way and I didn't want to ignore him.

Seawaddle, the great black beast with streaming mists of darkness coming off him in waves, stood at the fence, his sides bellowing and his hooves prancing. But his dark eyes were calmer than I had expected them to be. I slowly put my hand out to him, wishing I had an apple or a carrot, and he nestled his velvety soft nose right into the center of my palm.

Whoever had been riding him, *if* someone had been riding him, was gone, and I had about four minutes to get to the tavern. I grabbed my cell phone out of my waist satchel and put a call into the horsemaster.

Glethan answered on the first ring. "What can I do for you, Verla? It's a lovely day, and my family is here enjoying it, thanks to you."

I hated to break his streak of compliments but I had to. "I'm glad, but I was wondering if you had let someone ride Seawaddle? He's out in the jousting ring, and he was tearing around like he had a live wire in his tail. I couldn't see through the dust, but it looked like someone was on his back."

"What? No! No one rides that majestic beast. I won't let them. He is much too unpredictable. I'll be there in two minutes."

I looked around, wondering how I was going to do everything I'd signed myself up for without missing a time or a person. "He trusts me. Meet me at the tavern. I'll get him to follow me through the faire."

"Are you sure, Verla? Does he have a halter on, at least?"

I hadn't even thought to look. "Uh, no, but I have his attention, and Fig is here with me. Just meet me at the tavern."

The sun was sinking lower in the sky, and the fact that two out of the four new beasts at the faire were possibly being messed with made my heart rate increase fourfold. I hung up with Glethan and got ready to convince a kelpie that not only should he follow me, but he should do it by my voice only with no rope or bridle to help me.

"Can he understand me?" I asked Fig. Sometimes he'd answer in my head and sometimes he acted like I hadn't said a word. I really hoped that he chose the first one this time.

He bobbed his head up and down, which I supposed I could take as a compromise.

"Will you help me herd him to where we're going?"

I saw the whites of my dog's eyes for the first time in our acquaintance and backed off. "Never mind. I'll figure it out."

First, I had to get the horse to follow me to the gate, then get him to stand still while I opened it and let him out. My hands were shaking and my breath was rattling around in my chest. But I managed to do those two things without an issue.

The kelpie was docile enough as he slowly walked out of the gate and seemed to understand when I told him I needed him to walk with me at a slow pace and that we were going to the tavern.

See? Look at that! I could handle these kinds of things. I just had to believe in myself enough to know that I was capable and trust my instincts.

I'd been working with a crone for the last few weeks to get my abilities nailed down. Every single thing she taught me I seemed to be able to do almost without effort. I was still skeptical of all of it and constantly wondered if she wasn't fueling me with her own power every once in a while. But this proved that I was on solid ground, even without using my magic.

I wasn't going to look this gift horse in the mouth. Literally, as I led him along each avenue. I cautioned people not to touch him and made sure they knew he was only for looking.

"Please step back. Please. He's going to meet his owner, and we'll hopefully be able to see what he's capable of later, but right now I need you to step back." I smiled at the sandy-haired kid who'd helped me at the phoenix demonstration earlier, then kept walking as he melted back into the crowd of curious people.

Feeling good about things, I picked up the pace a little. And not two seconds later, Seawaddle reared onto his hind legs and whinnied like his tail was on fire.

Of course that could have been because it really was on fire.

Chapter Three

OH MY GOOD GODDESS above! I shrieked before I could stop myself. "Water! Water!"

Before I could say it a third time there were streams of water flowing from everywhere and anywhere. They twisted and turned and coiled through the air to douse Seawaddle. And of course me. While I stood getting drenched, the kelpie was prancing and his neighing sounded a lot like laughing.

"We're good," I yelled, and it sounded like I was under water because I was. I threw a shield up that looked like an umbrella, and the water witches seemed to get the hint. The monsoon stopped, and they hit me with a blast of hot air to dry me out, almost knocking me over. I yelled again and the wind stopped, but I got crowded in as soon as it did.

"Step back, please. We'll need everyone to make room. Just a little technical issue there. Sorry about that."

Finn made his way to my side. His smile dropped for just a second while he seemed to be memorizing my face, and then he turned a big fake smile back to the crowd. "Technical difficulty, that's all! Thanks for all the help. Go about what you're doing. I promise Seawaddle is going to do some magnificent things for us in just a bit, but right now we need to move him into position."

"What are you saying?" I whispered harshly.

"For once, please just go with it, Verla. I can't fight on all fronts by myself."

And so I also smiled and put a hand under the kelpie's chin to reassure him. I had no idea if it worked, but he did follow along, so that was something, at least.

"Go get Dalvon from the tavern," I said quietly, for Finn's ears only. "We're going to have to meet somewhere more private." I caught Finn's gaze and silently begged him to just go with this for me.

He shook his head. "Okay, but you call out if anything goes wrong. Anything at all."

"Of course." I wasn't sure if I'd keep that promise, but at least it got him moving and me a moment of alone time to think my way through this.

What was going on? Were people just not keeping an eye on their kids? All three instances could have been just mischief, although nastier than I liked. I was used to kids trying to put each other into trash cans or splashing in the fountain that had no-trespassing signs. Not trying to steal a phoenix, riding a kelpie, and then setting his tail on fire.

I checked him over, running my hand over his withers to let him know I wasn't going to hurt him. I found no singe marks on his body, and his tail had already gone back to its normal drifting, streaming black.

Phew! I did not want to have to explain that to Trice on top of telling her that despite being on fire briefly, he was okay. Explaining was going to be bad enough, especially when I had no idea what had actually happened.

Within minutes, Dalvon met me in the old fake graveyard along with Trice and Gargy.

Finn was right behind them.

"Does anyone know what the heck is going on?"

Everyone started talking at the same time. So much so that I couldn't make out any particular words. I looked at Fig and he barked once, but actually it sounded like three times. That was his special three-tone bark that moved up the scale. And it usually meant trouble was coming. Or had already been there.

Fig nudged Dalvon.

"Okay, you're first, my friend," I said to him.

"It was a kid. His mom came and apologized to me almost as soon as you walked away. He kept denying it, but she was sure. My phone battery died, so I couldn't call you." He smiled at me in that way that made a person feel like they were waiting for a kick in the teeth. I was totally not going to do that to him.

"Trice? You're next."

"I'm so sorry, Verla. I was almost sure that Seawaddle had figured out how to unlatch his own door, but I thought I'd handled it. He loves the jousting circle, and when he gets out there his one goal is to go as fast as possible. He loves the dirt devils he kicks up." She ran her hand down the side of Seawaddle's face, and he had the grace to at least duck his head.

"So there wasn't a rider?" I asked.

"Not that we can tell, and we've asked around. He was just up to his antics." She petted him again and then gave him a stern look. "You need to behave, sir."

He whinnied at her and turned his head.

"Okay, so what about the tail catching fire?" Surely that couldn't be so easily explained away. I was glad I hadn't said it out loud when Finn spoke.

"Actually, that's my fault," Grayden said. "I was playing with one of Barnaby's nephews while waiting for you to come to the tavern. When I threw him up in the air, he got nervous and belched fire. It was an accident."

Huh. "Huh." Nothing like repeating myself. At least it was only in my head.

"Sorry," that came out in a chorus of voices.

"So I don't have to change my Days Without Incident board?"

Finn hooked his arm in mine. "Nope, none of these were really incidents, just little bumps on the road with this many people here with abilities."

"Huh." Surely, I could come up with something more intelligent than that. But no, I couldn't.

I let Finn lead me back to the Tavern on the Line, where everyone had gathered to eat. We'd start the Wild Hunt in a few hours.

Suddenly I was very hungry and very much looking forward to filling my plate with as much as this corset could handle.

Two hours later, dusk was falling and I was looking forward to a star-studded sky as a light breeze ran over the tops of the trees, creating a musical rustle that ran before us like the song of the summer.

"Verla, are you sure this is wise? We've had a lot going on over the last two months. And we had those mishaps earlier in the day. I just don't want to ruin your Days Without Incidents board so late in the day." Dalvon was back and stood next to me in the jousting area with Pheeney perched on his arm.

"Dalvon, I appreciate you and your concern, but it's a little late to cancel anything when it's almost over. Besides, we can't live under a haze of what could be, Dalvon. We have to live for the moment. Every year we've done this festival. I'm not going to change the events this year just because of a little trouble. I was already irritated that I had to change the date because of the last incident." I said the words, and I even meant them, but there was definitely a part of me cowering and whimpering on the inside. We'd seen death and mischief recently, outsiders trying to ruin my home and my extended family. Today had been honest mistakes and little accidents, as far as I knew. But was I wise to continue to host a night of family and friends here at our village of the misfit paranormals? It wasn't like I could send them home early anyway. How would I explain that?

Honestly, I had no idea, but something had to bring back the joy around here. We'd had a traditional, someone who does the right magic and has the right pedigree, try to take down our livelihood and our home for his own nefarious and self-centered purposes not too long ago. Talk about ruining my Days Without Incidents board.

Most likely all he'd receive would be a slap on the wrist from the high court. The possibility had ruined some of the morale around here. Rightly so. But I wanted to get back the high energy and the feeling of safety and community, not the feeling of banding together to make sure we all made it out alive. Today had been a balm to the soul with so many happy faces and so much laughter. The rest of the night would be just as awesome.

And so we were doing the Wild Hunt that we staged every year to bring in the first harvest celebration of Lughnasadh, honoring the Celtic god of light. Tonight we would mark the middle of the faire season right along with being halfway between summer and fall. We were a little over two weeks behind schedule, but it had been the best I could do.

Althea and I had put together the best twelve hours of activities, and Dalvon was here to kick off the evening portion with his bird Pheeney. The afternoon had gone well after those couple of issues. I had high hopes for the rest of the evening.

"Just enjoy yourself. It's been awesome so far, and it is going to continue to be awesome. I decree it, and you know what happens when I decree things."

"They know better than to go awry," my ex said. Finn must have walked up behind me at some point without me noticing him.

I would have known that scent anywhere, though, and it took me back to my first Wild Hunt night when we'd purposely gotten lost in order to steal a kiss or two out from under the watchful eye of his Uncle Morty. Verla Faeth, the rebel. Not so much anymore, but there had been a time before life got complicated, as it does.

"Exactly," I squeaked, then cleared my throat. "This evening will absolutely continue to be without incident. My board is consistently building the numbers, and I won't have today be the day we go back to zero. So let's go. Dalvon, release Pheeney and start the night time portion of this shindig with a bang."

All five feet of Dalvon stood as tall as he possibly could. His hair was the same color as the bright plumage of the bird on his arm, a brilliant red that even the moon couldn't leach the color from.

"Fly, my darling," he said, and the huge bird launched herself into the air. She circled a few times, cooing in that way she had so you could almost see the music in the air blending with the rustling of the wind through those tree branches.

All the villagers and their families and friends gathered around to watch Pheeney trailing what looked like stardust behind her as she dipped and whirled through the darkening sky. Earlier we'd had food and games and displays. This evening was more of the same, and then we'd have the Wild Hunt to cap the evening off.

I waved to Clarence, our male siren, and to Helamn and Faelix, our sword masters. I waved to Gargy who stood with his gargoyle wings outstretched over Trice, who had created him. Recently he'd taken to showing up more as a gargoyle than the man he could transform into, but he was always in the appropriate attire depending on the occasion. This evening it looked like that meant gargoyle as he looked ready to launch himself into the air and join Pheeney above us.

As soon as everyone was present, including Barnaby, one of my favorite misfit dragons, and Wes, the dwarf that I could barely fit in a car, I clapped my hands for everyone's attention.

"I know we've had some issues recently, and I know we are stronger than anything that can come our way. I also know that without you there would be nothing for me to feel in total and utter control of, so thanks a lot for letting me be in charge every once in a while."

They laughed and raised glasses of wine, or ale, or soda, provided by the Tavern on the Line in the faire.

"I want to tell everyone how much you mean to me and thank you for inviting your friends and family, or friends who are family, to join us here today to celebrate one of the most wonderful days of the year. First harvest is more than a day, it's the beginning of something even more beautiful than before. And I want you all to enjoy yourselves and make sure that whatever you do, you do it with style."

Figiggly wanted to run and play and maybe even howl at the moon, but he knew better than to get ahead of himself. We'd been working with Althea on training him even as we were putting together tonight's festivities. I wouldn't say he was one hundred percent trained, but I wasn't looking for perfect, just awesome—which he totally was.

And he was also ready to run with his friend Jabbers, who was right next to him and leaning on Althea.

"Shall we?" I asked Althea. We'd grown closer over the last three weeks or so. Working together, we'd put together testimony regarding our last incident with a traditional. Grayden Hunter had asked for our information to make a case that would stick. Because the fiend was a fully functioning wizard from a family that had been around longer than rocks, Grayden needed everything he could get his hands on to make sure the culprit didn't get to walk away without punishment.

"I believe we shall." She smiled, and it was such a pleasure to see.

"Then let's." I brought both my hands straight up into the air, gathered the energy that always seemed to swirl somewhere right behind my breastbone, and then moved my hands together in a resounding clap that sparked lightning.

It was something I had learned I could do completely by accident when being irritated with the blender. I did not recommend banging on the thing with lit fingertips and a mess of bananas, smoothie powder, and strawberries in it unless you were planning on wearing it a moment after releasing the energy.

At least I'd finally gotten all the seeds out of my hair, with Finn's help.

The lightning I'd just created rose into the sky like a backward lightning bolt and then burst into a shower of white sparkles. And that was Pheeney's cue to circle one more time, throw her wings into the air, and then burst into flames. Her remains came down in a cascade of glitter in every color of the spectrum, and some we were only seeing for this first time.

There were gasps and applause, and people were scurrying around to get to the various booths we'd set up for scavenger hunts and corn hole and miniature golf set up in the maze on this beautiful night.

I walked around and chatted up groups where I knew one person and the rest were family or friends. Not everyone was a misfit, but I heard more than one person who was not a part of the faire asking how to get an invitation in.

We'd all meet back here in an hour or so to watch Hal do a private magic show with the real stuff he couldn't show to normal faire-goers. Our Celtic band was going to play us some tunes, and Zane had cleared off the deck at the tavern to accommodate dancers galore. And then we'd run around like maniacs trying to pick up all the presents I'd be hiding in the trees once everyone skedaddled. It wasn't a real Wild Hunt in the literal sense of the phrase, but it was a good time and a wonderful time to have it.

Things were moving right along, and my mouth was watering for a center-cut brownie, so I turned to make my way back to the dessert table.

And that's when I saw that Finn's mother was there with my brownie on a napkin and a huge and welcoming smile on her face. I swallowed as best I could and tried to talk myself out of the brownie, but I couldn't resist.

Chapter Four

WHY DID FINN'S MOM have to be here??? Extra question marks were most definitely needed on that one thought. I would have considered an interrobang, but I didn't think an exclamation point in the middle would help me now.

It was as if I was drawn to her. I really didn't have room in my stomach for a brownie. I was trussed up in this corset like I was trying to squeeze my own life out. I could go without the dessert.

But my feet kept moving in Tessa Taragon's direction no matter what my mind was trying to get me to do. Like run in the other direction, pretend I heard someone call my name, spot another spontaneous fire. I was drawn to her and had been from the first time I'd met her.

Figiggly ran in front of me, that little brat, and sat right on the woman's foot, turning his head up to pant at her, begging for pets.

I didn't blame him. She had a calm around her, an aura that always made things feel balanced and even. I'd needed that so much when Finn had left but had deliberately kept myself from seeking her out because once those divorce papers were signed, I no longer had any right to infringe on her time.

"Verla, you are a sight for sore eyes. Come give us a hug." She stopped scratching my dog's head to open her arms wide. And why wouldn't she? I'd never told her that I didn't want to see her again because it hurt too much. I'd just slowly faded out of the picture and hoped that if she missed me, she would... Well, I wasn't entirely certain what I had wished she would do. But that thought was moot six years after the foundation of my world had broken.

"Tessa," I said, smiling and stepping into the hug. I patted her back a few times for good measure, then stepped back. No need to overdo it. "You're looking well."

"As are you." She peered into my eyes with her dark-hazel, all-knowing eyes. I forced myself to maintain the eye contact and empty my head so she couldn't get anything from me.

It must have worked, because after only a small frown she beamed out her smile again.

"I'm so happy you're still doing this. My brother Morty can be a huge pain when it comes to moneymaking, so I'm glad he didn't shut this down."

I laughed because it seemed to be the right thing. "Oh, I wouldn't let him do that to me, and if he tried harder, I'd just find a bigger stick."

Her tinkling laugh tickled my ears, and I wondered for about the thousandth time if that was part of her magic. You couldn't ever seem to be mad when she was around. Even Finn full-out smiled when she was near.

"It's so good to see you. You've been busy, I hear. Finn keeps me up-to-date when I ask things of him. I hope that's okay with you?"

How on earth could you say no to that? *No, it's not okay that you still ask after me. No, I don't want you to care, because it hurts too much. No, please don't want to know what's going on with me.*

None of those things came out of my mouth. Instead I took her hands. "I appreciate you wondering how I am. How are you, though?"

"Things are good. I'm set up in my own little cottage on top of my Wiccan book store over in Gettysburg. You should come check it out. I hear that you have some new powers that you might need help with."

How much had Finn told her? I did not want all the crap going on to get back to Morty. I'd been keeping a lid on it in my monthly reports because I didn't want him to think I couldn't handle things on my own.

"Um, yes, when this little guy came into my life, it seems I became something I had never considered."

"Ah, but the Universe knew, and that's why this little charmer was brought your way." She scratched Fig's ear, and I could have sworn he was going to fall over in a faint of ecstasy.

"Yeah, I just wish the Universe could have taken some time to let me know. I'm still trying to figure out my limits and what I can do. I seem to always find out something new when..." I cut myself off. If Finn wasn't telling her everything, I wasn't going to be the one to spill the beans.

"Right, when something happens that demands you use the power within you."

"Um, yes. You're not going to go tell Morty, are you?"

She laughed and my ears tickled again. "Heavens no, he and I mind our own business. What he doesn't know isn't going to hurt him, and with Finn here everything will be fine. He'd never let anything harm you."

Except himself.

I quickly erased that thought from my mind, but I didn't think I had done it quickly enough when her frown appeared again and she reached for my hand.

"You know he never stopped loving you."

I could not have this conversation right now. Could. Not.

"We needed to separate. It's fine. He had things to do, and I got to come back to my home and live the life I'd dreamed of from the time I got dropped off. It's all good."

"Hmmm," she said but nothing more.

Quick subject change was completely necessary, so I blurted out the first thing that came to mind. "You'll have to meet Dalvon. I think you'll like him. And Buford. He's a demon but a good one. He was so awesome helping with some trouble we'd had. Oh, and Gargy and Pix and Seawaddle. You'll get a real kick out of the creatures. Maybe you could help us find a specialist to train the kelpie? You know so many people." I wanted to bite my tongue to stop the words from tumbling out. Apparently not only was I telling on myself but inviting her to be more involved, which would only mean that she'd be here more often. I had to stop before I asked her to bring her Wiccan shop here and take up residence on the other side of me in the village.

"I'd be happy to help in any way I can. I always have been. Sometimes my methods are a little misunderstood, but I get things done. Let's have coffee next week, and we can discuss what you're looking for. Maybe you can catch me up on what you've been doing for the last six years."

"That last part of the conversation would take about five minutes of your time. Same old, same old. Nothing new except for the last few months, since Fig got here."

"Still, I'd love to have tea or coffee with you. You could come down my way. There's this adorable little house that's a tea room run by some of the college students."

There was that smile again, and I just wanted to say yes to everything. I took in a breath to answer her, then let it out in a little *meep* when someone touched my shoulder.

"Finally," Finn said from my left, again sneaking up on me. How did he keep doing that?!?! That totally deserved the interrobang.

How did I keep missing his approach and not knowing he was there until after he spoke? His scent was ingrained in my nose and as soon as he spoke, he burst into my olfactory senses like the lightning I'd sent into the sky. So why wasn't I aware he was near me before he spoke?

That was something I was going to have to think about later, because he took my hand, bent over it while keeping his eyes on mine, and then placed a gentle kiss on the backs of my knuckles.

Tessa emitted a dreamy sigh, and I did everything I could not to smile.

"I'd like the first dance tonight, Verla, if your card isn't full." He stood and whipped out a bouquet of flowers that could have come only from Buford, the demon turned florist. There were roses and lilies, pussywillow and big green ferns. And in the center, there was a sunflower with a head as big as mine. It should have been chaotic, it was chaotic, but with a beauty I couldn't deny.

My eyelashes fluttered without my permission, and my mouth opened before I could think my way completely through my response. "I'd love that."

Finn's grin was wicked in his tanned face framed by his chin-length dark hair that he normally kept tied back with a leather thong. He'd dressed for the occasion in something he must have borrowed from Nedward the Bard. Frills lined his throat and flowed from the cuffs at his wrists. A dark-green vest showed off the width of his shoulders and followed the line of his impressive torso to where it narrowed at his waist. I used to spend endless hours tracing the contours and dips of that expanse of skin, singing soft songs and placing gentle kisses, then laying my cheek on his chest to memorize the rhythm of his heartbeat.

"As would I," he said, and I had to remind myself what that was in response to. Oh, right, dancing, and I couldn't afford to think about anything more than making sure tonight went well. Getting sucked back into the chaos that was Finn—and by extension, our brief marriage—was not on my agenda for the night.

Fun, enjoyment, bliss, and contentment, absolutely. Chaos and heartbreak and uncertainty, absolutely not.

No matter what, though, I smiled some more and couldn't get myself to stop smiling no matter how much I told myself I was being an idiot. This was all Tessa's fault.

I looked around...Tessa, who had left at some point. Where had she gone? When? And why?

Finn pulled my attention back to him by feathering another kiss across my knuckles. That was enough of that.

One night was not going to kill me. And one dance wouldn't break me. "Until then." I slid my hand out from his and clicked for Fig to follow along with me. Dipping my nose toward the bouquet, I threw one last look over my shoulder to see if Finn was watching me walk away in the stunning gown Tami had sewn for me a few days ago. It was a little Rapunzel, a little Maleficent, and all me, showing me and my sparkle to our best advantage.

He was watching all right, but his eyes suddenly went from very interested to a little bit terrified to a whole lot terrified. Had my dress ripped? Did I have something in my hair? Was I having a wardrobe malfunction and my boob was hanging out for all to see?

I turned back around to hide my embarrassment and found that not only had my bouquet gained about twenty more blossoming and fragrant flowers, but also that my tiny Figiggly had grown ten times his size to match the enormous chariot in front of us filled with hairy men, swords galore, and a horn that nearly blew the hair right off my head.

"We are the Wild Hunt!" yelled the huge guy who looked like something from a Viking tale. Then he signaled for the horn to blow. Three times.

Now this might not have been an issue, and I could have written it off as a trick or someone's family members just getting a little too into the whole celebration thing.

Except that the chariot was see-through, the men were see-through, the horn was see-through. And yet when the front man shoved a spear into the ground to mark his territory it most definitely was solid and deadly even if I could see the building on the other side, clear as day.

"Hello?" I made myself say. "Can we help you with something?"

He peered at me, and I realized he was almost opaque, not really see-through. The second thing I noticed was that he was definitely dead, judging from the way his throat was slit and apparently ready to ride the wild hunt with a gleam in his hanging eyeball.

Holy crap.

Chapter Five

CHAOS. CHAOS WAS THE name of the game as the chariot was joined by another and another, all filled with dead men in their opaqueness. They zoomed around the jousting arena and seemed to be seeing who could go the fastest. If nothing else, at least, when they made a wide turn it didn't actually break any of the fencing we'd replaced about two months ago. Instead, the chariots just shot through the hardwood and then bounced back into the arena once the driver realized he was out of bounds.

There were no horses pulling the conveyances, but they reminded me of Seawaddle and the way a black mist trailed behind him as he ran. This was a ghostly white mist that enshrouded anything it passed over or through.

As eerie and interesting as that might be, though, the bigger thing on my mind was what the hell were these guys doing here?

Finn pulled me closer, and I appreciated it for about a second and then had to get out of his grip to figure out what we did from here. I had trouble untangling myself from all his frippery, and I heard a distinct ripping sound when I was finally able to pull free. His left cuff was hanging from my cleavage like a flag of surrender. No way. No how.

"Stop!" I yelled, using some of that magic in my core to amplify the noise. Along with training Fig with Althea, I had also called on Mavis, an old crone who had been with the faire since before time knew. She'd retired to a care facility down the road but had been happy enough to have Finn pick her up every day and bring her to my house so she could give me some pointers on what I could do and how best to use it. She also didn't mind trying to tell my ex's fortune every once in a while by making a grab for his butt. She was a rumpologist and loved that her area of study allowed her to still at least try. She hadn't caught him yet, but I'd almost love for her to get a handful so I could know if I fit in his future anywhere more permanently than as a next-door neighbor.

I hadn't tried out all the things she'd said I could enhance with my core, because, well, some of them had made me blush and were not germane to my situation, but that didn't mean I wasn't curious.

Right now, though, I needed all these wild men to go back to wherever they belonged so I could get on with my low-level night of fun, not introduce a whole new element that would take fun to chaos.

The first guy, with his dangling eyeball and his slit throat, stopped before me with a grunt. "What is it you want, mortal? We are here for the wild hunt. We will have the wild hunt."

"You hunt all the wild you want, but it has to be somewhere else. This is a private party, and I don't believe an invitation was sent to you."

"We do not need an invitation. We do not need your permission. We hunt, and you will step aside or the token for this evening will be a bounty you cannot afford to pay."

"I am Verla Faeth, dammit, and I run this place. Do not backtalk me." I surprised even myself with that, but not as much as I seemed to surprise the three chariots full of hairy, ghostly men.

Finn had ripped off the other sleeve of lace and the frilly cravat and stood with short sleeves and that vest that was droolworthy. But he stood next to me, not in front of me, and I appreciated that.

"Verla! You are *the* Verla?" The big man squinted his one good eye at me. "But you are puny and small."

I had to admit I preened there just for a second. I couldn't think of anyone who had ever called me small or puny, or at least not in an almost complimentary way.

"We are here to find the Verla and assist in the hunt."

That took me off guard even more than the way his breath smelled of the grave. "What? Why? We don't need any assistance. We're just having a fun night with friends and family. We don't need any assistance." To say I was baffled would be an understatement. Althea and I had planned this down to the last minute, and nowhere in the plans did it state "call in legion of ghosts in chariots." And if it had, I guarantee you it wouldn't have been this unwieldy bunch.

"No, no, I know there was a call put out. We have it here. Sigrid! Give the parchment!" Much scrambling among chariots was followed by grunting and swearing, and a punch or two was definitely thrown. And then the main guy turned back to me with a parchment in his hand, an actual piece of curled vellum with spidery script. He handed it over before I could demand it from him.

Skimming the lines, I wasn't quite sure what I was looking at until Fig lumbered over in his gigantic form and stuck his tongue to the top right corner of the paper. "Go hence to Verla the Mighty Faeth. Assist as needed and wield your sword and your honor by her command. The Wild Hunt comes to Effington Faire and we must needs be of help to our kin."

"I...I...I..."

Finn took the paper from me and looked it over. Figiggly's tongue was no longer on the paper, but one lick must have been enough to change it from indecipherable to easy-reading material.

"What kin?" Finn asked, peering up at the huge ghost-man and the plethora of ones just like him.

"I do not question the orders that come from this one. I follow, and we are here for the wild hunt. Now show us where to go and what to do. We will take care of the infidels with the quickest of speed and depart back to Valhalla."

Where, oh, where was a fully functioning Valkyrie when you needed one?

But everyone had scattered. I didn't know how they couldn't hear all the commotion happening near them or why they weren't coming back. Perhaps something really was out there in the woods and the faire. Maybe it was hurting my family, my villagers, even as we just stood around and debated the wording of a piece of paper, no matter how soft and cool it was.

"No one told you anything else?" I asked. "You just came streaming out of the sky on your war chariot and had no idea what exactly you were getting yourselves into?"

He focused his one good eye on me, and the frown on his face told me more than I wanted to know. But apparently, he needed to say it out loud anyway. "We are not to be sent hither and yon without good reason. We do not question the demand because it is what we do. No one wants to drink ale and dally all day long. I get tired of fighting all the same warriors time after time. Heldigrad always tries to hit me with a left-handed sword blow right after he aims to headbutt me, and no one new has come to us in many ages. So when we're given the opportunity to fight a good fight against foes, then of course we come down here."

I felt like there would have been a *duh* put on the end of that sentence if he had been about a thousand years younger.

"Okay, so there's a threat, but we don't know what it is, and we don't know who it is, but you're here to help us defend ourselves, and apparently play chariots of mist in my jousting ring. Does that about set things up right?"

He shrugged. I looked over at Finn, who also shrugged.

"So, we have a threat and somehow my board has to go back to zero days without incident, but we don't know where it's coming from or what we're going to have to do to vanquish it?' I huffed out a breath. "I'd almost rather be in the thick of it before I figure out something has gone horribly wrong, so I'm not dying here of anticipation and thinking of every single freaking thing that could go wrong and probably end up being wrong no matter what I come up with."

Talk about irritating.

I paced a few steps left and then a few more steps right and collided with Finn's chest. I lifted my hands to steady myself and found his heartbeat under my palm. Before I could curl my fingers into his pec, I stepped back and paced the other way, but not before I saw the small smirk on his face.

"We need a plan, but I don't even know what we're dealing with."

A rustle in the brush behind me made me whip my head around, and an army of villagers came rushing out of the woods, knives, swords, bows and arrows, and even pitchforks at the ready. They hurled things and ran with yells like banshees in the dead of night.

Chaos reigned for about fifteen seconds until they all seemed to realize their weapons were useless. Heck, they were useless anyway, since I'd been very specific about only having dull swords and tipless arrows. The pitchforks might hurt a real person, but they slid right through the warriors like a hot knife through butter.

"Tone it down. Tone it down!" I didn't have to use my core magic that time, since what I really wanted was a minute to breathe on my own and not hear a single other thing in my vicinity.

Instead I sank my hand into Fig's fur and waited to see if he'd shrink. But nothing happened. He remained huge and at the ready, while I remained more confused than ever before.

We couldn't just stand here waiting for something bad to happen, though. That felt like we would be constantly on the defensive, and I much preferred the offensive.

"Okay, so we have the Wild Hunt here. They're not going to take our souls, and they're not going to cause undue mischief." I turned toward the chariots as several distinctive groans sounded behind me. "I mean it. This is a peaceful place. We're going to defend it, absolutely, but we're going to do it smartly instead of all willy-nilly. I hate willy-nilly."

"I don't even know you, lass. Why do you hate me? I thought we were here to help." The main man of the horde smashed his axe into the ground. "So much for assisting Verla the Not-So-Mighty Faeth."

"Seriously? Seriously, your name is Willy Nilly?" I couldn't help the small burst of laughter that escaped my lips, but Willy was not having any of it.

"We go now. I will not offer assistance to one who feels we bring so little to the fight and chooses to laugh at us. We will do the Wild Hunt elsewhere. Perhaps in the neighboring village. There have to be better pickings over there."

"Wait, no, I'm sorry!" I tried to grab his hand, but of course my fingers went right through him. "I had no idea that was your name. Willy-nilly here means something different. Please!"

He kept his back turned to me, but I did notice that all movement had stopped. Maybe if I put on the sugar a little more, I could do this. I'd done it before and was very capable of talking my way out of trouble.

"Willy—May I call you Willy, or is it Mr. Nilly?"

"Willy will suffice," he grumbled with great reluctance in his every word.

"Willy, I truly do apologize. I was taken unaware by so great an army and am more than grateful that you're here to assist us. We all are grateful." I threw my arm out and waved it back and forth to encompass all the people still standing with weapons ready. Then I patted my hand down to ask them to lower said weapons.

"I'm listening," Willy said, turning slightly.

"We just didn't expect such heroes to come to our aid when we didn't even know we needed aid. We aren't turning you away. I'm just not sure what to do with you since I don't know what we're up against." Before I could second-guess myself, I gathered everything from within me and threw it with my palms out and my fingers spread wide.

In my mind I had conjured a huge bubble that fit all the chariots and their occupants to keep them in one place and out of trouble. At least until I could figure out what we were dealing with, and what part they played in this whole thing. Maybe they were the issue and not something or someone else.

Cynical laughter followed my flash of bubble that actually looked more like a fish bowl when it surrounded the Wild Hunt. I whipped around to see if I'd missed a chariot.

But no, it was worse.

"Well, Verla of little Faeth, let me show you what exactly you're up against."

I knew that voice, and the way Trice screamed and her pet Pix blew fire I had a very good idea of who I was going to see when I turned around.

Lexton Cravensham. The traditional who had stalked Trice and tried to destroy her a few weeks ago.

This was not good.

Chapter Six

"WHAT THE HELL—" MY words were cut off when something flew through the air and slapped across my mouth. I automatically reached for it and, though I couldn't see it, I felt it writhe under my fingers. Was it alive? I clamped my mouth shut behind it just in case. Who knew what we were dealing with?

All I could see through my panic was that bastard Lexy who had tried to ruin my faire by poisoning the beautiful art Trice made. She'd walked away from him, and apparently, he wasn't used to being turned down, especially by a misfit. And so he'd taken his revenge. In all honesty, we had gotten the better end of that bargain since we'd gained Gargy, a wonderful gargoyle, Pix, a miniature lion with wings who blew fire and smoke like no one's business, and Pheeney, the amazing phoenix, along with Seawaddle the magnificent kelpie.

But I also had been told that this traditional—a paranormal who was born with the right powers to the right people—was at least going to be held until he got the slap on the wrist we anticipated.

How the hell had he gotten out? Grayden was away from us right now and at high court to sort out the details of the arrest. Or at least that was what I had been told last.

So were we dealing with an escapee, or had the Powers That Be given in to the traditional asshole's (there I said it, and I wasn't taking it back) parents' idea that a little mischief at a ren faire in the back hills of Pennsylvania wasn't enough to cause a ruckus in the haves since it was against the have-nots?

Had he been the actual cause of the ruckus early in the day? The explanations that had been given had felt a little too coincidental even for me, who wanted so badly to believe them.

Whatever this thing was on my mouth, it was making me nauseous. I was about two seconds away from either puking or passing out when Fig licked my face. The thing tried to hold on, but Fig's sigil of protection on his tongue was too powerful, and the thing gave up.

When it fell from my mouth, I was horrified to see it wriggle away. I lifted my foot to stomp on it, but Finn was already there with a walking stick. One of the special ones that Everest kept back for customers who knew what to ask for. The kind that hid a dagger inside it.

Finn stabbed at the ground, but whatever it was poofed out of sight.

Um, gross!

The whole thing had taken but a few seconds, but it had been distracting enough that when I looked up Lexy was gone. Shit. Shit. Shit.

Where was he? Was he the reason the horde had been called? Was this the threat that demanded a Wild Hunt be sent to my faire?

How could one person need an entire platoon of ghost men on chariots to take him down?

"Gather in!" I yelled. "Now!"

They came from all directions, my villagers, my family, their families and friends, and even with useless weapons they looked like warriors. But we weren't supposed to be warriors, we were supposed to be peaceful, fun-loving faire employees.

I took a deep breath. And then another. "Okay, look, I don't know what is happening or why we have this Wild Hunt with us. But that guy, Lexy, is a nuisance and more importantly a criminal. I need to find him and keep him from whatever he might be deciding to do. We know he's powerful, and smarmy, and not against doing whatever he wants to do, so no holds barred." I took a third deep breath. "I don't want you to get hurt, so I'm going to ask that you take your family and friends to the Tavern on the Line and stay there while I figure out what's going on before I pull anyone else in. I will absolutely ask for help if I need it, but I need you all safe first."

Not a single person blinked an eye. In fact, they all smiled at me. There were words of encouragement, and then they broke off into pairs and small groups, winding their way to the tavern. That was far easier than I thought it would be. I did ask a small contingent to stay behind and watch the fishbowl of growling ghost men. Volunteers cropped right up, and I moved away so that I could concentrate without the overall noise of grumbling coming from the glass enclosure I'd made.

I. Had. Made. Since when could I do stuff like that? I'd have to ask once this was all taken care of.

I looked around to make sure everyone had at least one other person with them. Everyone did, so I turned back to Althea and Finn, who had not yet left my side. Jabbers and Figiggly were in our tight circle too.

"Ideas?" I asked because, honestly, nothing was coming to me. Was Lexy here to destroy things? To make me pay for pressing charges? To get Trice back? Any of it was possible on its own, but also all of it was possible together.

Fig had shrunken to match Jabbers, which meant he was still about three times his normal floofy size. They were sitting right next to each other like their hips were glued together. That made my decision so much easier.

"Why don't the three of us work together? I'm sure he must be here after me to some extent and will want to find me or punish me first. But I don't want to drag you along if you don't want to be in the line of fire."

Finn shook his head. "When are you ever going to learn that we're here because we want to be? None of this is your fault. And we're not going to leave you alone."

Althea put a hand on my shoulder. "There is nothing that would keep me from helping with the faire's safety. I'll leave a message for Grayden, but I'm not sure what, if anything, he can do. I'll ask if they know Lexton is out and about, though. That might get us a third group of people if the special forces come in."

"Do it. I'd rather have more than not enough. Lexy caused trouble last time all by himself, but I have a hard time believing the Wild Hunt is necessary for one person. I wonder if he's not alone."

Willy tapped the glass behind me. "We are to do the hunting also. Let us out. We will spread out among your houses and shops. We have enough that we can each take a post around your faire and therefore be ready as necessary."

"Don't you normally just ride through and take souls? I'm still not sure why you were called." Not sure wasn't exactly true, more like totally baffled, and who was the one who had called them in the first place, and how did they know more than I did?

"The three fates know what is in store and sometimes will step in to lend a hand. That is all I can tell you. Now, we ride!" That blasted horn blew again and vibrated the glass to the point I thought it was going to break.

But it held, and I shook my head. "I need you to stay here for just a little longer. I promise you will get to do that hunt, but I don't want to send you out without some guidance."

He growled at me but said nothing more. Because he was acquiescing? Or because he was planning to get out as soon as I turned my back again?

The riders inside the bowl with Willy began shouting back and forth at each other. I couldn't hear what they were saying enough to make out the words, but I certainly heard the ghostly laughter and got the feeling that they were completely onboard for the mischief too. They had to remain until I knew what was going on.

"So where do we start?" I asked my team.

"I think getting Dalvon on board with us might be our best bet. Can he have Pheeney do a fly-over to see what the lay of the land is?" Althea snapped a gold chain on Jabbers and petted his ears.

I didn't have my chain with me, and I really hoped I wouldn't have to use the magic equivalent of an anchor on Fig. I put a quick call in to Dalvon.

"Can Pheeney go up and see if she can spot any issues?"

"Of course, Verla, it would be our pleasure to protect and serve this way. Would you like me to call on Gargy also? He and Trice took Pix back to their home. The little lion was getting too worked up, with the number of people in the tavern."

I bit my lip for a second, trying to think my way through that. Not good, not good. But I had to hold it together so as not to freak Dalvon out before I knew for certain what was going on. "They shouldn't have left. There's a reason I asked for everyone to stay in the tavern. I thought I'd made that clear." Damn. I started walking toward the village. Now that we knew it was Lexy out there, I was even more concerned for Trice. He'd been her ex-boyfriend and caused some serious trouble here before. "She should have stayed where I put her."

"Let us know what else we can do. I'll let everyone know to hunker down and await your next move." Dalvon signed off, and I blew out a huge breath.

"I'm not sure that expecting everyone to stay out of this is going to work, Verla," Althea said from my left. She was chugging right along with me up the hill. "Everyone is invested in this and wants to help."

We were halfway to Trice's cottage. Lights danced in the windows, and the wind picked up to rattle the branches instead of whistling through them gently. Overhead, Pheeney spiraled in the sky, and I waited for a report from Dalvon as I approached Trice's house, hoping she was safe with Gargy.

I raised my hand to knock, but Finn kicked in the door before I could finish the job. I gasped as I realized that hadn't been light glowing through the windows—it was a fire set in a circle around a bound and gagged and possibly lifeless Gargy, who was in human form.

Action was all I could think of as Figiggly launched himself over the ring of fire and Althea headed toward the kitchen, hopefully for water or a fire extinguisher. The ring was still thin, but with how old some of these houses were, it could burst into an all-consuming inferno in no time.

We three humans and the two dogs worked like a well-oiled machine. Fig ripped at the knots holding Gargy's arms to the chair, and then my beautiful puppy went after the knots holding the gargoyle upright. He worked at them cautiously and then caught Gargy on his back.

Fig had grown to the size of a hippo and jumped over the flames to avoid getting singed. I didn't know how he did it without Gargy falling off, but I was very thankful. For his part, Gargy, in true gargoyle form, came roaring off my dog's back like someone had lit a firecracker under him. Althea hit the fire with one extinguisher while she tossed a second one to Finn, and a bottle of water to me. I squirted to the best of my ability as the others stood in the middle of the chaos, shooting the fire with the chemical foam. My core tightened with the hatred and swelling need for vengeance, both mine and the perpetrator's.

Mine was definitely winning out, though, and when we caught this jerk, it was not going to be as easy as last time. Damn the special forces and the paranormal high court. This was war, and I had warriors ready like no one had ever seen in front of me, behind me, and in the sky. It was time to use them to the best of my ability.

Bring it on!

Chapter Seven

GARGY RIPPED THE BANDANA from his mouth with his clawed hand, shook his wings out, and ran toward the door. "We must catch the bastard who took my beloved and the Pix."

"Wait!" I yelled.

Finn stepped in front of the exit to the outside and wherever the woman and the little winged lion might be. To say Gargy was unhappy about that blockade would probably be an understatement, as he snarled like a caged lion. All six feet ten of him.

"I will not leave Trice and Pix in the hands of a madman. Get out of my way, Finn, before I am forced to move you."

"Hang on a second," Finn answered. "We need to know what happened so we can fight this smartly instead of always on the defensive. What can you tell us about how the fire started and who took them? How did they manage to grab them both and leave you incapacitated?"

"Whoever it was came in like a shadow. I was not able to see their face. They knocked me out, and the last thing I saw was Trice thrown over some barbarian's shoulder like a sack of grain. I must get to her. Now."

"We have Pheeney in the sky and a Wild Hunt was apparently sent to us for this very reason," I said, sighing when I felt a headache sneaking up from the back of my neck. "We need more information, and you're the only one who can give it to us. Please hold on a moment, and we'll be more prepared to help than just going out like gangbusters."

"Pheeney can talk to me while in the air. We'll get back to you. I'm not leaving her alone. Step out of the way, Finn, before I do more than growl." Gargy's voice was something to be reckoned with on a good day. When he was angry and possibly scared and feeling super-protective of the woman I knew for certain he loved, it got downright scary.

"Gargy, please, did the guy say anything? Was there more than one? Did he leave anything behind? We can assume it's Lexton, but I'd rather know for certain."

Gargy's crystal blue eyes narrowed and zeroed in on me. I hoped he remembered that I had helped him and that I would never want him or anyone in my faire harmed. But I also operated better with information, and we could do so much more if we knew what we were dealing with. I implored him with my eyes, while massaging my temples and trying my best to send out the most positive and encouraging vibes possible.

He shoved Finn aside anyway and was in the sky before I could draw my next breath. The flap of his wings sounded like the booming of a ship's sails in a terrible storm.

Finn righted himself and dusted his pants off. "What do we do now?"

Althea had been stalking around the room, opening jars and cabinets and the refrigerator. I wasn't sure what she was looking for, but if she found something I would not be against it.

"Anything?" I asked, then was interrupted by Althea gasping. She pumped the fire extinguisher handle and shot foam my way. I was quick to move out of range, but wondered why she'd gasped.

Then I followed the direction of everyone else's gaze and was both horrified and fascinated to find a message burned into the old wallpaper in the living room.

Verla only at wishing well ALONE

The words were singed into the wall, and though no fire accompanied them now, they still felt seared into my eyes.

"You know what?" I said to the room at large. "Let Gargy go. We're going to find this bastard one way or another, and I'm not following the rules of any coward who thinks he can get one over on us."

Finn took my hand and kissed my knuckles. I had no idea why but didn't have the time to think about it because another message appeared on the wall.

BRING LOTS OF CASH

"What are we going to do? And how much is 'lots'?" Althea asked.

"I have no idea. Put that call in to Grayden if you haven't already. And if you did, call him again. Find out if he knows where Lexton is supposed to be and why there isn't a restraining order on him. If there is, then how can we get it invoked?"

Of course those were ideas that would not help us right now, but it would at least set things into motion where the high court couldn't ignore them so easily this time. He'd kidnapped someone. I had a feeling that would warrant a little more than a slap on his delicate wrist.

"So, do you think he's here for me and Trice, or just Trice and I'm like a bonus?" I asked Althea and Finn.

"Could go either way. But I have a hard time believing he's going to give her up for cash, no matter how much you bring. And whoever did this didn't even specify how much to bring. How are you supposed to know?" Althea ran her finger over the singed words on the wall.

"We have no idea what his ultimate plan is. The money might just be the gravy on the cake. Maybe he wants it to get away. I have no idea how much that would cost. But why wouldn't he just get money from Mommy and Daddy?" I shook my head at myself. "It doesn't matter. What matters is me getting to the wishing well." Finn opened his mouth. I cut him off. "Alone but with Figiggly. Gargy will be in the sky and so is Pheeney. For that matter, we also have the Wild Hunt as a backup, but I want to see what he has to say before I bring in any of my weapons." Finn opened his mouth, and I cut him off again. "I need you and Althea to talk with the Wild Hunt on my behalf. Tell them to stay away until I know what we're dealing with."

Finn opened his mouth again, then let it hang there for a second.

"I'm done." I gave him a cheeky smile because this moment needed a tiny boost even if it was only for the length of a cheeky smile.

"On the way to the wishing well, make sure you tell Willy Nilly that I can speak for you. I don't want one of those spears to manifest in my chest if I can help it," he finally said.

Finn was being awfully understanding about this by not fighting me. I wanted to honor that. However, I didn't know if I had time for a side trip. "He saw you with me. He wouldn't hurt you."

"We shouldn't take that chance," Althea said. With her hands on her hips and a whip coiled from her belt loop, I had to agree. Props or not, I didn't want there to be issues with the set of beings who were supposed to be helping me, not attacking my crew.

Althea leaned over and pulled something out from under the sofa. She unfolded it and smoothed it out on the breakfast bar.

It was a map that very much resembled Dalvon's. One he'd been given of the faire when I'd hired him without a real interview. When I looked closer, it was apparent this didn't just resemble his map. It *was* his map, with his name and notes in his handwriting on it.

A chill went down my spine. I'd had a brief thought of Dalvon having set up all the mischief last time just to get the job, but I'd dismissed it. I'd hired him right away because he'd worked so well with Pheeney and had seemed like a great guy for a vampire who didn't drink blood.

Had I been wrong? Had he been in cahoots with Lexton all along? I was going to be sick.

No, I was not jumping to conclusions until I saw things with my own eyes. I'd deal with whatever happened whenever it happened. Borrowing trouble had only ever weighed me down, and I needed to be light to fight this right now.

"Okay, here's what we're going to do. I'll take Figiggly with me. You talk to Grayden, Althea. And Finn, you get in contact with the horde once I tell Willy that we need them on standby."

"And what are you going to do when you meet the kidnapper at the wishing well? What kind of money do you have on you?" Finn asked.

"Well, as part of the festivities tonight, I had planned on handing out gold foil-wrapped coins. That's going to have to pass as money, or ammunition of my own if I find that might work better." I shrugged. "We'll see what happens. Now, go do your things, my wonder crew, and let's get this bastard. No blood if possible, but if it's necessary, then at least try to get it on the grass. Washing it off pavement is never a fun thing, even for Calvin."

We split up as we went out the door, Finn toward the tavern and Althea toward the tree that seemed to allow the best reception for cell service.

After stuffing the map into my pocket and warning Fig to stay by my side, I went back to where I'd stashed the Wild Hunt.

"Willy!" I yelled because I wanted to hit something. Hard. He'd better answer me no matter how irritated he was with being in a gigantic fishbowl.

I shouldn't have worried in the least. He was in front of me with his cut throat and dangling eyeball a second after I finished his name.

"Verla the Faeth, you will release us!"

I gave him a quick sketch of what had happened, then spent five minutes talking him out of running off to the wishing well if only I'd give him directions since he didn't remember seeing one on his travels through the clear sky. That was not happening. And he wouldn't have seen it, since it was under a brick archway within the mansion on top of the hill.

I was curious to know how Lexton knew about the wishing well. I doubted that would be the first question I asked him, but I put it in the back of my mind for later, if there was a later.

Begrudgingly and with a healthy dose of rage from the dead man, I got Willy's agreement that he would allow Finn to be my mouthpiece for the next little while, and then Fig and I went trooping off to the mansion.

I had lived there briefly when I first came back to the faire as the manager, but found I much preferred something less ostentatious and more in the midst of my people.

Those were better, less volatile times. I really didn't understand what had made all these people and things start coming out of the crazy woodwork to attack my faire, but I was determined to take them on one at a time for as long as I had to.

So time to change that incident board and go wrangle myself a miscreant who thought kidnapping people and their pets while being a bully was right up his alley. I was about to strike him out with my ball of whoop-ass.

Winding our way through the paved streets of the faire, Fig and I approached the mansion. No lights were on, no telltale signs that anyone was in the building at all. But I wasn't heading for the building itself. I was heading for the arched entrance underneath, which led to the mansion's tunnel underground. The whole village had tunnels under the houses, to be used in times of danger and when hiding was a necessity. I had thought about sending everyone down there instead of to the tavern, but the tunnels still made me a little nervous. They were one of the reasons I hadn't just stepped down into Trice's basement and followed the tunnel to the mansion. Anything could be down there, an ambush, a mob, a rabid pack of something magical that could hurt Figiggly. At least by using the surface streets I could see what was coming at me and defend myself and my dog if I had time.

Gargy's flapping wings soared above me. I didn't wave him away, but I wasn't going to invite him in, either.

I also knew all the hiding places up here from working security when I was younger. We had towering bushes you could hide in or pillars you could fit behind.

I wasn't going to be taken unaware if I could help it.

Scoping out the front door of the mansion, I saw it was ajar, and the first nervousness of uncertainty hit me like a ton of pewter beer steins.

What was I doing? What did I think I was going to do? I'd had so much bravado when I saw the first message. I'd been on fire inside to eradicate this idiot and take him down as quickly and fully as possible, while making sure Trice was safe and his ass was behind bars for a good long while.

But now, standing out here in the whistling wind, knowing I had all manner of people around me but no one except my wonderful dog with me, made my knees shake just a little under my beautifully tailored dress.

I could do this. I knew I could. And Fig was not just a tiny puppy—he had power. He'd gone back to only five times his normal size. I didn't know if that was because he didn't think this was more danger than we could handle, or if he too knew about all the help we had within yelling distance.

Since there was a hidden back door to the mansion few knew about, I chose to circle around the building and go through there. It entailed pushing aside some of those bushes, but the effort would be worth it. Who knew what nefarious things Lexy had set up to thwart me? Did he really want money for Trice, or was that just a ploy to get me here so he could hurt both of us?

With the front door ajar, my gut told me the wishing well could wait another few minutes while I checked this out.

I really hoped with everything in my being that Finn and Althea were doing their parts and that everyone else had stayed safe at the tavern.

It was bad enough I'd had to drag Fig along with me, although I doubted the little dog would have stayed away even if I'd put him in his new reinforced play yard.

"Okay, we're going to go in quietly, and then we're going to poke around," I told him in a whisper. I could have tried the mind-talking thing, but I never really knew if he heard me unless he was the one who initiated the conversation.

I did not want there to be any miscommunications with so much on the line.

The door barely creaked as I opened it just enough to fit through. I forgot for a second that the opening would have to widen for Fig, so I turned around and assisted him as he shouldered open the door, sending it past the creaking stage and right into the squealing-on-the-hinges stage. I quietly closed it behind us, hoping the noise would be missed in a house this huge.

But then, a roar unlike anything I'd heard before filled the house, and Pix shot past me like a rocket and went around a corner into another hallway with those tiny wings of his flapping so fast they were a blur.

Chapter Eight

SO DID I FOLLOW Pix, or think that he'd managed to get away but Trice was still here? Who had roared like that? I didn't think it was Pix. But who else could it be?

I was not ashamed to admit that I didn't know where to go or what to deal with first. The place was huge. That roar could have come from anywhere and just reverberated through the house from the third floor on down to where we stood in the mudroom at the back of the first floor. It sounded again, and my heart pounded in my chest.

What *was* that? It could have been a dragon, a troll, a... So many things swirled through my head, I was having trouble grabbing on to any one of them. I still had Fig by my side, but we had to find Pix, and fast. I did not want to tell Trice I had lost her baby if he got hurt running away from their captor.

Gah, if we ever found Trice, that was.

"Fig, stick close, buddy. We're going to have to go up and then go down if we don't find Pix. I wish we could split up, but I don't want you at risk, and I don't want to be at risk either."

His tongue hung out of his mouth with that sigil of protection on it. I wished, just for a moment, that I had let Finn come with me. I could have released the Wild Hunt when I talked with Willy and they could have done their thing. I wasn't afraid to admit that not knowing what they were truly capable of was one of the huge reasons I hadn't let them run amok. But now I felt that it might have been worth the risk.

Why did I always have to feel so in control of crap that in the end only hurt me? There were no rules when it came to getting my friend safely back and nailing this jerk.

The back door slammed open behind us, and it was as if my very thoughts had called Finn to me.

"Are you okay?" he asked, huffing and puffing. For someone who was pretty fit, he must have been hauling tail to come in sounding like a set of bellows.

"Yes, but I have to find Pix, and I don't want to miss the meeting with the kidnapper and Trice. I have to get her back before something awful happens."

"Normally, Trice is pretty mild-mannered, but she can kick ass when she wants to. Do you really think she's behaving herself right now?" he asked, bent over with his hands on his knees. I wished I had a water to offer him.

As inappropriate as it felt in the moment, I chuckled at the thought of Trice giving as good as she got with Lexy. She had torn him a new one not two weeks ago and had been working hard on helping the system build a case against him, so the likelihood of her expressing that anger was a good bet.

"Exactly." Finn stood up. "Let's find Pix and then go for Trice at the wishing well. I can stay back, but

I can't let you do this yourself and alone."

"What's that supposed to mean? I am perfectly capable." Obviously. And yet, I was contradicting what I was thinking right before he burst through the door. But I didn't want to want him, and I definitely didn't want to need him. I'd survived for years on my own, thank you very much. Obviously not with these kinds of crises, but I'd done okay, dammit. I couldn't afford to let him back in like before. My heart wouldn't be able to take a second rejection like that.

So I fought him, even though the voice at the back of my brain was telling me what a huge idiot I was.

"Finn, I get that you want in on the action but, seriously, I've got this. I do not need to be policed by you. I know what I'm doing. My life is no longer tied to yours."

"You'd be surprised by what you don't know and how wrong you are."

The words I wanted to tell him got stuck in my throat when another roar shot through the house, followed by an even bigger roar that this time I *was* familiar with. For such a small creature, Pix was very capable of shaking the rafters of any building. He could also...

Yep, the thought that he could enshroud the whole place in darkness had just been about to cross my mind when he did just that.

Which was awesome to confuse the roaring thing and Lexy, but didn't make it easier for us to find anyone in this inky blackness. I couldn't even see my own fingers two inches from my eyes.

"What now?" I asked.

"Now you're asking for my help?"

I drew in a careful breath, then let it out just as slowly. "Please don't be a jerk, just help me, and whatever you think I don't know you can tell me later. Let's find the pixiu and Trice and get this exchange done."

"Here, here, here," I heard from above me in that squeaky voice that matched the body of my favorite little winged lion. The black cloud dissolved in an instant, and I blinked against the return of light.

Pix was telling us where he was! Finn beat me to the stairs to the second floor, but I wasn't far behind. Figiggly nearly knocked me over on the staircase to get in front of both me and Finn. We must have sounded like a herd of cattle going up, but who cared?

When I reached the landing, it was to see Gargy slumped against a vanity carved from oak, his forehead resting against the cabbage roses on the wallpaper. He was holding his right arm up at the elbow and his face was squinched into a mask of so much pain I flinched myself.

"Pix?" I walked into the room gingerly, not sure what else I would find. Had the thing that had been roaring hurt my favorite gargoyle? There would be hell to pay, I'd guarantee that.

Finn went to Gargy, and Figiggly put his paws on the windowsill, looking down to the yard below through the open window.

Had whatever was in here taken flight? I was definitely leaning more toward dragon, if that was the case.

"What happened?" I snatched Pix off the top of the vanity mirror where he was perched like a little bird.

"Uppies!" he squealed.

"You are uppies," I told him. "Now, what happened?"

He nuzzled under my chin. "Gargy roared and tried to hurt. I bit him."

No way. I looked over at Gargy and his normally crystal blue eyes were narrowed and a murky, dirty, pond green. What did that mean?

Finn took a step closer to the gargoyle, and I wanted to tell him to stop. We needed to know what had happened before trying to make contact. But if I didn't want him telling me what to do, then I was probably better off not trying to dictate his life either.

"Be careful," I said instead.

"I'm always careful." He reached a hand out toward Gargy and then jerked it back when Gargy snarled.

"Pix, what is wrong with him?" I asked, pulling the little guy away from my neck and staring into his eyes.

"Gargy owie."

"Did you give him the owie?"

He shook his mane until it fluffed out like he'd been hit by electricity.

"What happened then?"

"Another note," Finn said. He was crouched next to Gargy and had gently removed the clawed hand from where it was clamped on his forearm.

Trice is not behaving Sorry for trouble Meet by the stables

The words etched into Gargy's stone arm radiated with the aura of magic. An apology even as he hurt my friend. That was not going to make my punishment any less, dammit.

I crouched down next to Gargy. "Can we help you?"

He shook his head. "Go find her and bring her back. I'll be up in the sky and will let you know if I see anything."

His eyes were still dark, and that worried me. "Will you be able to fly with the damage to your arm?"

"It's just a scratch." He smiled, but it was tinged with some serious anger. And then he launched himself through the open window and into the sky like an avenging angel. Pix swooped out behind him, and both got lost in the darkened sky.

I almost hoped I got to this kidnapper first so I could keep him from the wrath of Gargy and Pix, but mine wasn't going to be any better.

I felt my insides roiling. Looking over at Finn, he didn't look much happier.

"Don't ask me to stay behind." He linked his fingers with mine. "Please don't ask that of me. I've been trying to follow along with what you want and how you want it, but I can't take a chance with your life just so you can have your way."

I pulled my hand from his. "You have a very strange way of trying to be nice to me, Finn. I don't need you to let me have my way. And every single time I've been able to take care of myself. I wasn't going to make you stay behind, regardless, but your approach to the situation makes me want to send you back to your uncle and not let you back in. Ever."

Shaking his head, he ran a hand over his face, and when he fisted that hand at his side, he looked like someone had hit him with a two-by-four. "I'm doing this all wrong. I know I am, but I don't know how to do it right." He breathed in, and then let it out in a gust. "There are things you don't know, and it's my fault you don't know them. But please trust me when I tell you that I'm sorry for how everything went down years ago. I was a young, inexperienced idiot, and apparently I'm still an inexperienced idiot, just older."

A tiny crack burst in my heart, but I had no time for this. "Let's table this. I'm sure once you explain whatever the hell that means that I'll just magically get you and your attitude, but at the moment I have far more important things to worry about. We have someone missing. Our past is hugely insignificant compared to that."

"Not as much as you'd think."

Now I was curious, or curiouser, I guess would be the right word, since his hints over the last few weeks had kept me awake some nights. But right now we had to find Trice, get this kidnapper, and hopefully put Lexy in jail for the rest of his natural-born life. I would absolutely go completely to the mat to press as many charges as I could possibly dream up this time. I was not going to leave it to the Powers That Be to do the right thing. They hadn't last time, and this was the situation we found ourselves in because of their leniency.

"So we head to the stables." I pointed my feet in that direction and prepared to gird my loins for whatever Lexy was going to bring to the fight. If he wanted revenge on both me and Trice, would either of us live to tell the tale? I had no idea, but it wasn't going to stop me from trying.

Fig walked beside me as we left the house, took the road to the right, and angled down to the stables where Seawaddle should be sleeping along with all the other horses we used for the jousts during our faire hours.

Of course Seawaddle was at the tavern now, since someone had tried to mess with him too. My mind clicked on the fact that the victims tonight were four of the new beings and the one who'd created them. That couldn't be a coincidence. And there was no way Dalvon would have hurt Pheeney during the demonstration earlier just to hide his crimes. I couldn't fathom that.

Nickering greeted Fig, Finn, and me when we got to the long barn structure where the horses were housed. Nothing sounded out of the ordinary, and I felt no danger near. Fig had gone back down to his little puppy size and trotted along with his swishy bottom and his tail curled over his back.

Were we out of danger? Or was the danger just not close enough? Or—I gulped at this thought—had Lexton taken Trice out of the faire in order to hurt her, reneging on any kind of ransom?

I did not want to ask that question out loud, so I kept it to myself as we went in the big double doors. My heels echoed on the concrete floor separating the two rows of stalls filled with our beautiful horses. We had grays and speckled horses, chestnuts, and one pure white with a black star at his fetlock. And then at the end was Seawaddle's stall in all his inky black glory. Even standing still in a stall, he always continued to throw off a black mist that trailed from his body. No matter where I looked and what information sources I'd tapped, I hadn't been able to find out if there was a way to get that to stop, or if it took away from his physical being to constantly have pieces of himself flecking off.

Who had put him back in here?

I was fully aware I was trying to distract myself from the fact that Lexton was nowhere in sight, and neither was Trice.

Damn it!

After a quick pet to the other horses, I pulled my dog and my ex out into the night air.

"Nothing. Anyone have any ideas on what comes next? He's not here, and I'm getting tired of running around the faire in these shoes and being led on a wild goose chase."

Finn crossed his arms over his chest. "I think we need to bring in the Wild Hunt. I didn't get a chance to talk with them before I came to you at the mansion. They were sent here for a reason. Keeping them locked up in the bowl might not have been the way to go about this. I know you wanted them out of the way and to try to do this without too much noise, but I think we're going to continue to be led around and around until Lexton either leaves with Trice and we never see her again, or until we catch him off guard. The Wild Hunt would go a long way toward that element of surprise."

Shit, he was right, which ultimately meant I was wrong. Normally, I had no problem admitting I was wrong. I did it often enough with my crew and the staff. If they brought me something I had overlooked, or something I had looked at incorrectly, I would readily admit I had not thought of it that way and immediately change my mind and my procedures to take new ideas into account. I wasn't a dictator, just a manager.

But this was my ex, the man who had hurt me more than I realized until he came trotting back in with the best peace offering I ever could have wanted. Figiggly had not only given me love, he'd also opened the way for my gift to manifest itself.

And for that I really should give Finn a little more slack, not to mention this faire would be his one day per his uncle, and so he had more invested in its health than even I did in the long run.

Craptastic!

"Okay, what's the game plan, and how do you propose we keep the Wild Hunt from being too wild? I'm willing to listen to what you have to say, but we need to be responsible and not go off half cocked."

The cheeky bastard smiled at me with one side of his mouth kicking up higher than the other. He brushed my hair behind my ear, kissed the end of my nose, and then we got down to the business of saving the faire. Although I was almost tempted to get down to another kind of business.

That would be a terrible idea, and I knew it, so I forced myself to focus on what he was saying instead of the way his lips moved around each word that fell out of his mouth.

And they were good words, full of wisdom and forethought and a bunch of tactical things I wouldn't have considered.

"You ready?" he asked, taking my hand in his again.

I sighed when he kissed my knuckles, but I wasn't sure if it was in longing or in resignation.

Chapter Nine

I WAS MORE THAN a little concerned about my reception from the horde once I went back to the bubble I'd put them in at the tavern. Willy Nilly had not been a happy camper when I'd forced him to remain behind with some of my own magic mixed with Figiggly's. Releasing them could either be the best idea to let them help, or the worst idea if they decided to turn on me instead.

I worried my bottom lip with my teeth the whole way there. Until I almost drew blood. And then I started chewing on my right thumbnail.

Finn took my hand in his again but didn't kiss my knuckles this time. I almost missed the gesture. Almost.

"They were sent here to help you, Verla. Things will be fine. Just explain the situation to them and then let them do what they do best."

I snorted. "What they do best is claim innocent lives as they ride through the sky and take your souls with them. Or didn't you read all the way through your mythology courses?"

Now he did kiss my knuckles. I'd be a liar if I didn't admit, at least to myself, that the simple kiss sent tingles throughout my whole body. Entire body. Roots of my hair, straight down to my toes. Or maybe that was just the nervousness I was feeling from having to release the Wild Hunt. Yeah, I was going with that. Much more practical.

"You're too worried. Something or someone thought you needed assistance, and they are lending you a hand. I know the magic world can be unpredictable, and that being a misfit only makes you more wary, but there are forces out there that we don't understand. Forces who don't care what your abilities are or how they manifest. They are simply in it for keeping balance in this world."

I almost asked him when he'd gotten this smart, but one look into his eyes, and I bit my tongue instead of my nail.

He smiled at me. "If you want I can talk to them, but I really think it would be better coming from you."

"That makes sense." I straightened the lowcut bodice on my dress and cleared my throat. What was I going to say that would sway them to my side after I'd just locked them up in a bubble, like putting fish in a tank?

Willy sneered at me from inside that fishbowl, even going so far as to stuff his dangling eyeball back into the socket so that he could effectively glare at me with both eyes.

Ooh, boy, this was going to be fun.

"Do you think I should apologize before I release them?" I whispered to Finn out of the side of my mouth.

"Nope, show them you're the boss, because you are, and let them deal with it. If they ever come back, they'll know not to just come galivanting in without first checking with you."

Ugh, I was the boss, and that was probably the best way to go about things, but my management style had always been a little less tyrant and a little more friendly business. However, these ghosts might not understand that. I briefly had a vision of that scene in *Lord of the Rings* where Viggo doesn't make nice with the ghosts in the cavern, he demands loyalty. I didn't really have anything to demand with, like setting them free, but that didn't mean I couldn't do my own brand of "Help me. Or else."

"Okay, I get it if you guys are probably a little irritated that I asked you to stay behind until I knew what was going on."

There was a lot of grumbling and a few calls for my head. I ignored them, and the fact that I very much did not ask them to stay behind, I put them in a bowl, for star's sake.

"And now that we know what's going on, I need your help in the direst of ways. This is a war zone, my friends, and I need your special assistance to bring down the enemy." I walked in front of the bowl, pacing back and forth, wishing I could ride Seawaddle like a true commander and maybe wave around a sword. Instead I avoided stepping on any uneven rocks in my high heels and keeping my dress from dragging across the ground too much.

But that didn't seem to detract from my message. The bowl of men vibrated with their huzzahs and war cries, to the point where I was pretty sure they might have made it to the decibel needed to shatter the thing.

Before that could happen, I snapped my fingers and they all tumbled out onto the ground in a mound of chariots and hairy men. They were quick to get back on their feet and line up before me.

They were tall. Taller than I had originally thought, or maybe they just had the ability to grow like Figiggly did when there was trouble. Either way, I'd take them.

"Here's the deal. We have a criminal in the faire. He tried to harm our villagers last time he was here and created what he thought would be monsters that he could then entertain privileged people with."

Some snorts and some growling, a few shouts. I hoped they were all in my favor.

"I think he's back, and now he's stolen a woman who is very dear to me. He set fire to her house, then knocked out the gargoyle we have on site."

"A gargoyle?" Willy asked. I wasn't sure if he was the only one who was allowed to talk to me, or if everyone else just was used to deferring to him and making him the mouthpiece. "You have a gargoyle?"

"Yes, we do, and he's flying through the faire now, but I bet he'd very much appreciate your help. Are you sure there's nothing more you can tell me about who sent you or why?"

"No, my lass, nothing. Where do you want us to start?"

A sudden burst of heat and a familiar Pix roar, one so loud my eardrums shook, had me turning my head toward the east and the huge fireball rising in the sky. It was so typical Pix.

"I'm guessing over there." Man, I hoped we would have a faire left when this night was over.

Another fireball lit the sky, and then a curtain of black rose like a tidal wave to envelope the northeast section of the faire. How had that little lion moved so fast?

A third ball of flames and another wave of utter darkness hit the jousting area off to the left. He must have been teleporting or something.

"Let's go. Everyone take a different road. If you can hold this person off until I can get there and not destroy anyone, I'd really appreciate it, but I'm not going to hold you to that. Go!"

And off went the three chariots. I nestled my feet more firmly in my high heels, wishing I had something to change into but not willing to take the time to go back to my cottage.

"I'm sticking with you," Finn said. "Dalvon went right with Pheeney, the Wild Hunt went left. Let's take the middle and hope we find this guy first. He has a few answers I'd like to beat out of him."

All I could do was nod and call Figiggly to my side. He was there in an instant but still smaller than I would have expected him to be.

"Wes," I called out.

My head of security under Finn came running around the corner and shuddered to a stop next to me. "Yes?"

"Call the fire department and the police and let them know there is nothing wrong at the faire. We have a permit for fireworks. Just tell them that's what we're doing and make sure they stay away."

"You got it."

He left, and Althea replaced him. "Grayden's not coming, but he just checked and Lexton is right where he's supposed to be. In jail. He had a vicious smile on his face when Grayden went to visit him, but he's not out here. Grayden's keeping an eye on him, just in case."

So if it wasn't Lexy, who the hell was it, and why did I have this sinking feeling in my stomach that I was about to get in way over my head?

I ignored the feeling because I would drown in chaos before I gave up. They'd have to pry this place out of my cold dead hands, and that would be quite the feat, considering I had every intention of not being crossed but haunting them for the rest of their lives. No matter who they were.

"Let's roll." I led the charge straight down the center of the faire from the tavern. We passed the chessboard, the throwing shack, and several stores. Finn grabbed a blade from the sword shop, and Althea took the whip from her hip. Her companion, Grayden's dog Jabbers, trotted along beside her just as Figiggly did with me.

We were coming in to kick some ass, and I wasn't even sure I wanted to take names. Just vengeance, thank you very much.

Another burst of fire appeared before us. This one did not reach into the sky but instead winged out from some hidden corner and illuminated everything within a hundred feet, yet didn't touch any of the buildings. That at least gave me hope that Pix wasn't actually burning anyone or anything with his flamethrowing.

I motioned for Althea to split off to the right and Finn to the left. I took the middle and walked in like I owned the place, because that was pretty much true.

In front of me, Trice was hanging by a rope tied around her waist at the candlemaker's tent. Four figures in black outfits had on fencing masks that looked a lot like the ones I'd just replaced for Helamn and Faelix. They had fencing swords and were slashing at Gargy as he stood in front of Trice with his wings spread wide.

The perpetrators must have had no fear because, honest to Pete's dragon, I would have cowered like a rabbit in a den of wolves with Pix throwing fire, Gargy growling and snarling, and Trice yelling obscenities. And then the Wild Hunt rode up over the top of the candlemaker's roof and sat at the edge of the action. If I saw Dalvon, I was going to have to make a quick judgment about whose side he was really on.

Wading in, I trusted Pix not to catch me on fire or blind me with a wave of darkness. I should have thought better of that last one as the darkness descended. It didn't just cloak this time, though. It felt like it was a deliberate smothering, like a wet blanket thrown over me that I couldn't get out from under no matter how hard I tried.

His roar followed the suffocating black, and the fire shot through the dark to land at my feet. It lit the area like a spotlight, and I found I was not alone. At first, I thought the people were ours, but the moon came out from behind a cloud bank and illuminated faces I'd never seen before.

About ten people—no, make that twelve—stood behind Lexton Cravensham, every one of them with a scowl on their face and some kind of weapon in their hand.

Was this what the horde was here for? The calling of the Wild Hunt? I did not want my faire to be a battleground, but—so help me whoever was listening—if these idiots thought I was going to play nice, they had better gird their loins.

"What do you want?" I asked the gang of people standing in front of me, because really it was a gang and nothing so gentle as a group.

If the Wild Hunt were supposed to help here, why were they still resting on the candlemaker's roof? How did I call them in?

How the hell was Lexton here and also smiling slyly in the jail with Grayden?

"Go on, Malcolm, tell her what you want! Make her beg like your brother told you to!" The Lexy double shoved a boy at me.

The boy couldn't have been more than fifteen, and he almost stumbled at my feet before righting himself, raising a hand in the air, and pointing his spread fingers right at me.

Chapter Ten

TWO THINGS CAUGHT MY attention at once. The first was that Finn was sneaking up and around behind this motley crew of what could only be described as teens. The second was that the look on Malcolm's face was filled with fear and regret. His arm shook as he held it out in front of him, as if the world rested on the back of those stubby fingers and it might crush him at any second.

So I was at a crossroads with a young man who looked like he was going to throw up because of what cruelty was being demanded of him. But I'd been fooled before by faked fear and, with this much at stake, I couldn't risk it.

"Back down now, and I'll call everyone off. We can discuss what has happened. We'll come to a resolution without anyone else getting hurt."

Gargy growled menacingly, and I shot him a look. I had said anyone else because this whole gang of little assholes was at least going to pay for the fire in Trice's house, kidnapping her and Pix, and most definitely carving into Gargy's arm. They weren't going to get away with no repercussions. I was just trying to keep any more to a minimum.

"We're not going to do that, you stupid bitch!" one of the hooligans yelled. Malcolm jumped and something about the way he looked at me reminded me of the kid who'd led me to Dalvon earlier. I peered closer, and sure enough, it was the same kid. The sandy hair, the freckles, the bright green eyes. Why was he addressing me instead of the Lexy double doing the deed himself?

As if in answer to my silent question, the older, dark-haired man walked up behind Malcolm. He had that same smile as Lexton, but his had far more menace. He was a dead ringer for Lexton, but how was that possible?

"I quite frankly am surprised that my dear twin brother wasn't able to win over you." He eyed me from the tips of my high heels to the top of my hair.

Kicking him very much crossed my mind.

"Your brother was weak and a wimpy jerk. Doesn't take much to break one of those."

His eyes narrowed at my words, and he threw his arm out toward me, flinging another one of those slimy things from before to cover my mouth.

I was prepared this time, though. I gathered my will, my strength, and exhaled onto the back of the creature, whatever it was. It collapsed in on itself and fell to the ground. I really hoped it wasn't alive, and that I hadn't just killed it, but there was only so much I could and couldn't do and still save myself and my people.

"Nicely done. Better than last time." He sneered. "Perhaps we should see if the third time is the charm?" He lashed out again. Fig jumped up and snatched the thing out of the air, winging it back from whence it came. It slapped onto the duplicate-Lexton's mouth—and wouldn't you know, the damn little shit couldn't get it to come off.

So sad.

As he fell to the ground, Malcolm lifted his arm again, less shaky this time, with much more determination on his face and only tiny traces of fear.

"You hurt my brother." His fingers crunched in on themselves, almost making a fist. He opened his hand in a flash and a lightning bolt shot out, but it went wide and then bounced off some kind of invisible shield or dome. I'd had no idea anyone had cast anything around us, but that totally explained why the Wild Hunt was stuck on the outside.

The lightning bolt crashed a time or two more, and then it split the air and the invisible dome.

The Wild Hunt crashed in and scooped up the ten other teenagers and the struggling Lexton double. Which left Malcolm and me facing each other. There was a tingle on the back of my neck and a shimmy in my limbs that told me I was face to face with something I might just understand.

And then Dalvon showed up with Pheeney. "Malcolm, what are you doing? Put your hand down. Don't you know who you're facing?"

A single tear leaked out of Malcolm's eye, and he refused to look at Dalvon. "Sorry about this." It was an echo of the note he'd written on Gargy, and my heart went out to him, even as I hardened it against whatever he was going to throw at me next.

But whatever he'd meant to form next fizzled and died in his hand. He scrunched up his face and tried again, but again it fizzled. And I knew for certain that I was standing in the presence of a misfit.

"You know, we like your kind here," I said gently and softly. "This is not a dealbreaker. You could come live among us and learn what your real talent is." Of course, that would be after serving time for kidnapping and endangerment, but it was the only hope I could offer him.

Finn stepped up behind the only remaining member of the group and waited to see what he'd do.

"No!" Malcolm yelled, and from somewhere out of thin air he grabbed a sword and launched himself at me.

I felt the impact in my biceps. I yelled in pain, then stumbled. Finn stumbled in almost a mirror position at the exact same time.

It was only the Wild Hunt and Figiggly who saved me. Fig jumped on Malcolm, causing him to drop the sword, and then the Wild Hunt took the young Malcolm into the night sky.

Holding my arm, I leaned against Figiggly and waited for whatever came next. I was pretty sure I wasn't dying, since blood was only slowly seeping out from under my fingers, not gushing. I was going to be okay. I was certain of that. But what had happened to Finn, and how were we going to explain this to the higher-ups in the paranormal world? To Lexton and Malcolm's parents? And how many more brothers did Lexton have on hand to come after me?

I wasn't sure I wanted to know.

And then, as if strolling along an avenue on a warm sunny day, Finn's mother entered the scene with an umbrella and a smile.

"Oh, Verla, that dress is stunning on you. And you were so brave. I knew I'd be able to count on you to do the right thing, but the Wild Hunt was getting restless, and we thought you might need help this time. I didn't want to intrude, since you've been handling things so well lately. But, well, it was necessary. Though I don't like that you got hurt and by extension so did your poor Voror."

She stroked Finn's head, and he looked up at her with pain in his eyes.

What the hell was a Voror? Was that Finn's power? How did it link to me? And what in the hell was she doing here acting all nonchalant when I had a stab wound and we had just had a bunch of kids taken away by the Wild Hunt?

I passed out before I could get any answers, and I didn't know whether to be pissed or happy that I went away before the reckoning.

I woke in the dim light of my living room. Fig was his normal size and nestled into the couch behind me. My arm smarted as I took a quick mental inventory and tried to remember all that had happened and how I'd even gotten here.

The wall clock chimed three in the morning. The true witching hour. I'd been out for a while. Dammit.

I sat up carefully, knowing that if my arm hurt now, it would only hurt worse if I tried to jostle it around by jumping up and looking for people.

Though I didn't know who I should look for first, or if I even wanted to find anyone right now.

There was a single candle burning in the kitchen, and I heard the low murmur of voices from around my circular table in the center of the floor.

"What do you mean you never told her? I thought that was why you left. That she couldn't understand what she meant to you and wanted to make her own choices. Have you lied to me this whole time?" Finn's mom's voice was low, but I could still hear every word. I got up from the couch and moved quietly toward them, straining to hear the reply.

"It was complicated," Finn said. Something rattled on the table when he smacked it with his open hand. "I was young and stupid, and now I don't know how to go about getting her back. And I think I brought this trouble on myself."

"Yes, dear, I know. You're going to have to make it right."

"And how exactly would he do that?" I asked, coming fully into the kitchen with my bum arm and my sleepy dog.

They both turned to me. Finn kept his eyes downcast. But his mother looked right at me.

"I am one of the three Fates, Verla. I'm the one who sent those ghosts here tonight, and I'm the one from whom you might need help in the future."

One of the three Fates. I wasn't even going to question they were real, but it was weird that I had never known what his mother was. Then again, I didn't even know what *he* was, so I guessed it wasn't as weird as one might think.

"Does this mean I should get the mother-in-law suite ready?" I asked it cheekily because the thought was not a bad one, and if more was coming, I might just need all the help I could get.

She chuckled, but Finn refused to look at me. My hand itched to pull his chin up to make him look in my eyes. I held off. Barely.

"No need for that, dear." Tessa chuckled. "I'll just be around if you need me. I don't know that you will, but there's someone who has a very vested interest in your life—someone other than Finn—who's pulling strings."

"And what is a Voror?" I asked, letting the thought of some puppet master go for the moment.

"A wraith." Finn's gaze remained glued to the table.

"A what? Wait, you were born a wraith? Or you turned into one?" I wasn't sure how they worked.

"Born, sweetheart." Tessa used her palm under his chin to bring Finn's gaze even with hers. "Born to protect you. His soul is connected to yours. His life's mission is to protect and defend you. And he'll never die until you do."

After those words that honestly hit me like a ton of bricks in the gut with every syllable, she got up from the table and walked past me. At the last minute, she turned around and used that same hand to turn my gaze toward her. "Give him some slack, dear. He thought he was doing the right thing. They always do. But he wasn't any more in control of this than you are."

She left and took my dog with her. So it was just me and Finn in the kitchen with a few candles lit and his gaze back on the table like it was the most fascinating thing in the world.

"A Voror?" I asked again.

He nodded.

"You had no choice who you were born to protect, I take it?"

His eyes snapped up at that. "I would have chosen you from a million people. Never doubt that."

"But you left and took my heart with you. How was that protecting me?"

He stuck his elbow on the table. "Just because I wasn't given a choice didn't mean you shouldn't have been given one. There's no rule that says we have to marry the ones we watch over. I should have told you before we even dated."

"And why didn't you?" I gulped because I was having a hard time assimilating all this in my poor little brain,

"Because I didn't want to scare you off. I didn't want to have you leave, either. I made you fall in love with me, and then it ate at me for all those years—I'd taken your choice away. So I divorced you to give you a chance to make your own decision."

My Goddess, my heart was racing so fast in my chest I was afraid it might jump right out of my throat. I swallowed in an effort to keep it where it belonged. "I'm just going to take a second to point out that has to be the stupidest thing you've ever said or done, and you've rocked some doozies. You divorced me and left me to give me a choice but didn't tell me or even ask me what I wanted? That would have been a choice, too. And one I would have preferred."

His mouth opened and closed like one of those electronic fish people loved hanging on the wall years ago. I wasn't going to help him with this one. I had the rest of the night to sit here and watch him gulp air, if that was what it would take for him to find an explanation that didn't make my point.

"Oh, one more thing..." Tessa peeked just her head back into the kitchen. "You're not actually divorced. Finn gave me the papers to file all those years ago, and I seem to have set them on fire instead. Oops. Clumsy spell work!" She smiled, then patted Fig on the head. "Stay here with these two, my sweet poochie. I think they're going to need some help. I'll just go sleep next door."

And she left Finn and me staring at each other with Figiggly's head in my lap. We sat like that for at least fifteen minutes. I didn't know what I wanted to find in his eyes, but he seemed to offer anything and everything I wanted. Kind of like Trice's vision of seeing the entire Universe in Gargy's eyes.

"I'm not even sure where to start," I said, then cleared my throat.

Finn shrugged. "Welcome to my world."

"And what exactly does that world entail?"

He shrugged again. "Just you. Always you."

"And what if I don't want that?" I was very much on the fence here. Yes, I'd loved him, and parts of me still wanted him, but there was so much to wade through here, and I wanted a whole lot more info before I did anything.

"Then I guess I'll need your signature again, since my mom made sure we were still married after all these years." He flicked my salt shaker and looked at me. "Happy anniversary, by the way."

Thank whoever was listening that I was sitting down. Something snapped in the air, and a huge tray of brownies appeared between us. The center floated up and out toward me. One of the four corners made its way to Finn. I snagged two napkins from the holder and winged one over to Finn to put under his brownie.

There was a lot to unpack here, but it might have to wait for another day. A crowd of people were singing outside my door, and then the Wild Hunt burst through into the kitchen.

"The Malcom has been taken care of for you, Verla the Mighty Faeth. You also had many enforcer-type people coming through the gate who took the other hooligans with them in chains. I was told the leader of the group would be sharing a cell with his twin before the night is over. I put in a good word for a dank and moldy dungeon, but they were not sure if they could accommodate my request."

"I'm not sure what to say." I felt like that was about the status of my world right now.

"Say only that you will allow us to come back another night, perhaps when there is more fun to be had?"

He looked so hopeful, I couldn't turn him down. "Of course, you can come back, but some warning would be nice next time. We like to know when guests are coming in."

"Of course and surely, Verla." With that he was gone, but the villagers were still singing songs outside like carolers.

"If we don't go out, they're going to wonder what we're doing in here," Finn said.

"True, but what *are* we doing, Finn?"

"I have no idea, Verla. All I know is I'd like to stick around to find out, if that's okay with you."

I had research to do on his kind, sorting through my feelings, meditating on how to deal with them, and apparently a marriage to either dissolve for real this time or take the initiative to rebuild.

"Consider yourself stuck." I smiled at him and then shoved the brownie into my mouth as I rose from the table. Only time would tell if things would work out. Right now, I had another victory to celebrate with my villagers, and I had to wipe my incident board back to zero.

Tomorrow I'd think about everything, but for this instant I deserved to bask in what we'd accomplished. Trouble might still be there tomorrow, whether I wanted it to be or not.

At least I knew we were strong enough to take it on.

A Dark and Stormy Knight

Chapter One

"BRING IN THE PONY, Verla!" Narcissio Paladin barked at me from the middle of the jousting field. He stood at around seven feet tall and was almost that broad from shoulder to shoulder. I don't know why I had thought he'd look more like Ichabod Crane when we'd spoken on the phone, but I couldn't have been further from the real thing if I'd tried.

Instead, he was more like a tree trunk, and I really hoped he'd be gentle with the beautiful kelpie I was putting in his care. Seawaddle wasn't wild, necessarily, but I had to know this kelpie could follow some basic commands and listen to someone if I needed him to. So far, he had done what I asked him to whenever there was trouble. I just wanted to make sure he could take commands when things weren't completely out of control.

He hadn't done anything wrong, but I'd also kept him in the stables whenever we had visitors, and I felt bad that he couldn't be a part of things. I'd asked our regular horse master, but he'd deferred, so I'd called in Narcissio at my boss's recommendation.

Well, on my mother-in-law's recommendation and with my boss's okay.

Narcissio's corded arms rose in the air like he was about to direct some massive orchestra, and his long thin nose almost quivered as I brought the "pony" to the arena.

Except this wasn't a pony. Seawaddle was a kelpie, a horse from folklore that was made to lure people to their deaths as it rose from the depths of any body of water. They were known for enticing the person to ride them, and then plunging down, back into that water, until the person drowned.

Some said the victim was then transported to the realm of the fair folk, or fairies. There, he or she would be imprisoned to do the horse's bidding until eternity came to an end, which of course meant forever. I had no idea if by doing the horse's bidding it meant that they were supposed to shovel shit and always have carrots in their pockets, but I was very happy not to have to find out.

Because Seawaddle had come to the right place when he'd been created. He hadn't led a single person to their death in all the days he'd been here. To say I was thankful for that would be like saying I was thankful there was such a thing as a corkscrew when I wanted to open one of my favorite bottles of wine. Total understatement.

He was a misfit like the rest of us. A paranormal creature who was designed for one thing, but incapable of doing it, or unwilling to. And we had plenty of people and creatures just like him at our Renaissance Faire.

But since this was the top horse master in all the world of paranormals, I was not going to argue with Narcissio when he said "pony." One just didn't do things like that. Especially when he'd been so intrigued by having the chance to train a kelpie that he hadn't demanded we pay him his usual fee—three virgins and a goat. The price was so archaic I wouldn't have paid it anyway. Not to mention that I wouldn't even know where to find a virgin, and I wasn't going to ask Peggy to give up her goat, Herman. But not having to tell that to Narcissio was another bonus. A gift horse I wasn't going to look in the mouth, if I wanted to get cheeky about it.

I led Seawaddle out to the dirt in the middle of the arena, quietly talking to him with every step. "Now, I promise he's not here to break you. I just thought it would be great if you knew how to perform some stuff when it was asked of you. I hate to see you locked up all weekend every weekend. I know you'd like to be out and about when all the people are here, but we can't do that if I don't know how to talk to you." Which was funny, since I was talking to him now. He probably didn't understand a word I was saying, but perhaps my calm, and my tone, would translate to him better than anything.

I had asked his owner, Trice, if she wanted to help me out here, and she'd told me that after the recent shenanigans she'd gone through she needed a break. For the record, I was more than happy to share the kelpie between us, and Trice was happy enough with that. Seawaddle didn't seem to mind, either.

I just added him to my daily animal to-do list, along with my wonderful Cerberus. Figiggly was an awesome helper who had come to me in the form of a tiny chow with a bushy coat that made him look like a fluffball when he wasn't defending me or the faire.

Speaking of Figiggly, he trotted around and through Seawaddle's legs as we continued our slow progress toward the center of the field. The contrast between the slightly off-white dog and the magnificent black beast on the other side of the halter was something to behold. The horse was enormous, with streamers of black mist floating off his body. Figiggly, on the other hand, was a fluffy menace who could get as big as the horse if he wanted to, but only when there was trouble. Which seemed to be often lately. I had hope that things were settling down now, but I hesitated to count on it.

We finally arrived at the center of the huge arena despite me dragging my feet for the last ten yards. On weekends we used it for jousting and games of prowess. There was caber-tossing and javelin-throwing, rock shotput and horse races. Every weekend we put jesters out in the field to entertain one and all. And then, to finish with a flourish, the ultimate joust ended the day with a few bumps and bangs for the cast and lots of laughs and gasps for the crowd we proudly served throughout the faire season.

But Halloween was coming up in two months, and I had promised a spectacular show. So spectacular, in fact, that we were already sold out for our last Ren Faire weekend of the season. And if we were going to deliver on that promise, I really wanted to be able to show off Seawaddle.

So I'd hired Narcissio and hoped he could do his own brand of magic with the lovely kelpie. As long as he didn't try to break the beautiful beast. I realized that was probably the hundredth time I'd thought or said that and knew I had to let go of the reins if I wanted this beautiful beast to shine. Literally let go of the reins. Literally. Like now. Gah!

Prying my own fingers off the leather strap, I made myself loosen my grip and hold the lead out in my palm. "Here you go. Just be gentle with him."

The man who had a towering reputation with taming and training any number of horses throughout the ages—and I did mean ages, since last I'd heard he had served King Arthur in Avalon back in the day—gave me a gentle smile under his long, quivering nose. "My dear, I haven't been around this long without knowing what I'm doing and what each beast needs. Please don't interfere, but do stick around. I want you to be happy with my services and to be able to continue with the training when I'm gone. It won't happen without me training you also."

Okay then, though I wasn't exactly in the mood to be trained. We'd just come off a big weekend, and Finn's mother was still here. But my ex-mother-in-law at the faire wasn't the end of the world.

Even if she wasn't really my ex just yet since Finn, my should-be-ex-husband, had never made sure the papers were filed to end our marriage. So my current mother-in-law being here was both wonderful and awful. It served to make me more aware of how far astray I'd gone from the woman I thought I'd be when I said "I do" all those years ago with every intention of never taking that back to be replaced with "I just can't."

I startled when Narcissio took the reins from my hand and put his hands on either side of the horse's face. I had to be present right now, not thinking about the past or, heaven forbid, the future.

The trainer locked eyes with the kelpie, and they seemed to be communicating on some plane I would never understand. I'd tried to talk with Figiggly in my mind, as I assumed they were doing, but we still hadn't sorted that out in all the weeks I'd had him. He'd talk to me when he was ready, but I was never able to start the communication. I'd stopped trying, to be honest. Not even Althea, my friend and dog-training helper, had had any quick tips on how to get him to open up to me.

I loved him, though, and would probably start trying again once things had settled down around here for more than two weeks at a time.

My Days Without Incidents board that I'd started about a month ago had not been cleared yet and reset. I should have done so on the day after our last debacle, but I just couldn't bring myself to start for the third time when I was not sure if I'd have to go back to zero. Again.

Narcissio let go of Seawaddle's bridle and his face at the same time. The man raised his hand in the air and the bit came out of the kelpie's mouth, and then the whole contraption sailed through the air to land gently at the trainer's feet. His other hand went out to the side, and Seawaddle pranced in place as if held at a starting gate. The streamers of black mist intensified as the horse raised his head to the sun and neighed.

And then he started out at a stately walk, head high, each foot placed solidly on the ground as if he were taking a stroll down a runway. Narcissio clucked his tongue, waving his hand in the air in a winding motion. Seawaddle dipped his head and then he trotted, picking up the pace just a tad. The trainer snapped his fingers and Seawaddle nodded again, moving smoothly into a canter. He'd made it about halfway around the ring at this point and looked so awesome doing it.

I held my hands in front of my chest as Althea joined me on one side and Glethan Draftsman, our regular horse master, joined me on the other side.

"That's something else, it is," Glethan said. "I couldn't even get him to come out of his damn stall most days."

I bit my lip. "I hope I didn't offend you by bringing Narcissio in."

He slapped me on the back, and as always, he didn't seem to know his strength. For a leprechaun, he was super tough and had a hand like a ham. "Nah, never. I want to see this boy do well, and having him penned up all the time doesn't help anyone, least of all him. But I have to know I can trust him to come when I call, and not jump a fence and take off. Narcissio should be able to do that for us."

I released the breath I'd been holding. The ren faire was a great place to live, and the people who lived here were like family. But that didn't always mean they liked every decision I made as manager of the faire. In fact, they were like most families where people got along the majority of the time but things were never actually perfect. And I liked that very much. Just not on the days where the dissatisfaction was directed at me.

"Okay, well. We're both going to have to learn how to talk to him, then," I said. "Narcissio said he'd be training me right along with Seawaddle, but I think he should train you too."

"Wouldn't miss it," Glethan said before walking over to lean back against the fencing.

I turned to Althea. "Do you think he's being honest? I don't want him to be mad at me." I shoved my hands into my pockets just as Fig came over to sit his fluffy butt on the toe of my boot.

"He's fine. We all want Seawaddle to be able to come and go and not be a danger to himself or others. Just let Glethan be, and don't push too much. Take him at his word."

"Okay." But I still bit my lip some more as I watched Glethan watching Narcissio.

Seawaddle had gone from a canter to a gallop, running full into the wind, the streaming mist coming off him in sheets that looked like fog ghosting behind his muscular body. I stood there in awe and wasn't sure I could have said anything even if I'd tried.

"He's going to create a vortex any moment if you don't get him to slow down."

My shoulders stiffened and my balloon of happiness popped over my head, showering me with something like hard acid rain.

Family. Or what used to be my family.

Finn, my should-be-ex-husband, stood to my left. At some point, Althea had moved to stand closer to where Seawaddle would run right by her. I watched as she trailed her hand through the black mist and giggled.

And I got to stand there and have my ex-husband tell me I wasn't doing something right. Again.

"I'm sure Narcissio has it all under control. He's the best there is, and your uncle was the one who approved him after your mother recommended him," I said. "He's not going to allow a vortex to happen."

Finn laughed and put his hand on the shoulder Glethan had slapped. "I was just kidding with you, but wouldn't that just be the cherry on top of the sundae of what's been happening this summer?"

I did not find it funny, so I didn't even bother to fake-laugh, but he did have a point. However, when I thought about it some more, I realized that our troubles had only really started when Finn had come back, not at the beginning of this summer. The first few weeks of this faire season had been completely uneventful. And then Finn had arrived one night, and we'd ended up with a dead body and hadn't stopped dealing with messes since then.

Peering at him for another moment, I wondered yet again why he'd come back after all these years. His uncle's letter had only said Finn needed a job and asked for him to be put on maintenance and security.

But Finn had previously worked with the paranormal special forces we'd called in a few times for crimes that couldn't always be handled by the regular police.

So why had he left that job? Why was he here? And why now?

If Finn felt me looking him over and trying to figure out what his game was, then he didn't let on. He moved toward the fence to exchange a few words with Althea, and then they both settled in to watch Narcissio lead Seawaddle through a pattern of maneuvers. The kelpie pranced around a barrel placed in the center of the jousting field. He sidestepped his way over to Narcissio, then jumped a few hurdles that had been put out. And then he went back to running.

He picked up speed to the point of being a blur with a hundred-foot trail of black smoke behind him. He flashed out of sight between one stride to the next.

I gaped. Where the hell did my horse just go?

Chapter Two

EVERYONE STOOD STILL FOR about three-point-five seconds, and then chaos reigned supreme. So much for my freaking days without an incident board. At least I didn't have to wipe it clean again, but damn it. People scattered left and right, while others started yelling. A headache pounded at my left temple.

Where had the kelpie gone? Had an actual vortex been formed? One that he'd been sucked into? I didn't think I could handle that. Then again, I wasn't sure I could handle anything additionally out of order, because I'd been through so much lately. I was definitely riding the edge of sanity, and I did not want to fall off the other side.

But thinking like that wouldn't bring my precious kelpie back.

I glanced over at Narcissio and then to Glethan, but neither of them appeared to know what had just happened any more than I did. Awesome.

Looking up, my heart clenched as I took in the way the previously blue sky had turned a shadowy dark gray. We might not yet know what had happened, but I had a distinctly sickened feeling we were about to find out.

From across the field, a series of huge, undulating columns of inky black touched down from the clouds roiling in the previously clear sky. The sinister whirlwinds stalked along on what looked like spider legs striking the ground, one deadly step at a time.

One struck no more than twenty feet away from me and left behind a shade, a shadow that looked like a blob as the inky, dark effect tried to take over my vision. What in the hell was happening? And when was it going to stop? Or was I supposed to stop it?

I felt totally out of my depth until I saw Seawaddle in that blob.

He galloped in my direction, neighing and tossing his head back. He ground to a halt right in front of me, but before I could check to see if he was okay, something rolled off his back and hit the ground with a thud.

As much as I wanted to immediately examine the kelpie, I couldn't ignore the body that had thudded to the ground.

Blank eyes stared up at me, from being stunned or hurt, I had no idea. As I reached down to touch the flesh at the man's neck, Figiggly insinuated himself between me and the person. My dog barked once before shoving his nose into the space between the person's head and shoulder. Was he sniffing for a pulse? Because I'd never seen him do that before, and I didn't want to see him doing it now.

I tried to pull him back, but he growled at me. Probably for the first time ever, my dog growled at me, and I had no idea what to do with that.

Taking a step back seemed a good first move when Fig grew to three times his size and straddled the body with his nose in the man's face and his tail down.

My brain seemed to explode with image after image. A fight with swords, a full-sized dragon, a castle, and a damsel standing in the window with her long blonde hair waving in the breeze. Was I hallucinating Rapunzel at this most inappropriate time? Why?

"Pay attention," Figiggly growled in my mind. Oh, now he wanted to talk? After he'd growled at me?

"To what?" I asked back in mind-speak, not without a little attitudinal edge to it.

"The battle," he said back without a single hint of angst. It was like he hadn't even noticed my sneer.

"I did. We just don't have time for this." The words zinged through my brain and the still image seemed to go into cartoon mode, each image layering on the next and making it flicker like one of those old-time reels of cinematography when color was not a thing.

A knight in tarnished armor faced a man in a robe, a flash of lightning struck the ground between them, and the knight thrust his sword forward as the robed man held up his hands and seemed to deflect the lightning at the knight. The woman in the castle window bowed her head, and the dragon screeched at a decibel that made me clench my teeth. I wished the film were like an old *silent* film.

The knight raised his sword and the lightning bolt flashed back at the robed man, burning his outer garment and leaving him in a heap on the ground in a shirt and trousers…much like the guy on the ground in front of me.

I blinked and shook my head to clear it of the images, then looked down to confirm what I had just realized.

And sure enough, the man who'd been struck by lightning was lying at my feet. But his shirt was now covered in blood, and his eyes were completely blank. Had he sustained the injury while my mind was filled with images? I tried to think back if he'd been covered in blood when he dropped off the kelpie, but I couldn't.

"What the hell is going on?" Finn said, and I was grateful that, at least this once, it wasn't me.

"I think we have another dead body," I said as Figiggly stepped away from the man on the ground, came back to my side, and leaned into my leg. I wasn't sure how I felt about that after the way he'd growled at me and been saucy in my head, but since he was my best friend, I tried to forgive him on the spot. Maybe it had just been nerves. Maybe there was more going on here, and he had had to be blunt in order to get my attention.

We'd go with that, at least for right now.

"Is it a dead body?" I asked Fig out loud. He nodded his puffy head as he sat on my foot and mewled like he was hurting. I wanted to check the corpse for a pulse, but after the way Fig had growled the first time, I wasn't sure if I wanted to try it again.

Finn leaned down to check instead, and Fig didn't move a hair on his little body.

"Oh, yeah, he's dead. But who is he, and where did he come from?" Finn asked, mirroring the very things I was thinking.

Had Seawaddle actually opened a vortex and then come back with a dead guy riding sidesaddle? I admitted to living in a different world where paranormal existed and thrived when normal people didn't realize it, but I'd never had anything like this happen before, so this was strange even for my faire of misfit paranormals.

"Well, what the hell are we supposed to do with this?" I asked. The next question I had was cut off by a scream to my left, over toward the Tavern on the Line.

I glanced at Finn, and he shook his head. "You stay here. I'll go see what's going on."

I wasn't going to be left behind with a corpse, though. I had a feeling this guy wasn't going anywhere, and if the vortex decided to snatch him back, I hoped someone else would find and turn in his killer. Because, for once, I didn't want to be the one to do the sleuthing. "Glethan, please stay with this…man…while we go see what other new freaking crap is going on."

Fig and I ran along the path behind Finn, who only looked back once with a frown on his handsome face. He could make any expression he wanted. I was not going to be ordered around in my own faire. Well, technically, it was his uncle's faire, but that was semantics right now, since I was the one in charge.

Hurtling around the last corner, I came to a dead stop when I almost stumbled across another figure on the ground. What the hell? Were there just random dead people all over the faire? More than anything, I did not want that to be the case. What kind of vortex had it been? One from a graveyard?

I hadn't even had a chance to register what I was seeing before the something jumped up and started brandishing his sword at me. What in the living hell was going on? I needed to come up with a new phrase. I was tired of repeating myself.

"Back, you foul beast. What is the meaning of this displacement? Where is the dragon?" With his armor clanking and his visor down, I had no idea what I was dealing with other than that he sounded male and was about my height. The rest was a mystery. Was he the guy from the Fig image collection cartoon?

Those questions were ones I couldn't answer, and honestly I wasn't sure I wanted to tell him anything I did actually know and certainly not with the way he was swinging the sword. And who was he to call me a foul beast? I might not have spent thirty minutes on my curls this morning, but "beast" was a little strong.

"Uh, I'm going to need you to calm down for a minute here so we can figure out what happened." I hoped the words would be enough, and I wouldn't have to ask one of the other guys nearby to tackle the knight, or whatever he was.

The knight clanked around in his chainmail and breastplate, then lifted his conical hat and tipped it slightly back to squint his eyes at me. He had a rugged face with a shadow of a beard. He looked a little older than I would have expected, but he did look human. That was something, at least.

But he didn't swing again, so I was going to take that as a good sign. The first one in the last few minutes.

At this point, I'd take anything I could get.

"Who are you and what have you done with the foul beast?"

He could insult me if he wanted to, and I wouldn't like it, but it wouldn't be the end of the world. No way was he going to do the same to my horse. I really hoped he was not talking about Seawaddle, because we'd have to exchange words if he was going to be mean to my kelpie.

"What foul beast?" I shook my head. "You know what, that is not nearly as important as finding out where the heck you came from and how you got here."

"Show me the dragon, you wretched woman!" And then he did swing the sword. I was not quick enough to avoid it, but he'd aimed high so he merely whisked the hat off my head instead of taking my head from my neck.

I wanted to be thankful for that, but instead I was infuriated. Unfortunately, I had no weapon to defend myself, so I stamped my foot and aimed my hand at his chest. I called whatever energy I could around me and released it on him. The flick worked, maybe a little too well, since it sent him spinning off to the left. He didn't drop his sword, though, dammit, and came back up, ready to go another round.

Maybe the metal of his suit of armor had dulled some of my magic. I still didn't know how everything worked in the world of magic regarding my abilities, and if this guy was from another dimension or time, then it could be that my magic wouldn't work the same way on him.

With a quick turn, he clanked and metal rang as he crashed down a path, shoving Finn out of his way as he made a mad dash toward the Tavern on the Line. For just a second I thought about running after him. But I knew I'd never be able to catch up with him, even though he was weighed down by pound after pound of metal and I only had on a corset and skirt. Not to mention the boots that might be made for walking, but definitely not for running.

Digging my phone out of my pocket, I quickly left a message for Zane, who ran the tavern, and hotfooted it in the direction of the errant knight. My faithful companion, Figiggly, trotted along next to me. He hadn't yet grown any bigger like he did when the guy fell off the kelpie out of nowhere. So I wasn't too worried about things, more confused and concerned as to what was going on. Although, with everything that had happened in the last month or so, I couldn't say I was surprised.

I glanced behind me when Tessa Taragon called out my name. Finn's mom didn't look a day older than she had when Finn and I walked down the aisle strewn with rose petals. Excuse me, when we'd first gotten married, since we were still married.

Yeah, I was trying not to think about that, but it wasn't working. It sat at the back of my mind almost every second of every day. Of course, it didn't help that Finn had the cottage next to mine and frequently seemed to be outside right when I stepped onto my back deck. He hadn't brought up the subject of our continued marriage either, and so it just sat there like a big huge...

Dragon!

Holy Moley! I had my mind set on getting to the tavern and had been thinking so hard I wasn't paying attention when I almost walked into a huge—as in enormous—dragon crouching behind the building that housed the torture museum.

The beast had thick black scales that glistened in the sun starting to peek back out from behind the dark clouds. Yellow eyes were slitted in the dragon's massive face, and they narrowed further when he caught sight of me and my entourage. A burst of flame shot out of his mouth, flying right over our heads.

I glanced over at Fig, and he still hadn't grown. Why not? I got that the knight might not have been a big enough threat for my dog to triple or quadruple his size, but a huge dragon shooting fire at us felt like it might be worth a couple of grumbles and at least growing into a mid-sized dog.

But nothing happened. Fig just sat there with his blue tongue lolling out and a grin on his furry face.

"What is so damn funny?" I asked him as the dragon shot out another burst of flames. This one struck the roof of the torture museum, making my heart stop for a second. But then nothing happened. The roof stayed intact and didn't even smolder. Fig sat on the toe of my boot, wagging his bushy tail over the hem of my skirt.

Another burst of flame, this one aimed at me. At the last second, I cowered even though I'd just seen that the fire didn't touch what it was aimed at.

But instead of being burned as I shook, nothing happened. Fig didn't even flinch as we were engulfed in a nearly transparent orange bubble. There was no heat, no burn, nothing other than a slight breeze that ruffled my bangs and a sweet smell of... bubblegum? I was not going to say the dang words again for anything! No hell would be mentioned. But I was afraid we might be in for a bit of trouble.

Chapter Three

THE KNIGHT CAME CAREENING around the corner of the building with a high-pitched scream that sounded like a knife on metal in my head. I put my hands over my ears and tried to process all the things that were and weren't happening when Finn came dashing over from the forge with a sword in hand.

The dragon blew another shot of fire to engulf him in his tracks, but he just continued rushing the thing. The knight chose that moment to step in front of Finn. When their swords engaged, the knight's folded over like one of those balloon swords Jasper the Jester made for fairegoers.

I wasn't going to ask about hell again, but man did I want to.

Finn took a step back just as the knight did the same.

"What have you done to my steel, woman?" the knight demanded. He tried to drive that very steel into the ground, but it bounced up from the force and smacked him in the face. He did not look amused, but I giggled. I couldn't seem to help myself.

"Are you ready to talk now? It seems your weapons don't work here. I think we might all be better off if you stop trying to fight and instead tell us where you're from and how you got here." I felt like a host on a game show, asking him to introduce himself.

He huffed, and the dragon did the same. They eyed each other as if they were mortal enemies but didn't try to engage, with us or with each other.

I was glancing back and forth between the two, trying to figure out what to say first and who to say it to. It was obvious they had expected their fire and sword, respectively, to do damage. The fact that they weren't was baffling to everyone.

The dragon was the first to break eye contact with the knight. It lowered its head, and a fat teardrop hit the ground at its feet. And then another and another. A tiny creek formed under those sobbing eyes, and I wasn't sure what to do next. How do you console something that's about four hundred times your size and previously bent on destroying you?

"Stop your caterwauling." The knight stumped back and forth in front of the dragon. "You are the reason for this travesty."

This particular travesty? Or the one back wherever they came from? I didn't get a chance to ask because the dragon belched another ball of flame and then curled into a ball on the ground. It barely fit between the stalls people used during the weekends.

"I thought I was free," it sobbed. "For once I wanted to be free and go to see my mother, maybe my kids, perhaps even a cousin or two. I thought this was the answer to all my prayers, and yet, once again, it's not, and I'm the bad man. Always the bad man. That's me. No one ever wants to know why I'm here. I'll tell you—it's not to keep anyone in, I'll have you know. I'm Merlissa the Magnificent, and I can't do a damn thing to save myself."

Okay, so no more using "it." She was obviously in emotional pain, and I wanted to help her, but how do you help a dragon? Especially one who was sobbing and curled up on herself like she'd just been fatally injured by a bubble balloon sword?

As surreptitiously as I possibly could, I took my phone out of my pocket and shot off a quick text to Barnaby, one of our two blacksmiths at the faire. I didn't need the misfit centaur for this one, but a fellow dragon, even if he couldn't shift beyond his tail, was someone I really hoped could help.

Putting the phone back in my pocket just as stealthily, I moved to stand next to Finn, who still had his sword up and ready for battle.

"I think you can put that down now, Finn. We seem to have some issues that aren't going to be solved with violence."

He gave me the side-eye and harrumphed, but I kept eye contact with him and waited for him to lower the steel. It took him a few seconds to actually drop the tip to the ground, but I waited him out.

"Better," I said. "And I appreciate your willingness to do bodily harm, but I think we're dealing with something totally different here."

"What do you want me to do? Just stand here until the dragon cries herself out? I can't imagine she wants an audience."

I doubted she did either, but I wasn't leaving the knight with her. And I certainly wasn't going to leave two complete strangers in my faire alone when I had no idea what they were capable of. No matter who they were, what they weren't able to do, or how they'd gotten here. I felt bad enough leaving the dead body back at the jousting ring, but I had faith Glethan wouldn't ignore my orders and would keep watch until we could figure out what was going on here.

"Okay, so now that we're in our corners..." I let that fade off as Barnaby came galloping around the edge of the building.

He skidded to a stop a few feet from the dragon and stared in what I could only interpret as awe. As if afraid to touch glowing iron because of the heat, the man who manned the forge very slowly extended his hand toward those black scales glinting in the sun. He hesitated about an inch from actually making contact as the dragon lifted her head to stare at him.

"What is this sorcery?" the dragon growled. "How do you look as a man but smell as a dragon?" She whipped her head around to stick her snout into Barnaby's palm. Taking in a heaving breath, I stood frozen, hoping against hope she wasn't going to open that massive jaw and crunch down on him.

Instead, she sniffed again and again, her eyes getting narrower and narrower. For Barnaby's part, he stood completely still and looked like he'd just seen the eighth Wonder of the Ancient World. Finally he nodded, and she backed off.

"Where do you come from?" he asked. "How are you here?"

She blew a zerbert at him and turned her head away. "I have no idea how I am here. I was going to ask the same question. And yet, I don't really care because at least I'm no longer where I was." She whipped her head around to rest her gaze on the knight. "A place where this cretin would have killed me, or at least tried to, without knowing the first thing about what he's doing. Jackass."

The knight sputtered as he drew his useless sword again, but Barnaby got in his face and shoved him in the chest. The sound his armor made as he fell to the ground resembled a newly divorced and angry person in the breaking-objects booth.

No one stepped forward to help him up, since we were pretty much all completely transfixed by the dragon.

"See? See what I mean? He doesn't even try to talk to me, just comes bearing down with that pathetic piece of steel and starts hacking. One of them got me years ago, and I've never completely recuperated, not that anyone has asked."

She swung her tail around to the front for us to see and, sure enough, the tip was gone.

I felt for her, I really did, but I had to ask. "What do you know about a dead man? Dark hair, blue velvety shirt, brown pants?" It was all I could remember of the dead body that I really hoped was still back at the jousting area.

Or maybe I didn't hope that. Maybe I hoped that wherever he'd come from had reached out and reclaimed him so someone else could worry about who had done him wrong. Also, I had no idea if the underworld connected to all worlds, or if each world had its own so it wasn't possible to cross him to the other side after death. I didn't want his soul to get stuck here if he belonged somewhere else.

The dragon shook her massive head and took a tree branch to the eyebrow. It didn't seem to faze her, though. "No, I haven't killed anyone in my whole life."

"Lies!" the knight said from the ground, still on his back like a turtle who'd been flipped over. "Lies, I tell you! It is known throughout the land that you are a killer!" He rocked back and forth trying to get traction to flip over, but it just wasn't happening.

I finally looked at Finn with his lowered sword. "Help him?"

Finn narrowed his eyes at me but went to help anyway. Figiggly joined him, using his nose to nudge the guy over to his side, where he promptly fell flat on his stomach with some more clanging.

I did everything I could not to let my snort of laughter escape. For once, I could proudly say I was successful, but the dragon was not trying at all. She laughed and more smoke came out of her nostrils. That too smelled like bubble gum. So very strange.

"How do so many die where you live if you are not the killer?" the knight finally asked, once he'd righted himself and taken his helmet completely off to tuck under his arm.

The dragon made a strangling noise, and then dropped her head.

"See, you cannot defend yourself because you can't lie!" the knight crowed. "It is as the legend foretells. And all legends are true!"

I was getting very tired of this idiot and his exclamations.

Turning to him, I looked him and his dinged and tarnished armor up and down. He had dirty blonde hair that might have actually been dirty, or that was just the color. His brown eyes were narrowed, and his chin tipped up with his nose so high in the air he might have drowned had it been raining.

I had always been one for the underdog against jerks like this who thought they knew everything, so

I guess this time I was going to be rooting for the underdragon.

"I think before we get any deeper into the insults and the tongue-tied issues, we should get something to eat while we try to sort things out. We need to get you back to wherever you came from and then you can finish things up back there." And maybe I wouldn't change my Days Without Incident board since this was all actually from a different place, and perhaps time, and I could very well make it seem like it didn't count here.

I did not wait for anyone to agree with me, or even check to see if they were following me. Then again, I didn't really have to, since I could hear the knight jingling, and Finn was grumbling, and Barnaby was talking in a low voice to the dragon.

I chose the wider roads in the faire to lead them over to the concession stands and called ahead to have Bob, the genie without a bottle, start some hot dogs. Nothing else would be done as quickly or with less mess, and Bob was here, whereas I had just remembered that Zane had gone out to some underground caverns a few towns over.

When we reached the hot dog hut, Bob was already there with his condiments out on the bar and a smile on his face. That smile faded a little as fear crept into his eyes when he caught sight of the huge dragon.

"It's okay," I assured him, even though I knew no such thing. "We're just here for a snack to keep our minds sharp for a problem we need to solve."

"Uh, okay. I'm not sure if I made enough hot dogs to feed a dragon, though..." He trailed off and then gulped and swiped a napkin across his sweat-beaded forehead.

"Barnaby, I'm assuming, because of her reaction to you smelling like a dragon but looking like a man, that she's not able to change. Can you take her to the mudman pit, so she can rest away from this idiot who's trying to kill her, and verify?" He nodded, and he and the dragon left.

Since I wasn't sure if all breeds and classes of dragons had the same powers or understandings, I figured I could leave it up to him to get the skinny, while I tried to get the knight to unbend long enough to sit down at the wooden picnic table.

I waved a hand to the seat across from me. "You can sit. We need to have a civilized conversation. No more threats, and no more yelling, and no more exclamation points. Just talking, for the moment."

He cocked an eyebrow at me, one that was much lighter than his hair, so I was thinking he was in serious need of a shower to be his normal golden-boy self. I wasn't going to offer him one, or anything else other than the food, so it didn't matter. Well, the food and the seat, but he'd better be ready to give me some seriously helpful information. All while I stayed upwind from him. Just in case.

"I will stand. I do not need to talk with you. I must complete my task. Only then can I be on my way."

"Hold on a second." I put my hand up like that would actually stop him. But it did at least make him pause in the act of turning to leave. "Where are you going to go, and how are you going to get there? You came through some kind of vortex, I think, or at least the dead guy came through the vortex on the back of my kelpie, and then fell into the dirt almost at my feet. Next, we saw the dragon and heard you, and all hell broke loose. Of course not literally, because that was a disaster the first time, but figuratively, and that's not a whole lot better."

"A vortex, you say?" He inched closer to the table. He was definitely listening. It was more than I had hoped for on our first verbal sally. I really thought it would take more. I had wondered how I was going to come up with more, but this was working just fine. As long as I kept him talking and moving toward the wooden bench.

"At least that's what we think it was. The kelpie, which is a horse, in case they don't have them where you come from, was running laps in the jousting arena. He went so fast he disappeared, but when he flashed back, he had something on his back. That something rolled off and turned out to be a dead man."

"There was no way to save him? Was he burned?" he asked, finally standing with his knees firm up against the bench. Now if I could only get him to actually sit down.

"I didn't see the reason for his demise, but his heart wasn't beating anymore, and I am pretty sure it should have been beating. Your place does have hearts, right? And they beat?"

"Where precisely do you think I come from?" he asked, not answering my question. I narrowed my eyes at him, but let it pass because maybe this was the conversation we needed to have more than the one I was directing.

"Another world? I honestly have no idea. You don't speak in a way that completely convinces me you're from a time long ago and time-traveled here. However, you also seem to have a creature I've never seen so incredibly large before."

"I heard that!" the dragon called from the other side of the hot dog hut. "I am not incredibly large! I'm magnificently large, and that means something back in Avalon."

"Avalon?" I repeated and then gulped. "As in King Arthur and the knights of the round table with swords in stones and the whole shebang?"

"I do not know of the shebang," the knight answered. "But yes, we are from Avalon. As far as the time period, I cannot tell you when it is since I have no reference point. Time can be very fluid in Avalon." He finally sat across from me. I snatched my own hand back from reaching out to touch him.

Down, girl.

But come on! Avalon! This was so awesome! And weird!

And now I was the one using way too many exclamation points. Perhaps it was contagious.

I cleared my throat before taking in a deep breath. "Okay, let's start over again. You live in Avalon, the realm of King Arthur. You're not sure of what year it was when you came here, and you're trying to kill a dragon to do what?"

"To save a princess. Isn't that always the task, Reginald?" Narcissio said from behind me.

Chapter Four

I DREW IN ANOTHER breath when Reginald fell off the bench and cowered inside his armor as if Narcissio was holding a hammer of the gods and was about to strike him blind or something.

"Is the body still at the jousting ring?" I asked. Probably not the best question to start with, but it was pretty important to me, all the same.

"No, I've had Glethan take the body into the horse barn and place it in one of the stalls until we could take care of it more appropriately. I came to find you, once that was taken care of, to see what else might have come through the portal the pony created." He hovered, all seven feet of him seeming to arch over the knight on the ground, even as he talked to me. "And so I find Reginald. Interesting."

"Okay, look, I know it's semantics, but that is not a 'pony,' it's a kelpie, and I have an idea of what came through, but I didn't know it was a portal," I said.

"I thought it was a vortex," Finn piped up.

I was grateful he'd mention it. While I didn't need a bunch of hands in this mess of a stew, knowing I wasn't alone helped. Fig was quiet, too, though I did wish he'd tell me if he knew anything.

"No," Narcissio answered, finally turning away from the cowering knight. "A vortex is entirely different and not so easily created. Seawaddle was able to create a portal, though, and that's something we'll want to address in the training."

Training was the last thing on my mind right now. "Hold on a second, because I think first we need to address how to reopen the portal." Because we definitely needed to return all the people—and especially the dragon—back to their own time and place.

"We should be able to open the portal without much issue," Narcissio said. "The direction and time might be something we'll have to estimate. Since I know Reginald from my time in Avalon, I have a good idea of when that might be. I don't think Reginald will be missed much if I'm off by a year or two, will you, Reginald?" He stood over the poor knight again and actually growled at him. "Who were you trying to kill this time, and how much money were you promised?"

Part of me wanted to save poor Reginald, but then my mind replayed that scene Fig had sent to me with the overlaid images, and it made more sense now. Reginald had been the one to lift his sword and aim the lightning back at the wizard guy, who was probably the corpse Narcissio had Glethan move into the barn. Well, at least that was one mystery I didn't have to solve. And since it hadn't happened at the faire, I was not changing my board...

I coughed and cleared my throat, but it wasn't until Finn put a hand on the other man's arm that

Narcissio finally unhulked and stepped back from the shaking tin can.

"Now hold on, Narcissio, because Reginald was defending himself. There was a wizard and lightning, and Reginald simply deflected it back to the man who'd sent it." I wasn't sure if I was saying that to Finn or Narcissio, but I let them both be the recipient. That way I didn't have to repeat myself. Hopefully the explanation was enough to get him to work on how to reopen the portal and away from scaring Reginald. I was not a fan of the fact that the knight had killed someone, but at least I was pretty certain it was only to protect himself. I wanted to focus on what the heck needed to be done to get my world back in order. Not having to change my Incident Board would be a pure bonus.

We'd see how that worked out, if at all.

"So how do we open the portal again?" I asked, biding my time since we were still waiting on the hot dogs to be finished. Narcissio walked around everyone, pacing himself with measured steps and looking up every five to ten seconds to take in the scene before him.

Finally, he stopped. "We will need to go to the jousting field and have Seawaddle perform the same steps as before. Reginald can carry the body back with him, as the corpse should not be left here. And since he is the one who killed the man, he can take responsibility."

"I did not kill him!" Reginald stood from his crouch with a cacophony of jingling and jangling. "He was trying to kill me. He is a wizard, there to enchant the damsel and steal the dragon preventing her escape."

"Dragon?" Narcissio once again stood over the knight, but this time the knight did not back down.

"Yes, dragon. The damsel has been trapped for years. No one has been able even to reach her to rescue her."

"And I'm sure the reward is substantial," Narcissio said in a low voice.

"As it should be. The dragon is fierce and has killed many men." Reginald tried to cross his arms over his chest, but that armor was not letting him keep any of his dignity. He finally settled on balling his fists at his sides.

"By dragon, do you mean someone like the blacksmith here at the faire? A shifter that can change between man and dragon?"

The fiendish light in Narcissio's eyes scared me a little. Okay, well, maybe more than a little—let's try a lot. And I was extremely happy I'd asked Barnaby to take her to the washer women's station next to the mud pit instead of having her stand near the knight who wanted to kill her. And now the man who looked like he just wanted to get his hands on her.

To train her? Own her? Kill her?

I had no idea and, quite frankly, I was not going to ask.

Narcissio whipped back around to me. "Did you see this dragon? Is it here? What does it look like?"

"Um..." I couldn't think of a way out of answering his question, which I felt might be in my best interest with the way his eyes were fiendish. And I still needed him to train my kelpie, so I was honest. Kind of.

"She does appear to be a real dragon and not a shifter. I don't know much else about her, since I couldn't understand her. That's why I had to bring Barnaby in."

Finn opened his mouth. I shot him a look that meant death to any who talked.

He was the one who cleared his throat this time. Good boy.

Narcissio, though, didn't appear to be buying my story. He squinted his eyes and hunched over me again where I sat at the wooden picnic table. Seeing him out in the field with Seawaddle was one thing. Having him this close made him look far less like a powerful horse master and far more like a villain in a slasher movie. His nostrils flared and his nose quivered. He clasped his hands behind his back and stalked away. I breathed a small sigh I hoped no one heard, then gasped when he jerked back around and seemed to transport from where he was about ten feet away to right up in my business.

"If this dragon is black and a female, then she should be able to talk, and I will need to see her immediately."

"I, uh, can probably arrange that." I swallowed the rest of my words because he leaned in until we were almost literally eyeball to eyeball.

"There is no 'probably' in this case, Ms. Faeth. I will see the dragon, and if I must find her on my own, then you will not enjoy the consequences of the search."

"Hey, now." Finn somehow managed to contort himself between the big guy and myself. Of course, that put my nose in his back and his rear end almost in my lap, but I didn't mind so much in this instance.

Narcissio straightened and backed away a few steps.

"Better, but I'd like it even more if you were another three feet back," Finn said. "Let's try that, and see if it makes me less ready to punch you in that quivering nose."

My hero. Not that I really needed one, but I knew when to be thankful and when to fight my own battles. This was definitely not the latter.

Although I didn't quite know why Figiggly seemed so complacent in this whole thing. I glanced down to find him asleep on the ground under the table. So much for a familiar that was a guard dog.

"Okay, now, why is it so important that you see this dragon?" Finn asked before I could.

I breathed better without his backside in my lap and peered around him to get a reading on Narcissio as he contemplated the question. I didn't know why it was such a hard one to answer that it took pacing back and forth again. A simple explanation as to why he'd looked like he was possessed by a demon would have sufficed.

I folded my hands in my lap, glanced over at the knight, and was taken aback by the sheer terror on the man's face. What was he so afraid of? But when I looked in the direction of his gaze, I didn't have to actually ask the question out loud.

Somehow, Figiggly had not only woken up and gotten out from under the table without me noticing, he had also grown about ten times his size and was currently nose to nose with Narcissio, who looked like he wished the ground would open up and swallow him whole.

"Fig."

The dog growled at the man and did not take his eyes off him. What was it with people and animals not listening to me today?

"Figiggly Faeth, what is going on? What happened?" I looked at Reginald, who only seemed to want to shrink in even further on himself, and Narcissio, who appeared to finally have met his match.

"Stay out of this, Verla," he said in my head. *Now* he decided to talk to me. Well, wasn't that nice?

"What is going on?" I said the words out loud again because I was not playing the mind games when we had so much to deal with.

He growled again and looked like he was not going to answer me. We'd see about that.

I rose from the table. He kept growling but did back off this time. He came to stand next to me before I threw my leg over the bench to get out. Which left me in that awkward place where the bench bit into the back of my legs and my stomach hit the table itself. Ow.

But even though he had listened to me with the first instructions, he was not budging this time. Fortunately, I didn't need him to. We'd leave it at that.

I sat back down like that was what I wanted to do, but I did put my hand through Fig's collar and let him know mentally that we were not done with this. I had no idea if he'd heard me, but at least I'd said it.

So now what to do with this situation?

"Narcissio, I'm going to ask you to go back to the jousting field and oversee the body that came through the portal." When he choked and opened his mouth, I held my hand up. At least he paid attention to this command even if it didn't come out of my mouth. "Please don't argue with me. I want you to make sure that nothing happens to the dead man. I will bring the dragon with me to you when we're done eating. I need more information before we proceed." It pained me to even think the next part, but it had to be said, which felt worse. "If you don't do as I ask, then I'll have to have you escorted out of the faire. And I'll find someone else to train Seawaddle."

His mouth snapped closed as he turned on his heel without telling me what he was planning to do. Since he was heading in the right direction, which was in the opposite direction from the dragon, I felt that, at least for now, things would be as I wanted them to be.

"Hot dogs are ready," Bob said with a smile on his face as he came out of his hut. He glanced around like he didn't understand why no one was running at his announcement and wasn't sure what was going on.

He wasn't alone. I had no idea either.

Chapter Five

THE DRAGON WALKED ALONGSIDE Barnaby as they returned from their stint at the washer women's area. They were talking like old chums, and I could only hope Barnaby had gotten some information out of the beast to help me figure out what in the world was going on.

The knight had chosen to put chili on his hot dog after he'd looked at the food like he wasn't sure what to do with it. Bob had helped him pick out the topping and had assured him it was delicious.

As the knight took his first bite, I waited for him to wince or choke, but since he didn't immediately spit it out, I turned away, figuring he was fine while I handled other things.

Which left me with this big huge beast that I didn't know what to do with or what Narcissio wanted with her. What was I going to do if I couldn't get them back to their own world? It was a big enough issue having a black horse streaming black mist around the faire, and at least the gargoyle now knew how to change into a man, and the Pixiu was rarely seen and so little it wasn't that hard to hide him.

But a dragon the size of a house—and that couldn't turn into a woman—was not going to be easy to hide, no matter what I did. Not to mention I didn't have a building big enough to hide her unless I tried stuffing her into the winery.

The dead body I could handle, and the knight I could force into assimilating into our culture, if I had to, but the dragon was a no-go.

With that in mind, I let everyone eat, picking up my own hot dog with just ketchup, hoping against hope that something brilliant would come to me.

After a few minutes filled with people devouring hot dogs, I decided to engage the knight again. He was going to get sick if he ate any more chili, and I needed more information.

"Tell me about this quest you're on," I said to the knight. Of course, my timing was far from perfect, as he had just stuffed the last bit of dog into his mouth and was trying to answer me while he chewed.

"Finish it first, and then we'll talk." I handed down the last of my bun to Fig, who had resumed his regular size after Narcissio left. I'd sent Finn after the man to make sure he didn't deviate from the path I'd put him on in order to go look for the dragon on his own. I expected Finn back any moment.

Bob handed the knight a paper napkin. He looked at it like he wasn't sure what to do with it, so I used my own to wipe my mouth, and he followed suit.

After patting his belly and thanking Bob, he turned back to me. "There is a princess in a castle. She has been taken prisoner by this dragon, and I must save her. My kingdom and those around us depend on her safe return."

The dragon snorted but didn't say anything as she shoved another three hot dogs into her mouth. Hopefully, she'd be full soon, because Bob might be running out of hot dogs, at this point.

"Ignore her and finish your story. Why is the princess so important to all the land?"

He harrumphed, then turned his back on the dragon to address me and only me. "She is the fairest in the land and a jewel in the crown of Avalon. It has been several years since she was taken from her bedchamber, and she must be returned."

"Don't forget the reward and the accolades," the dragon snidely put in.

"Reward?" I asked with a raised eyebrow.

"Well..." He shrugged. "A small stipend for bringing her safely home is not too much to expect after the perils of fighting this beast." He hooked a thumb over his shoulder and shrugged again.

The dragon growled, but Barnaby spoke to her in low tones, perhaps telling her not to talk. I said something anyway.

"Speak up if you have something to say." I aimed my comment at the dragon, but she just looked away and munched a few more hot dogs.

"She can't," Barnaby answered for her.

"Can't or won't, Barnaby?"

He shrugged. "I'm not sure, and she hasn't been able to answer me, either. Any question I ask makes her throat close up."

"Finn, what are we going to do?" I turned to find him staring at the knight and then looking at the dragon and then back to the knight.

"Do you know anyone who has been killed by the dragon? Are there bodies slumped on the tower with bite marks or half eaten?" he asked the knight.

I was just as interested in his answer, so I turned back to find him red in the face and clearing his throat. Interesting...

"It's a simple question," I added. "Surely, there's a body or two flung around on the way to the castle. Some bones? A carcass or seven?"

The dragon spat out a burst of bubble-gum-scented flames that never even touched the knight—just sailed right over his head.

He turned away and looked out over the food court, like something big was happening that I just couldn't see. "I did not come across any, but I wasn't there long before I was dragged into your world. That man in your jousting area is dead because he was in my way. Perhaps we should go find out why he tried to kill me, and that will tell you what you need to know."

Sounded good to me. Bob had just come out and tipped an empty serving dish to show me the hot dogs were all gone. I was going to have to put in an extra order and maybe explain to Morty, the owner of the faire and Finn's uncle, why we had gone through so many hot dogs by midweek. So far, I'd been moderately successful at downplaying what had been happening at the faire since his nephew had come here with a smile and a dog, but this one I might not be able to gloss over so easily. Especially if I couldn't figure out how to send these two back to Avalon...

Time to think on that later. Right now, I needed to know why the dragon kept snorting at the knight's answers but wouldn't defend herself, and her hesitation to explain why she wouldn't have killed the knight.

To do that, I had to go back to Narcissio, the dead guy, and the jousting ring. And take all these people with me. It wasn't my best day, but it wasn't my worst either, so I guessed I'd take it.

"All right, enough eating and talking, for now. Let's go to the corpse and get you all back to your time and place. I need to ask a few questions of your mom, Finn, if you wouldn't mind getting her. As one of the Fates, I'm hoping she might be able to help me with the portal."

"I don't think I should leave you alone with all this," he said.

I patted him on the cheek with a smile. "I appreciate your concern, but I promise I can handle myself, and look at the dog you brought me... He's his cuddly, cute little self, so the danger must not be that bad or he'd be huge like he was before." I shouldn't have said that last part because a scowl marred Finn's face instantly.

"That's what I mean. You might be safe now, but we should tread lightly with a guy who trains beasts and is who-knows-how-old."

"Who *is* the old man?" the dragon snapped. She towered over me, moving far faster than I would have thought possible for something so freaking big.

"He's a trainer. His name is Narcissio," Finn answered before I could stop him.

And with that she dropped to the ground. Her rear end flattened a table and her legs stuck out to tangle in the ropes of the mock ship-front of the beer garden. Big fat tears rolled down her cheeks as she dropped her head into her front paws. I could have sworn the noise of her wailing reached the center of Philadelphia, over seventy miles away.

I snapped my attention to Barnaby and watched as he tried to comfort the obviously distraught dragon. But was it because she feared Narcissio, or not?

I had a feeling it was time to find out. I could have asked her, but I was pretty sure I'd get better answers if I put her right in front of Narcissio and watched the two of them. And the only way we were going to be able to do that was to go find him and make him talk.

It would have been nice to feel more confident I could do that, but maybe if I couldn't, then Tessa could. It was certainly worth a try.

We trooped along the path to the jousting field in a sort of ragged line. I had the knight go first and then Barnaby before the dragon. Then there was me and Fig, pulling up the end like a caboose on a train of doom.

Wasn't that a great thought?

I sighed when the field came in view. Maybe now we could get all the pieces to fit together and find some answers, or at least get some clarity. And then hopefully we could get these two back to where they came from, along with the dead guy. If the dragon and the knight fought it out to the death once they returned to their place and time, that would no longer be an issue of mine.

As soon as I had the thought, I felt sick to my stomach. The knight might be dark and stormy, and the dragon hard to make talk, but both of them had value, and I would hate for either of them to kill or maim the other. Crap! I despised when I was put in such situations.

Not that I'd often had to save a dragon from a knight, or a knight from a dragon. At least not in a way that was anything more than a parlor trick at the faire.

I dropped back a few seconds, and Fig stayed with me. "Can we talk?" I asked.

He looked up at me with his puppy-dog eyes and his lolling tongue, and I thought he was just going to keep trotting along on his little legs. But then he tipped his head to the side. "What do you want to talk about?" he thought at me—I didn't know another word for the talking that went on in our heads, so we'd call it what it was.

"Should we keep walking?" I asked.

"Sure. I can walk and talk at the same time. What do you need?"

"I don't think we have time for what I actually need, but I do want to ask if you think the dragon or the knight is the villain in this story."

Fig growled low in his throat in a way I had never heard him do before.

"Was that a laugh?" I asked.

"You're far smarter than people give you credit for. Yes, it was. I don't think either is the villain. I feel like there's something more going on here that we just haven't seen yet. It might take talking to the dead man to truly know what happened and who is to blame. I have no doubt you're up to it. We just need to get them to spill all their secrets. You're good at that, at least."

"Thank you?" I was pretty sure that was a compliment. Maybe a little backhanded with the "at least," but still a compliment. But why did he sound so much more mature than he had been just a few months ago when he'd come to me as a puppy?

"Sure thing, doll. Now let's go see what's happening at the jousting ring and go from there."

Doll? When did we move from interacting as dog-mom and dog-child with him sounding like a little kid to him acting like he was the one in charge and calling me *doll*? We'd have to talk about that. If we had time, it would happen now. But he'd already trotted on ahead on those little legs, so I couldn't ask him. I did walk a little faster to catch up with him, which put us at the fence at the same exact time.

We joined Finn, who was looking around as if he had lost something. The knight and the dragon were also there, but that was it. I didn't see Finn's mom, Seawaddle, or Narcissio, and my stomach dropped. Had something happened?

"Where are they?" I asked the question as calmly as I possibly could. I did *not* want to get riled without reason. It was hard enough to settle down when I was riled *with* reason. No sense in working myself into a lather before I knew what we were dealing with.

The bright sky darkened again, and those damn columns of darkness started stalking across it. This time, though, they were joined by streaks of huge lightning. The legs of incandescent light struck the ground again and again but left no marks. Who was doing this, and how? Or was it the portal? Either way, it was definitely the last thing I wanted to see.

Chapter Six

MY BREATH CAUGHT IN my throat as the lightning stalked closer and closer. We all ran in different directions to get out of its way, but it split into a series of bolts and followed each of us like we had bull's-eyes on our rear ends.

Fig was by my side, growing with each step. This must really be something awful if he was going to be enormous for whatever was coming our way.

I sure could have used better breathing during my run, but between the lightning, the fright, and these freaking shoes, it wasn't going so well. Lightning struck next to me, and I started to zig and zag. If Fig had been smaller, I would have scooped him up and run with him. As it was, I could probably ride him like a horse with how hulking he was getting. Yikes.

Finally I made it to the stage in the jousting ring and the only shelter I could think of. Sliding under the draped skirt attached to the wood, I hoped against all else a bolt wouldn't light the stage on fire. Had I just pulled a hysterical-horror-movie-girl thing by hiding here? I was stuck, so it didn't really matter now.

What did matter was that Fig had not joined me, but there was someone else breathing heavily under here with me.

"Who are you?" I whispered into the dark, like the lightning could hear me. Something sizzled above my head. Maybe I was ruling things out much too fast.

"It's Tessa, sweetheart. I ran as soon as I saw the lightning. I'm not as young as I used to be or as athletic. Phew." Something started to glow softly and then brighten in increments until I could see her face. She held a ball of light in her hand. Within seconds of seeing it, I remembered I could probably do the same thing.

Stretching my hand out, I started to pull the energy, but she stopped me.

"I'm not as easily detected as you are. Let me take care of it."

A yell sounded outside and then a groan. Finn, oh my gods, I'd left him out there along with the knight, the dragon, Fig, and everyone else. So much for being the heroine of my own story.

"We have to go get Finn." I frantically tried to pull the skirt aside so I could scramble out.

Tessa's non-lit hand clamped down on my arm. "He'll be fine as long as you're safe."

"What? No. I am not going to leave him out there with this freak storm and just hope he might be okay because he doesn't have to worry about me running around. That's ridiculous."

That hand clamped down harder, and I suddenly felt very sleepy.

"Stay."

"I'm not a..." I blinked and then had trouble reopening my eyes. "Not a dog."

"I'm aware of that. But you're also not a Voror like Finn. And as a Voror he cannot be killed as long as you live. Stay put here, please. We'll be able to fight off whatever is out there without you being in harm's way."

Except that Fig could be hurt too. I was not going to just cower here, letting everyone else be in danger. Maybe Finn wouldn't die, but he couldn't fight alone. And I was more than capable of keeping myself safe.

I waited for her to leave, keeping my hands folded in my lap. When I was sure she was gone, I tugged on the skirt at the end of the stage. It refused to move.

"Shit!" I said it out loud even though I was only talking to myself.

"Do you mean shite, my beautiful lady? Foul language from such a beautiful mouth is far more attractive than I had been led to believe."

My head whipped around faster than that girl on *The Exorcist*. And when my eyes adjusted to the near darkness, I realized I was face to face with the ghost of the guy I'd seen dead earlier on the field. The one from a different time or dimension. Actually, I was pretty sure it was both.

"Oh, uh, well..." Super beautiful words, that was me.

"I did not mean to tongue-tie you. I would bask in your beauty if you would allow me the privilege."

"Well, see, I'm a married woman, so I don't think that's a good idea." Hey, I was still technically married. He didn't need to know the details. His frown prompted me to hustle through the next part. "And I really need to get out to the jousting area.

There's lightning across the sky, and my friends and family are going to get hurt."

I wrestled with the skirt again, but the damn thing still wouldn't move.

"Perhaps I can be of assistance." He floated through the curtain, leaving just his well-formed rear end and legs sticking out as he hung horizontal in midair. I would not look. I. Would. Not.

"Perhaps you are married, but it seems to me that you are not against continuing to view the menu items you cannot eat..."

This was so bizarre. It was like mixing old language with new concepts, or at least newer ones. Did they even have menus back in the day? I didn't know and didn't have the time to ask. So I skipped right to the important part. "Can you get me out?"

"I believe so." He zipped all the way through the skirt and within seconds I saw the first glimmer of natural light as he tugged a piece of the skirt free from the platform. He pulled again and more light shone through. But then, without any warning, he was speared by a bolt of lightning. He sank to the ground, then into it.

I did everything I could to hold back the scream boiling in my throat. I needed to get out of here and see what I could do. There was no way that was a random shot. If it could decimate a ghost, what could it do to a real person? Voror or not, just because Finn couldn't die didn't mean he wouldn't be hurt or maimed. Plus, that was the magic of this world. And if the lightning was from the other world, then there were no guarantees. As I'd thought earlier, perhaps the rules were different in the land of Avalon. I wasn't willing to take the risk.

"I need you." I sent the thought out to Fig and hoped that for once he'd hear me without him having to be the one opening the line of communication. I knew he did when his barking got sharper and moved closer. Thank the good Goddess. Now, we were in business.

As quickly as my tangled skirts and boots would allow me, I yanked the rest of the skirt off the wood and hustled out from under the platform. Tessa's magic was strong, but the ghost had proven stronger before he died, thank goodness.

Taking a deep breath, I strode out into the field. Whatever the hell was going on I was not going to cower and wait for whatever happened next.

I was going to be the thing that happened next, dammit.

No one tried to take over my faire like this and got away with it.

Despite my big-thinking talk, I hesitated before creating a ball of energy around myself once I'd reached the center of the jousting ring. I saw no one around me and, though the sky still roiled with thunderclouds and lightning, no flashes came down to the earth again. I wondered where Finn and his mom and Barnaby and the dragon were, but that was all I could do—wonder—because I had a battle to fight and a faire to save.

Pulling energy to me from everywhere nearby, I did my best to encompass both myself and Fig, who had just trotted up from the left. At least I wasn't completely alone now.

The bubble was closing when a shot of lightning hit Fig in the tail and singed his hair. Now, I was pissed. No one hurt my dog.

"Whoever the hell you are, get yourself in my sight right the hell now!" I screamed it to the heavens, and I'd do it again if they didn't immediately follow my directions.

The bubble of energy swirled around me like a self-feeding fountain. Replenishing and falling to the ground, it was a constantly moving thing, transparent but still sparkling with all the colors of the rainbow. This one was different than any I had created before, for some reason.

But when a woman strutted out from the barn, holding Narcissio with a whip around his neck and dragging Seawaddle behind her by his bridle, I no longer had time to wonder about the difference.

"You called?" she said in a smoky voice. Her eyebrow was cocked over one eye, and the smirk on her face made me want to do something completely unethical to wipe it off.

Who was this? And what did she want with my little faire in the middle of Pennsylvania? There wasn't anything special here. We were a faire of paranormal misfits, yes, but we'd been here for years without a single weird occurrence. And now, with so many things happening one after another, I wasn't sure what had changed to make us a place where all the nasties should converge.

"What do you want with us? Why are you here?" I demanded. Her stunning face went as stormy as the sky. I probably could have started out more evenly—at least not so shouty—but quite frankly, I was not in the mood to soothe my way into anything at the moment.

"Is that how you welcome all visitors to your pathetic little faire? I wonder why anyone comes back." She eyed me up and down.

I scoffed at her. "You are most definitely not a visitor we want here, and I'm pretty sure you didn't pay for admission at the gate. That makes you an intruder. I want you out. Now."

"Tsk, tsk. That's not how things work, my darling Verla." She sneered my name, sending a chill up my spine. What did she know, and how much did she know? And how did she know it from a different world and time?

I let my breath hitch in my chest for just a second, and then strengthened my resolve. Fig started growing by my side, expanding to the point where I had to push out the circumference of the bubble or have him exposed.

"Fig, I can only hold this for so long and at a certain mass."

"I'll go out and rip her apart," he responded in my mind.

"No." There was something about having him do that kind of violence that felt so incredibly wrong. Like it would change his being and his purpose. I just couldn't let him do it.

"Verla, she is a threat and must be handled. Let me out. I will tear her to shreds." He turned his head to look at me as he thought the words, and there was a fire in his eyes that made me shiver in dread.

"No. We take her together, and we do this the way we have before. No shredding!" What the heck was wrong with him? How had he gone from my floofy little dog with a sweet disposition but the ability to be a big dog when necessary, to wanting to shred things? He'd never even shredded a sock in my house, much less a person at the faire. We were going to have to talk about this, but obviously not now. Now, we needed to take care of some unwanted business in the form of a dark-haired woman and her evil tendencies.

"Nothing more to say? You call me out only to stand and stare at me from your bubble of protection? How very mundane of you, my dear. I was told you were a little more lethal than that." She jerked both hands down and forced Narcissio to his knees and Seawaddle to bow next to her.

For his part, Narcissio looked ready to spit nails at the woman's audacity, but my poor Seawaddle just looked at me with fear and anxiety in his eyes.

This woman was going to pay.

But how?

"Let me go, Verla." Fig again but I was ignoring him.

"And what is your name?" I asked the woman. Her hair had started floating out around her like she had her own personal windstorm going on near her head. The brilliant vermillion dress that fit up top like a second skin and then flowed down from the empire waist was something I'd seen on many a historical romance novel. Honestly, it was beautiful, but not on someone so icky.

That wasn't entirely true, since she was actually lovely, but I was giving her no fashion points when she'd come to destroy my home and my livelihood. Or had she?

"I am called many names." She laughed gaily but with an edge of venom.

"One will do. And while you're at it, if you could just let me know why you're here, that'd be great too."

"I'll do both. My name is Helena to most, and I'm here to take you and your faire into my possession. There are things in my future I do not want to bear, and so I've decided to change addresses. This looks like as good a place to land as any. When the portal opened, I just stepped right through in an effort to start over. But to start over I have to have a place, and I want yours."

What in the world?

"Well, you can't have mine, and it's not mine to give away, even if I wanted to."

"I don't need your permission, Verla Faeth. I know more about you than you think, and I know what you can do. But I also know what you can't do. That will be your downfall after everything is said and done."

What was she talking about? How did she know about me from another dimension?

I didn't have time to ask, as the dark and stormy knight, Reginald, came running after the dragon, who was flying low to the ground. Her scales glinted in the overcast sky as she settled next to the beautiful woman and blew out a burst of fire at the knight. Was this the princess he'd been trying to save? The one who was supposedly being held captive by the dragon?

But when the dragon settled, Helena reached out a hand to her and the dragon flinched like she'd been scalded with boiling water. She took a step to the right, just a small one, but she was jerked back by an unseen hand.

The knight bowed before the wretched woman to the left, staying out of the dragon's reach.

"Beautiful Helena, I am here to save you. I will be your knight in shining armor."

She looked him up and down with that same snide expression on her face. "I highly doubt that's considered shining armor, and you're pathetic. I don't want you or your help. I want your death, actually."

And another bolt of lightning shot from the sky to spear into the top of Reginald's helmet. Chinks in his armor began billowing smoke as he toppled over into the grass.

"What in the hell is wrong with you?" I screamed at the top of my lungs. She'd just killed someone right in front of me. I was working hard not to hyperventilate. I couldn't even focus enough to do anything but yell.

"Nothing, dear girl. I've told you there are things coming up soon in my life I do not wish to be a part of, one of them being marriage and being consigned to the depths of the world of the dead. I've holed myself up in a castle for years and chained this dragon to me in order to keep anyone who was coming to get me away. But my father is getting trickier with his methods, and when I saw the horse creating a portal, I was not going to miss my chance to get out from under the underworld, as the saying goes."

"Wait. What?"

She had the absolute audacity to roll her eyes at me. "Shall I break it down into smaller bite-sized chunks for you? I am a princess, and my father has arranged a marriage where I would become a daughter of the underworld. I'd have to do all that nasty stuff with the River Styx, and probably knit atrocious afghans for the residents of the dastardly place, and cook dinner every night over the fires of the damned. I won't do it. I won't. Instead, I will live here and become you. I've lived in that tower for years while stupid suitors have tried to rescue the damsel in distress. They should have been trying to rescue the dragon I made stand guard while I killed them all."

Holy crap!

Narcissio opened his mouth, but she jerked on the whip, and he choked. Without thinking, I reached a hand out to save him and ended up with some magical backlash. My hand broke through the barrier I'd made, and that was the thing Fig had been waiting for, obviously. He dashed out from inside the broken energy field and ran at the woman and her two captives like his tail was on fire—which, thankfully, it was not anymore.

We were standing half the field away from each other, but with every bound Fig blurred and was a whole lot closer to her than if he'd just been running normally. What the heck was that?

She threw a bolt of lightning at him from her hand, and he dodged it, thankfully. But he got struck by the next one. He fell to the ground and started shrinking. Was he going to get sucked into the ground like the ghost?

Feeling like I was going to puke and rage at the same time, I ran for him. I took much longer since I didn't have the blurring speed advantage, but I still made it there in record time. I curved myself over his tiny body and waited to feel him breathe, move, talk to me in my head...something. Anything. But there was nothing.

The keening wail that burst from my mouth shook the very heavens. I cried and cried, sure that my heart was disintegrating in my chest and leaking from my eyes. My Fig, my precious Figiggly, was gone, and someone was going to pay dearly for this.

"You heinous bitch," I growled, rising and bracing myself for something I'd never done before.

Purposely striking out, not to protect myself or others, not to de-escalate the chaos around me, not to save anyone. I was going to strike out to kill, and I would have no mercy or regret.

"Verla, I need you to do exactly as I say," someone whispered in my ear as I raised my hand to see if I could bring my own lightning bolt of agonizing death.

I tried to move my head to see who was there, but I was forced to keep looking forward at the horrible woman who was smirking at me.

"Do not fight me, please. You know I would do anything to save you, and you know I love you, so I need you to trust me."

"Divorce papers?" I mumbled out of the side of my mouth. It was Finn's mom standing behind me. I'd be able to place that voice almost anywhere if it had been a normal situation.

"Okay, so I didn't file them when I told you I would. I'm sorry, but I knew for certain you two belonged together if you could each just get out of your own way. But this is different. And if you can't trust me, then at least you can know for certain that I've always tried to do what's best for you." She was whispering quickly, and no wonder, since the woman across the way was looking at me like she was waiting for something. And if I didn't do it quickly, she would strike out at me, and I had no new defense set up.

"Okay," I finally conceded.

"Clench your hand at your side," she said.

I did as she said.

"Now raise your arm straight out and keep your fist closed."

Did that too.

"Open your hand and concentrate all your hate and anger and sadness into that one spot in the entire universe. Pull everything you are and were and will be into that one small area, and unleash it."

I tried, I really did, but when I tried to think of past, present, and future, everything got jumbled in my head. I squinched my eyes closed as image after image raced through my head—Finn and I on our wedding day, the little picnics he used to bring me just because, interviewing for my job at the faire with his uncle Morty, managing this place and shaping it into something I loved, the day Finn came back towing an adorable little fluffball of love with him, me figuring out murders with the help of my friends, and trying so hard to bring justice to those who were harmed recently.

And so I lost the moment and the force of my will. I must have opened my hand too soon, because nothing happened. And because nothing happened, the woman at the end of the field took the opportunity to not only laugh at me but to send out another bolt of lightning aimed right for me.

Chapter Seven

I WAS NOT FAST enough to outmaneuver a lightning bolt, but Finn was fast enough to jump in front of me and catch it right in his upper arm. He went down and took me with him.

What was it with these freaking Taragons? First his mom telling me to do as she says, then her son diving right into the fray.

And where was his mom? Nowhere I could see as I let my gaze roam over the field. It was just me and Finn and my poor dog resting on his side in the grass, not moving. I couldn't help it. I sobbed some more. My Fig. My little Figiggly. The one who was at my side almost constantly. The one who'd let me cry in his fur when things weren't going so well. The one who made me laugh and protected me. My unexpected gift that had turned into a lifeline.

And he was gone because of the dark-haired freak from a different time and place.

I would not let Finn die too.

"I know you can't die until I do, Finn, but I need you to let me take care of this. Your mom is around here somewhere, and I do trust that she can do things I can't, but this one is mine."

He was smart enough to just nod at me and stand up. He held a hand to his injured arm.

"Are you going to be okay?" I asked.

"It's just a flesh wound," he said. "I'll take care of it."

His mom, on the other hand, whispered in my ear again. "I still have things I can do, Verla. You can take her down if you want, but I can help make that possible."

I whipped around, because I had not seen her that close. And I still didn't see her, no matter where I looked.

"I've cloaked myself, dear. The Fates have the ability to do that. Comes in handy when searching out certain situations that need more attention than the loom."

Okay then. Finn's mom was able to go invisible. That was good to know, but a little weird. Hopefully she never tried to sneak around when I was singing off key in the kitchen.

"Do whatever you want. Just leave her for me." I started walking toward Helena and that smirk fell off her face. I wasn't sure if I was a threat or if Tessa was doing something I couldn't see, but I was coming for her, and I didn't care about anything else. Especially with my dog dead.

I stopped the tears that wanted to flow by bringing forth my anger to reign over every other emotion.

The walk seemed to take forever. I looked down at the ground for a moment and realized that was because the field was moving like a backward conveyor belt. Every step I took was the same step, over and over again. I never got any closer.

Who in the world was doing this now? I tried jumping to the side and running, but neither seemed to put me any closer.

The smirk might have fallen off Helena's face, but she began to laugh at me, and for some reason that was worse than the smirk.

The laughter seemed to make her forget herself for a moment, though, and Narcissio was quick to take advantage of her inattention to him. He jerked his head away from her and sent the end of the whip sailing through the air and out of her hand.

"No!" she yelled, even as he grabbed her arm and threw her over Seawaddle's back. He nudged the kelpie forward, and Seawaddle took the hint, but the dragon started moving, too. It didn't look as if she wanted to move but was more dragged. Was she attached to the woman with invisible bonds? I was tired of not being able to see anything.

"Refocus your energy, Verla." Tessa said from somewhere near me. "You can see into the magic around you if you refocus your lens. *Think* your way into this."

I had never been good at thinking my way through anything. I tended to make snap decisions and go with them, trusting my gut. Sometimes it worked, and sometimes it was a disaster, but it had kept me alive and partially thriving for all these years. Even most of the magic I'd done up until now had been more about going with my gut than actually trying to direct things to the way I wanted them.

So how was I going to refocus a lens I'd never known was there?

I thought of Fig again and wished he was here to help me. But he wasn't. No one could do this for me.

I was going to have to come to terms with that and fast.

I closed my eyes for a moment, taking a breath and letting it out. When I opened my eyes again, I saw a glimmer of something. The dragon was pulling against the direction Narcissio was trying to go on the kelpie. There was a struggle going on, as both were strong not only in magic, but in physical ability.

But I saw nothing magical about it.

I shut my eyes again and concentrated. No one was going to hurt me right now, and I needed this time. Just a few heartbeats to get myself together. I took them and thought of seeing magic, of seeing the way energies swirled through the air. Of the way each person was a part of the bigger whole, yet an entity all their own. How they connected, and how the magic of the universe trailed through the earth in the ley lines.

I paused the lives of every single person on the planet for just a minute to give myself a breather. It was something I'd been working on with the old crone, and though I'd hoped it would work this time, I hadn't been sure. But it did, and for that I was grateful.

This time when I opened my eyes it was like being in a wonderland of color. All the everyday colors faded to a black-and-white background to be overcome by the swirls and patterns and shades of magic. There were ropes from some things to other things. There were threads tying flowers together, a web that spread over the faire like a shelter, roadways of energy traveling on the ground to intersect at the Tavern on the Line. Very aptly named, since about seventeen of those roads all connected right up the hill.

I was absolutely fascinated. I wanted to run and touch everything, feel the way the magic ran through my fingers, because I had a feeling it would be like passing your hand through a waterfall, one of energy instead of liquid.

But then my eyes moved to where my beautiful dog curled in a fluffy ball on the grass. Since he was already off-white, his color didn't change much except that his blue tongue, where the sigil of protection was, the one he used to find out if things were safe by licking them, was a dark gray, and there was no more magic in him. It spread around him in a pool like blood and made me choke on the tears I had been trying to fight back.

My poor Figiggly. Not even a year in my care and look at what I'd done. I hadn't protected him. I hadn't been able to keep him. I hadn't been able to even keep a dog around long enough to fully experience that kind of love in my life.

I was never going to be enough.

The magic was beautiful, and the designs and patterns were lovely, but I'd give it all up in a hot second to have my Fig back. All of it.

I almost sat down and cried right there. Forgot about everything else going on and just laid my head down because what was the point when everything I loved and valued always left me.

Almost but not quite, as I heard Narcissio calling me from far away. And then Tessa joined me and sat next to me on the ground. I didn't know how she was able to evade my stopping of time, but I was more grateful than I could say to not be alone in this moment.

"If you can't see the light, then I'll sit with you in the dark," she said.

"Isn't that a meme from the internet?" I asked without looking up.

"Someone might have taken that and made it one, but in the world of the goddess, and as a Fate, I will tell you we totally thought of it first." She bumped shoulders with me, almost knocking me over onto my side. Instead, I hit a firm barrier and looked up to find Finn seated on the ground on my other side. He was gray too, but coloring didn't matter when it came to the man I loved. Still. Dammit!

"You're far more powerful than I ever thought possible, and most likely I'm only around to hold you up every once in a while, instead of being your soul protector." He too bumped my shoulder, and then held my hand in this space out of time.

I looked to my right, but Tessa had moved through the jousting arena to stand over Fig and then she bent down and picked him up to cradle him in her arms.

And Finn and I sat there for a minute. I'd stopped time to give myself space while I worked through how to do what needed to be done. Somehow, Finn had been able to step through my magic and bring his own.

I needed to do what was necessary, what needed to be done. I breathed easier knowing I had help.

What needed to be done was that I untether the dragon from the princess and keep Narcissio from taking them to the depths of some creek or stream. My kelpie had not killed anyone as of yet, and I was not going to have him used for that purpose if that was what Narcissio thought he was going to do.

It might not damage the kelpie to perform the task that many in his line were built for, but I wasn't going to allow that to be done to him against his will.

Finn stood and dragged me up with him. He wrapped his one good arm around me from behind, then rested his chin on the top of my head.

"What do you see?" he asked. "I just see everything stopped in motion. I have a feeling it's more for you."

"I see all the ley lines leading to the Tavern, and the way the dragon is roped to that princess. I see nothing within my Fig." I gulped back a sob. "I see a gossamer-like thread between you and your mom. I see tiny tendrils of magic touching flowers and the earth. I see Seawaddle has a tie to me, but it's a loose thread, not tight and constraining like the one between Helena and the dragon."

"What about us?"

I had so hoped he wouldn't ask, but now that he had, I couldn't evade answering him, and I wasn't going to lie. "There's a kind of three-strand braid between my heart and yours." When he sighed, I wished I had left that last part off.

"That's what I thought." He gave me a quick squeeze, but I had no idea what it meant. "So now how do we fix all this?"

"I'm going to need some scissors or a knife to cut that dragon-and-Helena tie. I have to get Narcissio to let the woman go and figure out what to do with her instead."

"That's a lot of only you doing things. Any room in there for help?"

I was never so glad we weren't facing each other. I didn't want to disappoint him, but it was easier to say no when I wasn't looking in his eyes. "I think I have to do this by myself. I think I have to do a lot of things myself, and instead of constantly wishing that wasn't true, maybe I need to just concede that that's my way of life and accept it, even celebrate it, instead of always trying to fight it, or change it." I stepped out of his embrace swiftly so he couldn't try to keep me in one place.

He didn't even hesitate to unclasp his hands around my waist and let me go. It was better this way, anyway.

"Can you go to your mother and help her? See if there's anything that can be done for Fig? I know it's not a big thing to do when there are so many other things, but it would mean the world to me, and I trust you to take care of him. And I want to thank you for bringing him to me, if only for the short time I was able to feel like he belonged to me." Finn nodded, and I wondered if I was only talking about the dog, or about Finn too.

Either way, I couldn't concentrate on that right now. Any second, I would lose the ability to keep time from moving forward, and the world would resume its normal frantic pace. I had to work out what I was going to do and how I was going to do it before that happened.

I said a quick prayer and raised my hand.

Only to have it covered and have myself turned to face what looked like a mirror but was actually a woman. Who looked just like me but in different clothes…

Chapter Eight

WHO WAS THIS PERSON and what was she doing here? I could feel her solid hand touching my hand, so I knew I wasn't hallucinating her. Her eyes were the same color as mine, and where everyone else was gray, she was as colorful as I was. Fully technicolor.

"Who..." I cleared my throat and tried again. "Who are you?"

"I'm here to help, Verla. I brought the scissors you need." Her voice was even eerily similar to mine, or at least the one I always laughed at when I heard myself on a recording.

"I...the scissors?" I gulped.

"Yes, the ones to cut the magical ties. You can sever any connection you want with these scissors."

"Where did you find them?" It was probably a stupid question, but I had nothing else to say as my eyes kept roving over a face that was so much like the one in the mirror but only on good days. She had my skin. The hair was a tad more styled and managed; the dress code was definitely more trendy-mall-girl than I had ever been, but she was like an upscale version of me.

Who the hell was she? Did I have a doppelgänger? Was the next princess of the underworld messing with me? Their magic was different, and even though she was still slung over Seawaddle's saddle, that didn't mean she wasn't capable of doing things with her mind.

I tried to step back, but the woman held on to my hands and smiled at me. A nice smile, one with no malice in it. And when I looked down at our joined hands, I saw the tether between us. It was tattered and torn, like a skein of yarn that had frayed and was coming close to snapping, but it was there, and I didn't know what to make of it.

She used a hand to tip my chin back up so we were looking eye to eye. "I'll answer whatever questions you have as soon as we right things. I promise not to leave until we talk, but right now, we need to get the world back on its axis correctly, or far more will go wrong in this world. We can't have that." She smiled gently at me, and I was pretty sure I gave her a paler version of it myself.

"Okay. But I have a lot of questions."

"As do I, but first we need to take care of things here. Now, where shall we start? Here are the scissors."

The metal of the scissors was cool and seemed to come with the thought that these were a very powerful object and not to be placed into the wrong hands. And I wasn't the wrong hands, for once.

Taking a breath in through my nose, I blew it out my mouth and tried to think my way through what the order of things should be. I didn't have all day, and could see Finn and his mom holding Fig between them. Both had stopped moving and were now part of the time stop I'd put on everyone. It was only this other woman and me moving in the world.

"What's your name?" I asked without turning toward her.

"Charlotte, but my friends and family call me Lottie."

"Okay, Charlotte—"

"Lottie. Please call me Lottie."

"But..."

"Please."

"Okay, Lottie." I cleared my throat. "I think, first things first, we need to cut the ties from the big, bad girl to the dragon, and then get her off the horse, and take her from Narcissio."

"Why not just let him take her to drown her?" Lottie asked, and I was about to go back to Charlotte, if she really didn't understand the implications of forcing the kelpie to do the one thing he had not yet done and become a killer when he wasn't before.

Not to mention, I still didn't know what happened to the people they drowned. Would he be tied to her forever? I couldn't do that.

"Do I really have to explain that to you?" I asked, peering at her to see if she was playing with me.

"No." She looked me in the eye with a gaze I'd seen numerous times in my own mirror. It unnerved me. "You don't want him to become something he's not just to serve a purpose that isn't his own."

Fine, we'd leave it at Lottie, then. It wasn't exactly how I would have put it, but it was close enough, and I could appreciate that. "So what do we do now, and how am I supposed to use these shears?"

"They can cut any tether you want. Any rope, or chain, or thread, can be severed with these things, and it won't come back. Take them, and do what you think is necessary."

She had presented them to me handle first, so I turned them around so my fingers were wrapped around the handles. They weren't big, and if they were normal scissors, then they probably would have been okay for cutting paper but not much else. I turned them over and over in my hands as I thought about what to cut. So many possibilities, but only one certainty. Did I only cut the tie between the dragon and Helena? Or did I use them fully and also cut the tie between Finn and myself? Would he die without it, or finally be able to live his own life without having it so inextricably tangled with mine? What must it be like to know that your life absolutely depended on someone else's? Never knowing if some freak accident would kill you, even if you weren't involved in it?

But then I remembered all those movies and television shows where a simple conversation would have solved a problem. Where someone thought they should take over all by themselves without asking for input from the person it would also affect. I shuddered. I didn't want to take away his choice a second time. Unknowingly taking it the first time or having the Fates do that for him, was enough. However, I might bargain for another use of the scissors if he wanted out.

And that left me with the tie between the dragon and Helena. I stepped forward and opened the scissors. The woman who looked just like me was next to me, waiting anxiously to see what I'd do. I could feel the emotion rolling off her and glanced over to find that a swirl of green magic was wrapping itself around her heart and floating in the air toward me. What did that mean? By using her scissors would we then be anchored to one another?

I stopped right before I would have closed the scissors on the rope between Helena and the dragon. "What are the consequences of using these?"

Her head snapped up and she zeroed in on me. She'd been so intent on watching me cutting the tie that I took her by surprise. "I don't know," she blurted out.

"Wait. What? How do you not know? Are you the owner of these? Did you steal them from someone else? How do we even know this is going to work?" I dropped the shears to my side but not to the ground. They got warmer in my hand, to the point where I almost wished I had a glove on. But I didn't drop them. I held them at my side, hoping they wouldn't burn my skirt.

"I'm not sure what they'll do. I know what they do when I use them, but I don't think another unfated hand has ever held them."

Well, what the freaking hell was I supposed to do with that, then? "I can't..."

Her eyes narrowed. "There's no need to concern yourself. Just use them and get this over with. You can't hold time forever. In fact, I'm not even sure how you're holding time now. But it will catch back up with you. You want to be done before everyone goes back into motion. Now cut the ties that bind you, and get this done."

There was no malevolence in her eyes, no malice that I could see, but I still didn't like not knowing what would happen. However, she was right that time would not keep holding. I could feel little movements on the periphery of my hold. If I didn't let it go soon, I would be exhausted and no good to anyone.

So far, my gut and my instinct had led me in the right direction. But I'd also had Fig with me through it all, and I didn't have that backup or protector anymore.

Did it matter, then, what happened? I would at least have saved the dragon, and I'd deal with the woman on my own.

I opened the shears back up. Placing them around the rope, I snapped them closed and cut the tie between the dragon and Helena—and the whole world exploded into chaos.

Chapter Nine

TIME ZOOMED FORWARD, EVERYONE moving in fast-forward while I stayed in slow motion. Helena broke Narcissio's grip, falling to the ground but getting back on her feet in a flash. The dragon turned on Helena and hit her with a burst of fire that blackened everything about her, from her hair to her dress to her face. Soot rained down around the woman, but she didn't burn. Was that because of her powers? Or because I'd changed the rules of magic here when I'd used the shears?

No matter what the situation, I stepped back for a second and looked around at my people. Finn was flat on the ground, Tessa hovering over him. Fig was still curled into a ball, his eyes closed and my broken heart next to him. Narcissio remained atop Seawaddle. He grabbed the blackened woman and slung her across the saddle.

With the burst of time, he was already out of my reach and heading toward the creek before I blinked.

Dammit! I should have thought of that before doing anything.

I ran after them as fast as I could, but I knew without a doubt I would not be able to get to them before he plunged the trio into the depths of the water.

"Use your tie!" the woman next to me said. She was keeping pace with me, even though it looked like she'd probably be able to run a lot faster than I could.

"Help me! Save him!"

"I can't," she said, bowing her head and stopping her pursuit.

I ran past her because I wasn't giving up for anything. I concentrated on the tie between myself and Seawaddle. I couldn't see the magic as clearly now with the normal light of life and time back in play, but they were still there. I hoped they'd be there for me to follow the ley lines another time, but for now this was the only tie I needed to concentrate on.

I put my hand on it as it spun out from my heart to the broad chest of the kelpie. Running and holding onto the tie was going to be difficult, but I'd done worse. I gripped it in my hand and called out to the horse, hoping that, unlike with Fig, I would be able to communicate first.

"Seawaddle, stop. Turn around and come back. Buck Narcissio and the woman if you have to, but get back here."

At first there was nothing, and I was thankful I'd kept running. If I didn't save him or couldn't get there fast enough, maybe I'd at least be able to tell myself I'd tried my best and hadn't given up.

But then I felt a tingle in my hand, a subtle shift in energy. It grew stronger, traveling back and forth like the cartridge in a printer. Maybe that wasn't the best analogy, but it was all I had.

I put the call out again, and the surge got stronger. I started gaining ground. I could see Narcissio and the kelpie up ahead, standing at the edge of the creek. Seawaddle was as stiff as a cardboard cutout even as Narcissio was kicking him in the side to step into the water.

"No!" I yelled, sprinting the last few yards. I grabbed the lead on Seawaddle's bridle and jerked it out of Narcissio's hand and over the kelpie's head. "No, you will not do this to him."

Narcissio jerked his gaze to me, a ferocious scowl on his face. "Let go now. I know this woman, and she cannot remain here. She cannot be let loose. She needs to be removed. She is a menace and a destroyer of everything around her. I have first-hand knowledge of the destruction she's capable of. Long ago, she was promised to me in marriage, and she not only balked at the betrothal but was angered enough when I did not want to marry her that she took my true love and turned her into the black dragon."

I swallowed hard because, while the story hit me in the heart for him, I was still going to stop him, no matter what I had to do.

Narcissio continued without taking a breath. "The kelpie is made for this work. Do not stop me." Being that he was seven feet tall, and a huge man on top of just being tall, I was not completely surprised when he jerked the reins back. I was, however, surprised that I didn't let go, nor did I fly over into the creek with the force of his pull. I stood my ground.

I wasn't going to question how that happened. Maybe later, but now I had things to do.

"I will stop you. You're not going to turn him into a killer when he's not been one before now. I won't let you."

"Won't let..." He shook his head and dismounted to stand right in front of me. You never really know how short you are until you're faced with a man as big as a tree.

But I didn't back down. I felt a presence behind me and knew Finn's mom was nearby and invisible. Where was my doppelgänger, though? And how did this all fit together?

"I won't allow you to do this to the poor animal," I continued. "Everyone here is not what they're supposed to be, but they're the best versions of themselves. I will not let you change him. I warned you at the beginning that you would not break him. I'm here telling you now that I meant that. I will fight you, if I have to, in order for it not to happen. Bring it on. I'm ready." I grounded myself and waited for the first blow, either physical or magical.

Instead, he laughed. "I was warned about you. I told them I highly doubted you were as troublesome as they'd made you out to be, but I see they're actually underestimating you and your powers. Very interesting, if you must know."

What? Who was talking about me? But I focused. "I don't need to know anything except that you're not going to take this woman anywhere on Seawaddle's back. I won't have it."

"As you wish, then. Since this is your property and your rules apply, then I cannot make the kelpie do anything." He grabbed the woman from the saddle, and she sent me venomous vibes.

But then it wasn't just vibes, it was wave after wave of doubt, denial, hate, and evil. The revulsion pulsed in my veins along with a toxin that felt like it was eating me from the inside out. Looking down, I found a rope growing between us. A thread I hadn't seen was growing and growing, solidifying, and becoming a chain. I had no idea if the scissors would work a second time for me, but I'd be damned if I didn't try.

Angling down from above, I snapped the shears over the chain and was very satisfied when they severed the link with a most gratifying metallic clank. The chain spun back toward the woman and wrapped around her from head to toe. She screamed.

I stared in horror as Narcissio took the end of the chain and dragged her over to the edge of the creek and threw her in.

"What did you just do? Won't she drown?" That was my ultimate fear as a way to die. That and suffocation. And no matter how much trouble she had caused, I was not going to be a party to someone dying such a horrible death.

"You are much too soft," Narcissio said, standing between me and the water. "But to answer your question, no, she will not drown. She will sink to the underworld and be taken to her place among the people there. It is where she belongs. Where she has belonged for ages."

"So I just consigned her to death?"

"If by Death you mean capital letter D for Death, then yes, and she was consigned there many years ago. She has been out wreaking havoc for ages and ages. No one has been able to get to her or bring her back due to the dragon. Over the years, the myth changed from her exiling herself to her needing to be saved like some Sleeping Beauty."

"Holy hot dogs!" A woman with shining silver hair and yet unlined skin came to an abrupt halt next to me and grabbed my hands, then danced me around the clearing in a jig I had no idea how to follow.

"Whoa, whoa!" I said once she slowed down enough to double over in laughter. She hadn't let go of my hands yet, but I pulled them back during one particularly hearty guffaw, and she let go.

"Oh, Verla, you've saved me!"

"How is that possible, when I have no idea who you are?"

She roared at me, and it smelled like bubble gum.

"The dragon?"

She bowed in a way I'd only seen on television for those time-period movies. "At your service, my dear Verla. I will be at your service for the rest of my life." She grabbed my hand again, but this time she simply kissed it, then smiled at me in a way that shone from her head to the tips of her courtly and severely out-of-date shoes.

"But you just got done being roped to someone for a long time. Why would you want to be of service again so soon?"

Narcissio laughed at me, but I ignored him. Let him do whatever he wanted. I was serious.

"If I am in service, then I don't have to leave." Her smile dropped from her face and became very serious, looking into my eyes and still holding my hand. I noticed she was actively avoiding Narcissio's gaze, but let it go because I had no idea what I'd even say if I brought it up.

"But I don't need—"

"I am in a place where service would be something we could trade favors for," Finn's mom cut in from behind me. I turned to find her finally visible. I really hoped she was not going to do the invisible thing a lot if she was planning on staying longer. I did not want to have to guess where she might be.

"Of course, milady." The woman bowed over Tessa's hand and winked at me.

"We'll need another house," Tessa said. "I'll talk to my brother."

Better her than me. I didn't want to have to explain to Morty what was going on around here and was happy to leave that to her.

But looking around, I realized everyone was here but Fig. My beautiful baby was gone. For some reason that made me look for Finn. When our gazes met, he started walking toward me slowly, as if testing out the waters.

It took me less than a second to run into his arms and bury my head in his chest. I sobbed my heart out as he led me back to where the little fluff ball rested on his side.

"How am I supposed to be without him, Finn?" I had finally stopped sobbing and was only gasping breaths now. It hurt, though. It hurt so much.

Finn kept his arm around my shoulders, tucking me into his embrace where I so desperately needed to be. "I don't have the answers, Verla. I'm so sorry."

I sniffed. I'd never been a pretty crier, but I had to look like a disaster at this point. "I appreciate that. And I appreciate you bringing him to me. I just wish I had protected him better."

He kissed the top of my head. "You did the best you could."

A thought occurred to me, and I whipped my head around to see if I could find the doppelgänger. If she had shears to cut ties, did she also have something to bind them tighter? Could I pull Fig back from death by reinforcing our tie to the point where he couldn't leave me, like Finn as a Voror? As much as I was against taking away someone's choice, I knew Figiggly would be here if he could. No one could convince me otherwise.

"Where is she?" I asked.

"Who?"

"The woman who looks just like me. She brought me scissors to cut the tie between Helena and the dragon. Where is she?"

"I didn't see anyone with you, Verla." Finn stroked my back, probably to calm me down, but I was having none of that.

"Tessa!" It wasn't quite a scream, but it was close.

"Yes, darling?" she said when she materialized next to us.

"Tessa, where is the woman who looks like me? She was here. She gave me the scissors. Where did she go? I need her back." I wasn't sure why I didn't say Lottie's name, but that gut of mine was telling me not to speak it aloud.

"Someone gave you scissors? You used them?"

I should have clued in at the tone Tessa used, but I was way too focused on her answering my question instead of me answering hers. "Yes and yes. I already said that. Now where is she?"

"Well, Verla, she's a Fate, so she'd be in the Underworld, where we all live. She's the keeper of the archives of souls and isn't permitted to leave. Ever."

I still didn't clue in to her tone. "I need her back here. She gave me the scissors to cut things, but I want to bind them. I want to be able to..." Two things occurred to me at once. First, Tessa was not a happy camper about this doppelgänger coming topside. And two, if I could just see the threads of magic again, and find Figiggly's, I could pull him back all by myself.

Moving out of Finn's hold, I got down on my knees next to my baby and put my hands on his chest. There had to be something in there, some way to connect with him and bring him back. I just had to find it.

Chapter Ten

HE WAS STILL WARM. As I sank my fingers into his fur, I could feel his warmth. The same warmth that kept my feet from freezing at night if I'd forgotten to turn up the temperature in the house. The same warmth I'd felt when he wouldn't get off my lap. The same warmth I rested my forehead against when the day wasn't going so well but it was better with Fig.

And it would be better again because I was not giving up until he returned to me.

I pulled every bit of energy I could to me. Nothing was safe or sacred if it would help me right now. I filled myself up to the point where the hairs on my arms stood up, and I felt like I'd just downed a quadruple espresso. I was ready.

Hovering my hands over Fig, I looked for the thread between us, the one I could hold onto and reinforce like I had with Seawaddle. But it wasn't there. Nothing was there. It was gone, completely gone.

No, I could do this. I just had to...

"May I be of assistance?" At seven feet, Narcissio looked like a regular person as he crouched next to me.

I spread my hands out in front of me and had no words, so I just shrugged. The energy I'd been ready to unleash slowly drained away. I tried to recapture it, but I was just too damn tired.

Falling back, I sat down on the ground, not sure if I'd ever get back up.

"He's that important to you?" Narcissio asked.

"More than almost anything. He's my friend and my baby and my savior and my companion. He makes me laugh, scream, shrug, and shake my head. He frustrates me and fills me with love. He's my best friend. And besides Finn, no one and nothing has ever meant more to me."

Narcissio took my hand in his huge one and turned it over to see the lines on my palm. "Many, many years ago, I tried to learn the skill of palmistry, if just to pass the time. I had no idea where my true love had gone or why she'd left me. I didn't know how to find her or even if she was alive. And so I took up any and all hobbies and careers in an effort to make life bearable, since I couldn't end it."

My heart went out to him. "I'm sorry. The woman who wants to be of service here is that true love?"

"Yes." His smile lit up his face. "And we have much to discuss and decide now that we have been reunited. I never stopped loving her. I would have given anything for her return. And now that she's here, it's like my whole life changed in that instant."

"My situation is different obviously, but with a similar feeling. That's what happened when Fig came into my life. Finn brought him to me as a gift to ease the transition of my ex living next to me again. As much as I didn't want to want Fig in the beginning, I was helpless to resist him. He was so wonderful. I love him." Tears leaked out of my eyes again. I let them fall but held back the sobs.

"He loved you too."

"I know. That's why it's so hard to think he's gone. Everything I've ever loved has left me. This time I hoped it would be different. But it wasn't." I petted Fig's fur when I really wanted to grab him up and hug him.

"And if you could bring him back?"

"In an instant. I'd give anything and everything. No holds barred."

"I would ask a favor, then."

"Can you…?"

"Will you let me ask the favor?" There was a different quality to his voice, more formality like I was about to sign a pact over something I didn't completely understand.

I loved Fig and wanted him back, but I wasn't going to be an idiot and make a deal with a devil-type person without knowing what the stakes were.

"I'm listening."

"Can Brinlynn stay with you here? I need to attend to taking the two deceased knights back to Avalon, where they can be buried properly. However, I am unwilling to take her back to that world because of what they would do to her."

"That's it?"

He stared back at me, no nose-quivering, no frightening intensity, just a guy who was trying to make sure his true love was okay. "That is all I request of you. It would mean everything to me if I knew she was safe here. With you."

"I have to tell you that things have been really weird around here lately. I'll keep her as safe as I possibly can, but that's not a real guarantee she won't get caught up in something strange if we run into any other weirdos. Or if they run into us."

"Brinlynn is one of the best warriors in the known world, yours or mine. She was left when she was a young girl. Her parents moved without telling her where they were going, when she was working as a chambermaid at ten years of age. She fended for herself and passed for years as a boy to be a page, then a squire, and finally a knight. When Uther found out she had duped them all, he banished her. Arthur tried to help me get her back, but then the debacle happened with Helena, and you know how that ended."

"But now it's beginning again." I mustered a cheeky smile briefly to let him know I was on board.

"It is. And I'd like to know she's here with someone I actually trust for the first time in a long time. I believe you're her best chance until I can come back."

"Of course." I would have said it sooner, but I hadn't wanted to interrupt him.

"There are issues to discuss."

"Quite frankly, I don't need to know anything more than that. Even if you can't bring Fig back, I would still protect her here at the faire. It's what I do."

His smile transformed his face. I could see why someone like Brinlynn would fall hard and endure years of dragonhood to be with him again.

After a few more seconds of checking me over, Narcissio nodded. "I will need you to use the ley lines to transport us back to Avalon. I will warn you it could alert certain undesirables to the location."

"I. Don't. Care. Period. I don't. Whatever you need to do, do it."

"Verla..." Finn was by my side. He took my hand and massaged my fingers to get them to loosen from their fisted grip.

"I know what I'm doing, Finn. I'm not being stupid. I want to protect the faire, but if there's a way to undo what Helena did, then I'd like to give it a try."

"Okay." He kissed my knuckles. "You're doing the right thing. I just wanted to make sure it was for the right reason."

"I appreciate that. Now, let your mom take you to the healer and get that lightning-bolt-shot arm looked at. Later, you and I are going to have to talk about doing stupid things like jumping in front of me to save me. And the Voror thing, let's definitely talk about that..."

Narcissio cocked an eyebrow at the two of us. I ignored him. There were some things that did not need to be made public.

"So what do you need from me?" I asked Narcissio.

∞

The list turned out to be small and all things I only had to ask one of my colleagues for to get it done. We had sage and crystals to cleanse and magnify. We had dill and garlic from Bob's kitchen to ward off any evil spirits. We had a haunting melody from the steam-pipe organ to cover the words Narcissio was speaking to get through to Avalon so no one would try to use them other than him.

And we had my sweet Figiggly, nestled into the new dog bed I had wanted to give him for his six-month birthday next week. I wasn't waiting. If he came back to me now, he could have anything he wanted. Anything at all.

Narcissio walked clockwise around the tavern deck. He chanted and threw dog treats into the middle of the circle he was creating, again and again. I'd stopped counting the number of times he'd trod the same path, because each one made my stomach tighten more.

What if Fig didn't come back?

I shut that thought off immediately. I would figure it out. If this didn't work, I'd try elsewhere. And I still had to find Lottie, if all else failed. Actually, I'd be looking for her regardless. There was more there than she was telling me, and Tessa had refused to answer any more of my questions. We'd see how long that lasted.

But first, my Fig needed to wake up.

Another five circuits—I couldn't help myself—and Narcissio looked tired. He'd been walking for what seemed like hours, and at some point I was going to have to let him off the hook and just know he tried his best, but it was beyond even his skills.

Finn had his arm around my shoulders. It was comfortable and comforting, so I didn't try to move. Brinlynn sat next to me, beaming at her man as he chanted and the organ played a tune that I was very much considering using at Halloween—a little spooky with bridges of hope.

I wanted that bridge of hope.

And then Finn nudged me. I wedged myself further into his side, not wanting to count anymore.

He nudged me again. I ignored him.

He tickled my waist. I pinched the underside of his arm.

He yelped and then the most glorious sound ever hit my ears. A bark. It was soft and a little hoarse, not full of his usual exuberance, but it was a bark.

I knocked Finn back in his chair, rocketing out of my seat. He just laughed and waved me on when I turned to apologize.

And then I was holding my puppy, who was licking my face. His tongue was dry. I didn't even have to ask for water because Bob brought a bowl and some pieces of hot dog. Where he got them was anyone's guess, but Fig wasn't the only one who was grateful for the treat.

"I love you," I whispered into his ear.

"Love you more, Dog-mom."

All was right with my world.

Narcissio kissed Brinlynn goodbye for what seemed like an hour before he stepped away. He called the four winds and the four humors, the four corners and four gods. To his right stood one of our horses with a cart. The two dead men had been placed carefully into the cart, and we'd had a small procession on the way to the tavern to honor them and their sacrifice.

I'd have to change the Incidents Board even though all the players but one were going to a different time and place. Not a big deal anymore. I had my Finn, my Fig, my faire, and now my family. Or at least that was what I thought. How else could a Fate look just like me?

Had she been given away too? What did she know about me when I knew nothing about her? What exactly did my story say in the Archives of the Fates? Were you allowed to ask for corrections and use white-out on certain episodes you'd rather not let anyone ever have access to?

All questions for another time. And I was looking forward to that time, now that I had my Fig back.

Finn put his arm around me as he joined me to sit on the deck. Fig stretched his little body between both of our laps. This was pretty close to heaven as far as I was concerned.

And whatever came our way next time better be ready for a serious fight. I wasn't playing anymore. Of course, I'd prefer to be left alone to go back to just being us at the faire, but Narcissio's warning had not fallen on deaf ears. We could be drawing something bigger to us by activating the ley lines.

And if someone was bent on terrorizing us, or trying to take what belonged to me, they'd better be ready for the fight of their life. I had one hell of a team, and I wasn't afraid to use it.

Witch Way to Halloween

Chapter One

I WASN'T ONE TO worry over things that had not happened yet. I let things flow as they would and then went with that flow. I was a smooth sailor, a non-worry-wart, a serene lake of what will be will be...

Ha! Who was I trying to kid? I always worried about things that hadn't happened yet—it was like my signature Verla Faeth move.

Okay, so I had been *trying* not to worry about things that hadn't happened yet. I wasn't doing the best of jobs, to be honest, but at least I was trying.

Right? Right.

But if I was worrying, it was only because I had every reason to be concerned with how things had been going at my Ren faire in Central PA lately. Our little slice of heaven here in Effington had not exactly been an effing ton of fun, with all the chaos that had been unleashed over the last few months.

Ever since June, we'd had a strange handful of incidents that had rocked my world. Though I had attempted to talk myself out of changing my Days Without Incident Board after the last one, I'd finally given in and started over again when I almost lost my faithful companion, the super-duper awesome Chow named Figiggly.

"Come here, my love," I said to him as he circled the bench near the steampipe organs.

"Verla..." He didn't actually say the word, nor did he think it into my head as he did sometimes when there was trouble. But I could tell he wanted to say it, probably with exacerbation. Maybe a small side of irritation. Perhaps a smidgen of "When will this ever end?" And I didn't care.

"Come on, Fig, you need a hug."

He grunted but eventually sat at my feet and waited for me to pick him up and cuddle him. For a Chow, he was still pretty small. And for a fabled Cerberus who helped me cross the dead into the Underworld, he was positively tiny. Not to mention he also lacked the two additional heads that fit the standard mythology of the Cerberus being a three-headed dog.

But I loved him anyway. And my life had only gotten better since he'd been given to me by my ex. Sure, the dog had been a token gesture for smoothing over the fact that said ex was moving back into the house next door at the Ren Faire. But in the end, he was worth every second, and the token had definitely worked.

Of course, I wouldn't have been able to say no to his move-in plans anyway. Because, while I ran the faire, I didn't own it. That honor belonged to my ex's uncle, Mortimer Jenkins, Morty for short. It was pretty complicated, if you couldn't tell.

I snuggled my head into the soft fur at Figiggly's neck and then kissed his nose. "You're the bestest boy, and I love you so very much."

If dogs could roll their eyes, I was pretty sure Fig's would have rolled back to look at the inside of his skull. As it was, he just grunted again. It made me laugh and, after the issues we'd been having over the last several months, I'd take any non-maniacal laughter I could get.

Murder, mayhem, sneaky people, and others bent on revenge infiltrated the faire at various times over the last few months. I still didn't know exactly why *now* when we'd never had this kind of trouble before.

However, I had my suspicions when I learned more about the seventeen ley lines that crisscrossed over at our famous Tavern on the Line pub. They hadn't been this active in years, from what I was told, but something had made them come to life, and I was going to spend the off-season learning what it was and find out if they needed to be re-smothered or allowed to flourish.

We had grown through this season of unrest, though, and any and every fight that had been brought to me and my merry band of misfit paranormals had been fought until we were the victors.

So, no, not exactly how I would have wanted to live, but at least we were all still alive.

And today was Halloween, the biggest day of the year at the faire. It marked the end of the faire season, a day I'd been impatiently waiting for more than usual. Then, after we shut down for the night, we could all sleep well, knowing tomorrow would be the beginning of a much-needed rest for all of us.

I was so looking forward to the downtime. I already had a bunch of lessons set up with the old crone, Mavis, who had been helping me learn more about the unexpected gift I'd received when Fig showed up. I'd become a crosser of the dead. I hadn't expected that, and it came with some other awesome powers that I wanted to make sure I knew how to use properly.

"You worry too much about things," Fig said in my head.

"You don't worry enough," I said out loud and then caught myself. Yeah, note to self, maybe don't look like you're having a conversation no one can hear but you... Fortunately, no one was currently paying attention to us, since they were much more interested in the ghosts coming out of the pipes of the steam organ. Most likely none of them were wondering what was wrong with me. But there was almost always that one person, and I refused to look like a fool if I could help it.

I lifted the dog off my lap, then put him back on the ground, making sure to hang on to his leash. Normally, he was allowed to prance around on his own, even through the faire with guests here. He'd learned the rules and followed them, most of the time.

But today we had completely sold out of tickets, with people wanting nothing more than to be here for the last day we were open until next June and for the biggest Halloween we'd ever had. And that meant we had many booths decked out with their creepiest swag, as well as lots of things set up that I did not want Fig to get his nose into.

Throughout the troubles, I'd passed off most of the bad things that happened as "practicing" for our annual Halloween event if a faire goer saw something out of the ordinary. It was the only excuse I'd been able to think of when I had a gargoyle flying around and pitched battles of ghosts being played out in the faire. So here we were, the early afternoon hours of Halloween Night, and people were expecting a spectacular show. They were getting it, from what I could tell as I wandered around.

But forgive me if I worried either I wouldn't deliver, or something more would happen and make me deliver a little too much.

So far, though, it appeared all was in order, and I was just going to enjoy that for as long as it lasted.

Actually, I guess I had kind of learned to go with the flow, like toilet water...

"That ghost is hanging around the toilet again." Finn Taragon, the bane of my existence and the love of my life—along with not really being my ex since he'd never fully filed the divorce papers—stopped next to me in all his wonderful finery. I took just a moment to truly enjoy all that he was when we weren't at odds, like we usually were.

"Privy," I reminded him without thinking about it. I was nothing if not consistent about making him use the right language when in the faire.

His dark hair was longer than I was used to seeing it, and his eyes sparkled in the late afternoon sun. I loved him, and we'd been married for more years than I realized, but I wasn't sure if it was right to keep him around me. His mother had finally told me he was a Voror, a wraith that lived only as long as the person he was watching lived. And that person was me.

Here at the faire, we were all misfits for the most part. But Finn was all in on the Voror thing and yet still here.

"Fine. Privy." He shook his head.

I ignored the headshaking. It wasn't my fault he didn't say the right words. But it sure as heck was my job to correct him, just like I did anyone else who worked here at the faire. If I took a little more pleasure in irritating him than I would with anyone else, that was between me and myself.

"Is it that same woman who refuses to let me cross her? Irene?" I asked. "She's going to have to go at some point. I can't move her without her consent, but she's a nuisance. If she'd just hang around and do nothing, I wouldn't have a problem with her staying, but the vandalism with water has to stop."

He straightened the cravat at his throat and pulled on his cuffs. Poor guy was at least cooler than usual, since I made him dress to the nines in faire attire every day, even when it was hot as Hades. With autumn finally kicking in, it made for nice weather as the leaves changed, so he wasn't sweating.

"I've tried talking to her, Verla, and she won't listen. I'm not sure what else you think we can do, but she keeps asking for the sin eater and refuses to go until her sin is eradicated."

We had a sin eater on site, but as I said, each of us did not do the thing we were supposed to do, so I couldn't exactly ask Althea to put the woman to rest.

"I'll go talk to Irene later, as long as she's not doing anything horrendous." *Please, don't let her be doing anything horrendous.* "She's not really bothering anyone, is she?"

"No, people are actually getting a kick out of her water tricks and think it's a mechanical set-up they just can't see."

"Okay, as long as she stays with low-level entertaining, then I think we're fine until the faire closes," I said. "Maybe since the veil is the thinnest today, I can get her moved on. I'll put it on my list."

"Good luck with that." Finn bowed to me, very formally, and a gaggle of girls to my right giggled as they oohed and ahhed. They were normal people who ran the food service counters or helped with clean-up, along with some of the faire-goers. I could see how they might be enchanted by the way my ex presented himself, but they didn't know the half of it. And I wasn't going to be the one to tell them.

Because the facts were that he was certainly something to behold, and he was still mine. I just couldn't bring myself to take the steps to let us be close again. Too much history, too much left unsaid, too much to wade through right now. But it would happen. Or at least I thought it might, if I could get myself to make a move, since I'd asked him to not make any moves on me. I had a plan this winter to really think about what I wanted and what I was willing to do to get it.

But this was not winter, and I had a Halloween spectacular to run and then a ghost to talk into being sent on to the afterlife, hopefully for the last time.

I was ready to walk around a bit more now that I'd had my rest on the bench and my doggy hug. I turned a corner at the candlestick maker and was immediately engulfed in a cloud of smoke so thick I thought someone was on fire. Before I could get myself in a tizzy, I heard laughter, and the smoke partially cleared to reveal a group of our season passholders drinking out of wooden mugs filled with bubbling and smoking drinks. Zane, at the tavern, had warned me he'd be doing this when he'd asked to order dry ice, but I hadn't realized they'd be so... frothy.

With a smile on my face for the revelry going on around me, I continued on. The dish-throwing shack was doing a brisk business. Kramer waved, and a dish that had been going toward the back wall seemed to stop in midair and start dancing. Everyone waiting their turn in line gasped and then laughed as it resumed its original course after a few seconds and crashed spectacularly into the back wall. Clapping ensued, and my grin got bigger. At this rate, a couple more cool things might have my cheeks hurting. But I'd take it.

My plan had been to make a circuit this morning to ensure everything was in place. I'd ended up getting waylaid a few times with issues, so I was only now getting around to everyone.

Pulling my pocket watch out, I realized I needed to step it up a little if I wanted to see everyone. We were still a few hours from closing.

I walked past the singing pumpkins Madame Tresell had put out and smiled as children stood in front of them in awe, singing the songs we'd taken from nursery rhymes and turned into slightly spooky versions, along with classics from movies like *Nightmare Before Christmas*. Next, I strolled by the bookstore and enjoyed the spirits playing in the rafters and aisles of the shop. We'd strategically placed projectors to mask the fact that the spirits were actually real.

A few steps past the shop, I found myself in the midst of a crowd. Our resident magicians, Jacque and Tyrone, were wowing the enraptured people. The show was literally on fire with more than just card tricks. Plus, they'd painted their skin a light green. They looked far more like the trolls they were supposed to have been than the way they looked normally. On any given day, they would have totally passed for normal humans, hence why they'd been kicked out of their tribe and came to the faire to be accepted for exactly who they were.

"Nice job," I yelled over the cheering crowd, and Jacque winked at me.

A flaming sword swirled in the air, twirling and twirling and looking like it might never come down. Marilyn, another magician—though I wasn't sure what her talent should have been—stood off to the side of the stage, flicking her wrist left and right, and the sword followed suit. I'd never seen her do anything like it before, but I'd given everyone leeway to do whatever they could to make this day amazing. It was very possible she'd enlisted help from one of the prop guys to put an invisible string on the sword she was manipulating from the wings.

And speaking of flames, Barnaby, our resident blacksmith and defunct dragon, must have talked with Hal, because he was currently firing his forge with his own breath. The coals glowed yellow and red as he breathed fire. I'd seen Hal do that once during one of his shows on the big stage. It took some sort of fuel like paraffin and a flame, but the best could hide how they did it. And Barnaby seemed to be a near genius. How cool was that? Maybe we could add it to his normal forge shows in the next season, if he wanted to take the time to perfect it on the off-season.

I made a mental note to let all of them know how awesome they were doing.

But now, I'd seen enough and was ready for a drink to quench my thirst. I made my way over to the Tavern on the Line to see how Zane was doing, Fig right on my heels. The bubbling and smoking drinks I'd seen earlier might just be the answer to the way my throat was starting to burn.

Not that I needed an excuse to drink something from the faire, but if I did, this excuse was as good as any other.

Turning the corner from the magician show, I came face to face with one of the Wild Hunt we'd had here a month or so ago. He looked lost and a little feral, even for a ghost of the fabled riders of the Vikings.

I put on a show when addressing him, since people were watching as he tried to chew the grass from the side of the pavement. "Heldigrad! I believe lunch is that way, you fiend."

I pointed and laughed, but when he looked up at me with wide eyes blazing with fire, I wasn't so sure it was an act after all.

"Heldigrad?" I peered at him to see if he was just playing out a part. Fig got off his rump to sniff the ghost, and the nearly transparent man in all his dulled armor turned on him. I had Fig's leash in my hand, so I yanked on it, and he came back to my side quickly as Heldigrad growled low in his throat.

Though we tried hard not to be too anachronistic at the faire, I still had to have some way of getting in touch with the clean-up crew and security throughout the day. I pressed my ear to engage the earbud and waited for a burst of static to dissipate before talking softly in a serious tone while making sure my smile stayed firmly on my face.

"I need someone to get Willy Nilly and bring him over to the magician's area. We have a rogue ghost. I'm not sure what to do to get him to stop gnawing on grass, or trying to gnaw on grass." Since he wasn't actually able to move anything in his current state. Or he wasn't trying hard enough. I wasn't sure which, but I didn't have to be sure about that to know something wasn't right.

I was not changing my Days Without Incident board on the last day of the faire. It was a promise I had made to myself this morning, and one I would only break under the direst of circumstances. To which level grass-eating ghosts did not rise. Yet.

Willy Nilly, the leader of the Wild Hunt, came soaring in on his chariot without a horse and stopped right next to his comrade. "Got him, Verla. He's been acting a mite weird the last few days, maybe something about being here instead of in Valhalla. We'll get him fixed up!" He grabbed Heldigrad around the waist and lifted him into the chariot, and then they were off in a flash. People laughed and clapped, and I did too, right along with them, even though my eyelid started twitching. I would not be nervous now. Would. Not.

I needed that drink more than ever.

Fig was quick to take the lead once I told him where we were going. We made it to the tavern without another incident—not that we'd had one the first time, since there was no incident and the board would not be changed. Zane was doing a brisk business, and that made me happy to see. He winked at me from behind the counter as he and four other people served up the smoky drinks one after another.

A slight cloud seemed to hang in the air, but it was no big deal, as it would go away soon enough.

Finally it was my turn at the bar, and Zane handed over the mug of froth and smoke with just a smile.

"Thanks," I said, then started gulping.

"My pleasure," Zane said in a voice I didn't particularly care for.

And then I saw his head float off his shoulders, to be replaced by the face of a huge wolf with not only fangs but horns, and he snapped his jaws not two inches from my nose.

What the hell?

Chapter Two

I JUMPED BACK AND came in contact with one of the many barstools lining the bar. Scrambling for purchase, I didn't find it. Instead I crashed into a table and went down. The big wolf vaulted over the bar and stood over me, huffing and puffing, and I used every last ounce of my energy to not scream.

The faire was uppermost in my mind, even while I was being threatened by a beast that no one else seemed to think was an issue. How could they not? The thing was drooling and slavering and scaring the bejesus out of me. Holy crap!

Was it going to eat me? Would I be like Little Red Riding Hood, faced with danger that I wasn't sure how to escape? Danger that could end my life. Like right now. Imminently, to be precise.

I wouldn't scream, though. I. Would. Not. Scream.

But a scream was definitely burbling in my throat and made me feel like if I didn't scream I might puke.

Jerking my head to the left, I found Fig sitting next to me, his normal size, and smiling at the beast before me.

"Fig! Get him!" I said the words out loud, if also under my breath. But he either didn't hear me or was ignoring me. I tried again in my head, but no response there, either.

What was going on?

Not two seconds later, I was lifted off the ground by huge hands. Was this my demise? Would I die at the hands of a wolf on All Hallows Eve? Really? It seemed like such a stupid way for my life to end after everything I'd been through.

"Verla. Verla! VERLA!"

Who was calling my name? When would I feel the crunch of my bones in the vicious-looking jaw that had backed up a little, but not enough to suit my desire? Why wasn't I using my newfound magic to fight this hideous monster off?

All questions that might remain forever unanswered as I waited, frozen, for the first chomp.

"Verla."

I snapped my head to the right and found Finn kneeling next to me on the wooden floor. People had backed away from the scene I was making even as I was trying to act cool. Maybe I'd just say I stumbled into a chair and went down. It happened and could be easily explained away as clumsiness until I could figure out what was going on and still save the faire's reputation. I did not want some patron to go on social media and howl about the fiends we kept here and how one of them had eaten the manager...

"Verla, snap out of it. Can you hear me, Sparkle-kins?"

I hadn't heard that nickname in so long I'd almost forgotten it existed. Until I looked up into Finn's eyes and saw how worried he was.

"I, um..." Could not get actual words to come out of my mouth. It felt like someone had wadded up cotton, dipped it in honey, and shoved it into my mouth. With glue. The kind everyone had sniffed when we were in elementary school.

"I don't think she's in a good place right now, Zane. Is that cellar still okay to use?"

I listened as Zane answered with something other than a growl, though I couldn't make out the words. And then I was being lifted and hoisted into a fireman's carry. I really wished my big old rear end was not so on display for the whole tavern to see, but it did feel nice to have Finn's arm over the back of my thighs. Better than I had expected—or wanted, for that matter.

I hung there for a moment, watching the belt on his pants writhe like a snake, then just closed my eyes. Something was going on, and I wasn't quite sure what. But I had the distinct feeling my eyes were seeing things that weren't actually there.

"Finally," Fig said in my mind as he trailed along behind us.

"What do you mean, finally?" I asked in my mind. Or at least I thought I did until Finn walked down the stairs, asking me what I was talking about.

I didn't answer him because I was concentrating too hard on not puking on the back of his pants. The view from here was something to behold, and I didn't want to ruin it by getting sick.

We made it to the bottom of the stairs without incident. Finn set me down on a loveseat that seemed to appear out of nowhere. I didn't remember there being one down here when we were dealing with Buford and his brother's demonic ways, but Zane was always more than welcome to change the décor whenever he wanted. Perhaps he was entertaining someone on this couch on his nights off.

Not that it was any of my business, or even remotely relevant right now.

But it was comfy, and I did wish for just a second that Finn would sit next to me and let me snuggle my head into his chest. Instead, he paced and paced, and paced some more.

"Can you just stop? You're making me dizzy. And since when are you calling me Sparkle-kins again?"

He did stop with his hands on his hips, showing me very clearly that he was very well put together in the chest area as well as other areas. So not only did the drink make me see things that weren't there, but also enhanced things that very much were? Not good. Not good at all. Or rather, it could be very good, but not good *for* me.

"Something is wrong with you," Finn said, and I nearly nodded in agreement but kept my head still at the last second. "I think it might have been something in your drink. I don't feel like you're hurt, or maimed, or in danger of dying, so that's at least something. But there's a slight tremor in the bond between us, and it's making me nervous."

Ah, the bond of the Voror. The one that made it so that Finn couldn't die as long as I was alive, but the second I was gone, so was he. I had very much considered slicing that tie when I'd had the scissors of a Fate in my hands, but in the end, I couldn't do it and really hadn't wanted to.

"Do you think there was poison in my drink?" I asked, hesitating to put the thought into words, but not sure what else to say.

"I don't think so. Yet, if it is, I hope it's only in yours and not everyone else's who drank that frothy and ridiculous thing. I'd better call up to Zane and see if anyone was near your drink."

I shook my head, and it sent off little charges at my temples that set my brain beating like some kind of festival in the jungle. Holding up my hand, I waited for the feeling to pass.

"I watched him pour it right out of the carafe. There's no way he poisoned me." I bit my lip. "Is there?"

"Of course not," Finn said and resumed his pacing.

"Then what—"

I was interrupted by clattering coming from the right side of the room and then a full-on centaur burst through the doorway that led to the underground tunnels that ran throughout the faire and the village we all lived in next door. Mostly they had been put there for safety years ago. They ended in the catacombs, where those who had lived and died at the faire went to rest their bodies while their souls crossed the river under my care.

Where did this centaur come from and who was— "Tyler?" I gasped.

"Tyler." Finn took a step toward the half-horse, half-boy, and the beast shied away, gargling words I couldn't understand.

"Tyler," I said. "Settle down, and we'll figure out what happened."

How could this be? Tyler couldn't even really run properly—much less trot—and had never shown himself to be anything equine, despite his father's centaur lineage. His mother, Marilyn the magician from earlier, had told me this over coffee a few weeks ago when she was contemplating what to do with Tyler's twenty-first birthday coming up at the end of the year. Should she contact Tyler's dad and ask him to stop by? Leave the man to his own devices because Tyler never even asked after him?

It was one of the many reasons she had brought her little boy here at four, and we'd watched him grow into a wonderful young man who had no talent whatsoever, but who very much liked heading up the maintenance crew and teaching new recruits how the faire worked.

What the actual hell was happening?!? Interrobang totally and completely needed in this very weird situation.

And then another being came through the tunnel entrance—Buford with his eyes blazing and his hands hooked into horrible claws. My brain kicked into overdrive as I realized that if Tyler was a centaur, then it was entirely possible that my nice friend Buford—who was a demon but couldn't do much in demony ways and was the sweetest person alive—could very well be quite the threat if he was also what he was supposed to be when he was born instead of his misfit self.

Fig sensed the danger before I could say a word and lunged at poor Buford, who stumbled back and hit his head on the wall behind him, knocking himself out.

"Quick, bind Buford, because when he wakes up he could be saucy." Though the words made it sound far lighter than I felt, it was the first really coherent thought I'd had in the last thirty minutes, and I was going to relish it even as it scared me to pieces. "He'll never forgive himself if he does something he wouldn't normally do. I think we have some serious issues here, and we're about to go into complete and utter lockdown if this isn't fixed."

And if it wasn't fixed quickly, I was going to have to change that damn board.

Finn cut his gaze to me, and I nodded. So did Fig, who was sitting at Finn's feet and growing. He'd reached about three times his normal size, and if he got much bigger, he wouldn't be able to fit down here, for one thing, and for another, he wouldn't be able to get up the stairs or into the tunnel.

Speaking of the tunnel, I couldn't handle anyone else coming through right now, so I rushed to shove the door shut and then barred it by stacking several boxes of alcohol in front of it. My impromptu barricade might not keep everyone out, but it would at least slow them down until I could figure out what to do.

Of course, I had no clue, so this could take longer than I actually had, but at least I'd bought a little time.

"What are we going to do?" I asked Finn. My voice was small compared to my normal volume, but honestly, I'd never been more scared in my life. Nervous, sad, frightened, yes, but not this full-on condition of being scared enough to want to hide under a bed and not come out until the monsters were gone. "The trolls are actually green, and the dragon is really breathing fire, and now Tyler is a centaur. Suddenly, everyone is what they were supposed to be, but what do we do about those like Zane who are not safe like they were before this happened?"

"All right, look, we have some choices and some things we can count on. The rest will fall into line once we get out there and see what's going on. Is there anyone in particular we should worry about?" he asked, and I felt like throwing up again. Hopefully this was not going to become my new go-to when things got rough.

"I don't know. I don't know what everyone is supposed to be, so I don't know what we're going to have to deal with."

And that might just be the steel beam that broke the horse's back...

Chapter Three

I WAS THE ONE pacing now, waiting for Buford to wake up. "How hard did he hit his head?" I asked no one in particular, but would take answers from anyone. I couldn't stay here forever because we had a lot of people out in the faire—both those who might be a danger if this trend of gaining your birthright made its way throughout the faire, and those who were in danger as patrons of the faire because they were completely human and could be targets if faced with the newly minted birthright holders.

Talk about my Days Without Incident board needing to be wiped. I would probably just have to throw the thing away if this got as bad as I was worried it might get. I had said I was a go-with-the-flow kind of person, but this felt far more like the beginnings of a tsunami then a gentle glide down an easy river...

Buford woke up with a snarl that made my hair stand on end. Fig grew another size bigger and stood in front of Finn with his own snarl. I so did not need a pissing match between a dog and a demon, thank you very much.

"Buford, if the real you is in there somewhere, I just want to let you know that I'm going to try to fix this, but you're going to have to remain shackled for the moment. I don't want you to hurt anyone or yourself."

"Release me, human, before I wreak terrible carnage on you and yours." He growled the words, actually growled them at me.

I wanted to take a step back. I wanted to actually run screaming from the cellar. But I held my ground. It was a close thing, but I did it. Of course, it helped that Finn had come up behind me and put his hand on my back. With Figiggly standing against my left leg, I was essentially caged in, facing a demon who apparently wanted to wreak havoc. I really hoped that the bonds we'd put him in would hold.

Without any warning, my brain quickly flashed to the possibility of him using a shard of a broken wine bottle to cut through the ropes tying his clawed hands. The bottle could come from a crate to his right. "Finn, tie his feet too, and let's move that box of wine out of his reach."

Another growl followed my words, and then the demon howled. I had a hard time thinking of him as Buford because my Buford was gentle. He'd dreamed of living at this faire filled with misfits for his whole life. He'd had a map of every attraction, a map he'd held on to for years and years, ever since his mother had given it to him during one of his few good memories of being a child.

This was not my Buford.

Finn did as I asked while I kept my gaze on the demon. Tyler, the centaur, clopped back and forth on the concrete floor, talking nervously about everything and anything, with a whinny thrown in every few seconds to add to the chaos.

"Do you want me to call your mom, Tyler? Maybe she can help? I'm not even sure how to get you up the stairs, but I'm really hesitant to send you back through the tunnels. I don't know what's on the other side or in there."

The boy-turned-half-horse nodded his head, and I took my phone out of my side pouch. I had another flash of Buford lunging at the centaur and knocking my phone out of my hand. I did step back this time, and Buford howled again.

I had to admit here that I had thought the first vision was a fluke and just me thinking about what could happen. But with this second one, and all the ways Buford was swearing so hard the smell of sulfur was rising off his now-flaming hair, I couldn't pass this off again as a fluke.

Why was this happening?

I winced when a quick burst of images ran through my poor spinning mind. Zane with a horrendously maniacal smile on his face, running his hand over and over the basement door with a piece of chalk. He winked at me in my vision and then a pop sounded and the whole bar went dark except for the pulsing green of the ley lines crisscrossing at every corner of the tavern.

"Finn, I think we have a prob—"

A scratching sound on the door at the top of the stairs was followed by a set of screams that made my blood run cold. The lights went out in the basement. Buford chuckled deep in his chest. And Tyler neighed.

A subtle glow began at my feet and then traveled up my legs and chest until I looked like some kind of glow stick that had just been cracked. I had no problem believing this might be the final snap in my ability to act like a civil human being when I really wanted to primal scream and get the freaking hell out of here and maybe never come back.

"Stay very still, Verla. We're going to be okay, and we'll get out of here. I just need you to stay very still. In fact, if you could hold your breath that would be even better." Finn's words were probably meant to make me feel better, but they didn't.

In fact, the whispered words sent a chill up my spine. What was going on that I couldn't see? And why wasn't Figiggly trying to protect me, or grow even more?

He stood at Finn's side instead, with his whole stance rigid and ready to attack.

"Lost your dog, sweetie?" Buford cackled menacingly. "I suppose it was bound to happen. No one stays for you, do they, darling? Perhaps it's time to look at who might be the common factor in all of these troubles. Perhaps it's you. Perhaps..." He cackled again and then snapped out of the room in a flash, shackles and all.

Crap. Crap. CRAP! Someone could take me to task later for all the damn caps.

"Finn..."

He lit his cell phone up with the strong flashlight, and his face at first looked ghoulish. But then I remembered that he was already what he was supposed to be, so he wouldn't be springing any surprises on me. Hopefully.

But that also meant that Figiggly—who should have been an arazeles—was protecting him now as a warrior protector, not me as his guide for the dead.

Which meant... HOLY CRAP!

Was I now a seer? Was I able to tell the future?

Quickly, on the tail end of that last question came another. Where was my deck of tarot cards?

Although, did I really need them when I kept getting flashes of the future completely without them?

Too many questions and too many things rolling through my brain when it was very possible that every single patron of the faire could be in very grave danger right now. If Buford was on the loose and Zane was practicing black magic instead of the white magic he'd chosen all those years ago, then we were in for some very bad times if I couldn't get a handle on this.

"Oh, Goddess, Finn, we're in some serious trouble."

"I kind of got that impression when Zane put a curse on me." Finn's arms were now roped to his sides and his skin was green. Well, not just green, it was also scaley and...

"Did he turn you into a fish?"

"I'm thinking more of a dragon if the burning in my chest is any indication."

"I am so sor—"

"Look, if you're going to apologize, save it. You had nothing to do with this, and we need all hands on deck to figure out how to stop it." His jaw tightened and then clenched. He looked like he was fighting something inside him, and I reached out a hand to help. "Please, don't touch me. I don't know what that will do, and we can't afford for anything else to go wrong."

Another scream sounded upstairs. I flashed on a dragon belching fire out on the grounds. Finn? Or Barnaby...because if Zane and Buford and Tyler were changed, then there was a distinct possibility that everyone who worked at the faire—all of my loveable misfits who wouldn't hurt a fly—could very well be wreaking havoc with whatever powers they should have had at birth. I'd thought it before, briefly, but seeing Buford flash out had hammered it into my head that this wasn't just a possibility but a very stark reality.

Finn shoved me aside. I couldn't stop myself from knocking into Tyler, who whinnied. And then Finn burped, and fire shot across the basement to hit the rock wall. He looked horrified at what he'd just done, but I snickered.

Completely inappropriate, of course, but I did it anyway.

"Well, at least you didn't eat the beans and hot dogs I tried to force on you last night, or this might have been a whole other issue."

He harrumphed but looked like he wanted to laugh, too.

"Come on, Finn. We've made it through every other thing that's been thrown at us here. And even if this is the very worst it's ever been, we're going to get through this too." I breathed a sigh of relief because I actually believed the words that were coming out of my mouth. Not to mention I had no flashing images to contradict my words. "Now. Let's go kick some ass, take some names, and find out what we're working with. Not everyone who doesn't have their power is going to be turned into something bad. We have many wonderful people here who either are going to help us, or will fight their instincts tooth and nail to at least not hurt us. I have to believe that, and so do you."

He nodded, and I nodded back.

"Tyler, tell me what you were seeing when you were heading this way."

My horsey friend stamped his hooves on the floor. "Not a lot. My vision was clouded, but I kept feeling this pulse in my veins like something was stalking closer and closer, and then I was galloping, and then I had four legs and two arms. Sorry I don't have more information."

"My dear boy, there is no need to apologize. We'll get through, and the Days Without Incident board will even survive this turmoil. I'm not without resources, and nothing, and no one, is going to stop me."

I said the words valiantly, almost like the speech Viggo Mortensen gave in the third Lord of the Rings movie, but inside I was quaking so hard I was very surprised body parts weren't starting to fall off.

What in the hell did I think I was doing? And how was I going to do it without Fig by my side as my boost?

My dog came over at that moment, though, and stood against my leg.

"I'm here. I can fight the urge to protect Finn if I concentrate really hard on you. I might not be a Cerberus at the moment, but I am still your loyal companion. That's not going to change no matter what the ley lines are trying to do."

"Who's my good boy?" I asked in that sickeningly annoying voice people used way too much with animals.

"I am." Funny enough the response was in stereo, not only in my head but also in the real world, as not only Fig had answered but also Finn verbally and Buford, who had flashed back in.

He was sweating so badly I thought he must be melting.

"It's the hellfire," he groaned. "It's flaming inside, but I'm dousing it with every good memory I have with you and the faire. If anything goes wrong, please know that I would never have wanted to..." He groaned again and then howled. "Hurt you." And he collapsed on the ground.

"Finn, what are we going to do? We can't leave him like this, but we have to get topside. I have to check on everyone." Anxiety and concern were taking over my brain and making my feet and legs twitch to get upstairs. And I was still glowing. And Finn still had scales and was blushing green. That might be hard to explain when we left here, but we'd figure it out.

"I brought chains." Buford raised just his head from the floor and nodded to his right. The chains were like horror materialized. Not only were they huge beasts that looked far more like the manacles we had in the torture museum than regular cuffs, but they also had spikes turned inward. One move and those things would pierce you over and over again with the needle-like nails.

"I can't do that to you, Buford."

"Of course you can't, my dear scared Verla. Such a tender heart, such a loving soul, both of which I can't wait to devour." He snapped his jaws at me and then started to cry.

"I'll do it." Finn stepped forward and batted Buford's snapping teeth away as he locked the chains on the poor demon, who was obviously struggling between worlds.

"We're out. Now. Pronto," I said. "No more messing around. I need to find out what is happening and stop it before it gets worse."

I headed for the cave system while everyone else headed for the stairs. When I heard Tyler's clopping moving away from me instead of toward me, I turned to glance back over my shoulder. "There is no way he's going to be able to get up those stairs, and whatever Zane is doing in the tavern is not something I want to walk through, especially if he hexed the door along with cursing you."

Finn's shoulders slumped, and he belched fire again, careful to turn his head to hit the stone wall in the same scorched place as last time.

"Watch that when we get outside. I don't want you setting anyone's hair on fire."

He snorted, and Tyler neighed. Fig, for his part, barked. I felt briefly like I should have some kind of call sound to make, but I didn't. My "yeehaw" as we entered the subterranean cave system from the tavern to the surface was just going to have to be enough for the moment.

It was about all I could muster as I moved toward what I really hoped was not never-ending chaos.

Chapter Four

WHEN WE EMERGED FROM the tunnels over by the throwing shack, I had really expected to see the earth and buildings on fire, perhaps a dragon or two swooping in and out of the trees and laying down streams of destruction. Maybe a round of screaming villagers being pursued by something with talons, sharp teeth, and a thirst for blood.

Instead, people were milling around in the near dark, laughing and holding hands, strolling along the gravel and paved pathways, enjoying the sights and loving it. I heard so many thrilled comments about this being the very best faire ever as I tried to slow myself from rushing along those very same paths. I didn't want to alarm anyone, but there were several people I absolutely had to check in with. The first being Dalvon. Of course he was on the other side of the faire from our current position.

I wasn't quite sure how I was going to explain my glow or Tyler's extra legs, but so far everyone just oohed and ahhed over both and clapped. If they weren't asking, I wasn't telling...

We quick-walked past the chessboard, where a set of leprechauns were jumping over and around one another. No harm, no foul, thankfully. People clapped and laughed.

Finn grunted beside me as we went by the food court. Moving as quickly as I could, I directed him around back and had him set the trash on fire in the metal bin against the wall. Once his belch was a roaring blaze, I tossed some water on it from the anachronistic garden hose.

Beggars couldn't be choosers right now. And I was seriously begging whoever might be listening in the almighty upstairs that this was manageable and doable. At least until I could get the gates closed behind our human patrons and figure out what came next.

As I walked as casually as possible along the paths, so as not to alarm anyone, it was hard to ignore the fact that the faire was a rocking success, though. I had to slow a few times to wade through the masses of faire-goers.

And it was all backed by the spookiest music ever, coming from the steampipe organ around the corner. Ghosts flew out of the pipes, and I had to believe they were probably real ones, and very possibly under their own command. I'd believe anything right about now. I stood for a handful of seconds just to make sure they weren't hurting anyone, but people were laughing and singing with the music, and not one person looked anything less than delighted.

So I moved on.

We came to another corner and one of the paranormals that I worried about if the change was true across the whole of the faire. Rebella had really gone all out on the maze she ran, creating spider webs as big as houses and a ton of fake spiders to match. At least I hoped they were fake, now. She'd planned to have some of our extras posted throughout, in witch garb from the sixteen-hundreds, and a cauldron or two at the dead ends.

As I got closer to the entrance of the maze, I heard screaming, and my heart stuttered. At first, I thought it might be in pain or fear, but as I listened more intently, I realized it was happy screaming and lots and lots of excited chattering.

Okay, then. Hopefully the guests would continue to be full of delight and amazement so huge they were screaming in joy themselves to match what I assumed was a recording to go with the planned frights.

Then a shadow flitted over my head, and I was instantly reminded of when Gargy had first come to the maze. My heart tripped in my chest for a second time, but when I looked up, it wasn't my resident gargoyle.

Instead, Rebella had wings, and she was hovering over the top of the maze. Part of me wanted to think she'd found someone to rig her up and this was a surprise she just hadn't run by me. My first thought was that I'd have to get with her tomorrow to find out how she'd managed it. Then I admitted to myself that she was a Valkyrie and...yeah, right. Wings. Cool. Or at least I hoped it was.

Right now, she was the one screaming in delight. I wanted to delight with her, I really did. But there could be complications. I did give myself one brief pause to think how amazing she looked and sounded, but then I had to come back to reality. A Valkyrie in the faire could be a serious issue if she decided that we were embroiled in a battle and started choosing who would live and who would die in that battle.

With trepidation in my heart—and a fire-breathing Voror, a centaur, and a Chow that kept flashing back and forth from tiny to big by my side—I waved to her to come down. She shot down from out of the sky like an arrow of lightning to land inside the maze a few turns away from us. I forced my breathing to even out and prepared myself to greet her with a smile. She had been one of the people I'd wanted to check on anyway.

"I'm thinking the maze is a very bad place for a horse and someone who is belching fire, so why don't you guys go see about Barnaby and Everest? Keep in contact."

"Verla, are you sure?" Finn asked.

"To be honest, Finn, I'm not sure of anything right now, but I do know that we have a ton of paranormals in this faire that could be in distress, and we can cover twice as much ground if we split up."

I had expected another pushback, at least from Finn, but the two men just nodded and left. I escaped into the maze before either of them changed their minds.

Rebella had outdone herself with the spider webs as big as a house and the huge spiders she'd made out of Styrofoam and black lace. I peeked around the corner of the first turn, and there was the star of this particular attraction. Rebella was crouched in the corner, maybe fixing something on the huge web she'd strung there.

"Everything looks amazing," I said cautiously, wanting to feel out the situation before I assumed it was all bad.

Rebella froze for a second then slowly turned around and stood up. "You're sure it looks okay?" she asked, tucking her hands behind her back and pinning her wings.

"Positive!" I breathed as much enthusiasm into that word as possible and pasted a smile on my face. "It has all this great character, and it looks almost real. And tonight you don't have to worry about using the floodlights when it gets dark. The fairegoers are expecting things to be spooky tonight, and we're going to deliver. Then you'll be gone for the rest of the holidays, so we'll keep it simple. That way there's less to break down." How did I mention the wings without making her fly into the sky and take off?

"If you're sure?"

"Positive, Rebbie!" Maybe a little too much force behind that exclamation point there, but I wasn't sure how to stop myself now that I'd started. "I'm so excited that you're going to have some time to yourself to get things done and still do them for you and your family. Plus, people are expecting costumes tonight and big scary things in not well-lit places. So make your costume fierce and your persona fiercer, and we'll own this day." I was pouring the excitement on a little thick, but I didn't know what to tell her about what was going on, and I didn't want to freak her out and make her worry. But the wings...

"Yes, ma'am," Rebbie said, bringing one of her arms out from behind her to salute. Those new wings popped out behind her in all their glory, and she tried to shove them back, without much luck. How did it feel to finally have the wings she had been born without as a misplaced Valkyrie? I knew slightly how she was probably feeling by now, being able to see the future. Wings, though—that must be a whole new experience...

"Those wings are beautiful! New?" I asked, just to see what she'd say.

She blushed and pushed them back behind her again, and then smiled. "Yep, new."

"They're lovely. I might have to see if I can get some new ones for other people."

"I really should go get things in working order. I'll see you later?"

"Sure..."

She turned away from me, and I felt marginally slighted, as well as dismissed. Okay, then. Maybe she was just thinking about getting into the role. Normally, I'd have caught up with her later to ask how they'd made the wings fly. But I already knew, and I'd promised not to hide anything from the faire workers. This was too important. And while I wasn't worried that she was going to start taking warriors that weren't really warriors out in a battle that wasn't happening, I still had to do the responsible thing here.

"Can I, um, talk to you for a minute?" I waited until she turned around again and was concerned to see her face crinkle into a frown and tears slip down her face.

"I'm going to have to leave now, aren't I? I have my wings, and I'm a full Valkyrie, so I can't stay."

"What?" My face must have crinkled too, but mine was not because of tears. It was horror at her assumption. "Oh, my stars, no. No, you don't have to leave, and certainly not because you've become what you were supposed to be at birth. I know we're mostly misfits here, but I would never turn someone away like that. You're a part of us."

"Oh, Verla, I've been worrying about that so much for the last hour." She grabbed my hands. "I don't want to go, but, oh my, what a pleasure it is to have these beauties." She swished like the fairy in *Scrooged* right before she clocked Bill Murray with a toaster.

"I'm sure, but that's part of my question. Why an hour? Is that when you got them? Did they just magically appear on your back?" And what had I been doing an hour ago? Right, watching ley lines pulse and move in a way they never had before.

So was this truly the ley lines' doing? And was it permanent? What would that mean for everyone?

I was getting too far ahead of myself.

"Yeah, I was helping one kid in particular navigate the maze because he seemed pretty scared, even though you can tell everything in here is fake. We turned a corner, a light flashed under a hay bale, and suddenly I had wings. They opened, and I lifted off the ground—which absolutely delighted the kid, by the way—and then I set down and led him out of the maze, where he told all his friends what he'd seen. I let the wings unfurl again and did a couple of tricks, but I didn't see the light again. Although it was very similar to the way you're glowing, but yours is more subtle." She cocked her head at me and looked me up and down.

Since I couldn't do that, I just looked at myself from the waist down, and yes, indeed, I was very much glowing, but not as brightly as I had in the darkened basement below the tavern. Was I carrying ley line magic with me? The thought made me shiver, so I shunted it aside for the moment.

"Yeah, I'm going to be honest. I'm not entirely sure what's going on, but Finn's out checking with everyone else in the opposite direction while I work this side of the faire. As long as you don't get any urges to choose who is to be slain and cart them off to Valhalla, I think we'll be okay."

"I'll be careful." She chuckled, and thankfully it sounded like genuine mirth instead of that evil cackle both Zane and Buford had blasted me with.

"Okay, but use your walkie if you get nervous. And just know that Wes could potentially be super big if he comes running."

"Got it, and good luck!" She took off into the sky, and another set of children went wild as she did a few flips in the air and then arrowed back down to the ground. Holy crap, that was cool!

But I had to leave because I had to check on Dalvon.

I made it to the aviary in time to see him stumble out the back door and throw up on the ground. I was horrible with puke, so I stood back and closed my eyes.

"Having trouble with your protein shakes?" I asked, opening my eyes again because I needed to see his state.

"Yes," he croaked, and his throat sounded like it was rusting shut. "I want blood, Verla, I've never wanted blood, but I want it so badly I can barely stand."

"Oh, sweetie, I'm so sorry." I crouched next to him, ignoring my own issues because he was far more important. "Listen, I know you don't want to drink and that you have a wonderful last act show for the joust, but why don't you sit this one out?

Something's going on in the faire, and I'm thinking I'm going to need to close down early."

My mind flashed to Dalvon, my resident vampire, a vegetarian. But in the vision he stood with a bird in each hand, and both were dead, but his eyes were glowing with a light like a blood moon.

I could not let that happen.

"I'm going to give you to Finn in a minute and call Grayden in. I'm sure we can get you something to settle your stomach, but I really think you need to take the night off. We'll get back to the faire in a few months, and it will all be okay." At least I hoped so, and that I wasn't telling lie after lie in my hopefulness.

"There's no need for that," Patrice said from behind me.

I turned to find her standing with Gargy in full gargoyle mode and Pix, her little fire-lion, perched on her shoulder.

"Why isn't there a need?" I took her in from head to toe, wondering what I might have to deal with in regard to her. "We cannot let Dalvon go in the opposite direction from what he's done his whole life. He'd die before drinking someone's blood."

Dalvon snarled, and I took that to be acquiescence.

"I understand that, Verla, and I know how these things work, but I also regained all of my powers, and I can make him a brew to hold him over with the river water you use to cross souls. It's not going to cure him, but it will hold him over until you can get things back in order."

"Back..." It came out more as a question, and I didn't know how to finish it. Figiggly whined at my ankle, small again and with his tongue stuck on Gargy's leg.

The blue symbol of protection of Fig's tongue met the sigil on Gargy's leg, and a nimbus of blue emanated from both of them.

"In order," Gargy ground out. "We've been talking, and we're aware that some people might want to keep this newfound bounty of powers, but there are many who will not. Right now, we need you to find the source and settle it down until we can handle it."

"Yes, of course." That made total sense, and I should have thought of it earlier. In my defense I had a ton of images and memories and thoughts running through my head—like twenty-six televisions on up there, and they were all on different channels.

"We just came from the privies, and we think you might want to start there. The whole thing is lit up green and there are ghosts popping in and out of the stalls, then zooming out the door and back in. They appear to be scaring people, unlike the other phantoms in the park." Patrice petted her little Pixiu and rested her head on Gargy's rock-hard shoulder. Would he be able to change into a man ever again?

I could not under any circumstances think about stuff like that, or I might just lose my mind.

I had a mission and an objective. It was time to hit the privies.

Chapter Five

I WAS ALREADY HEADING in that direction, so I left Dalvon and his birds to Patrice and her little homemade clan and started on my way to the public restrooms near the food court, with Figiggly trotting along beside me. I was allowed to think of them that way, if only in my mind.

Right now, I had a ghost to take care of and a whole ren faire to check over before it imploded.

With so many tickets sold, I had figured we might experience a thing or two that wouldn't go exactly according to plan. But I'd wanted everything else, especially everything paranormal, to go exactly as it should.

Of course, I now knew that had been a pipe dream, but for the moment I was on a mission and only worrying about half of the million things that were currently going wrong.

See? Progress!

Some of the kids wearing their witch garb came streaming out of the torture museum chattering excitedly, and I moved on so as not to get trampled by the crowd of extras. I almost got caught in the middle of another trail of people in court dress trying to get into the candle shop on the corner, and I laughed a little like a loon. All was well on the outside, and we were very obviously delivering on the promise I'd made for a fantastic Halloween. But the rest had to be taken care of, and that was where I came in.

Just as long as no one knew about the underlying ley lines that were messing with everything I loved.

And then to my left there was the jousting field. I'd set this one up myself but had no part to play in it. Brinlynn, a recent transfer to the faire and a warrior of the highest caliber, was riding on our resident kelpie, who'd agreed to not take her down to the depths of the nearest stream.

I really hoped he would keep that promise for now.

The crowd was loving the way she and the kelpie were pitching a fevered battle with the ghosts of the Wild Hunt. I'd promised the fabled warriors a place at Halloween after their help this summer, and I was not one to go back on my word if I could help it. They were going at it now, and I worried less about them since Brinlynn was not a misfit and neither were any of the members of the Wild Hunt. I did see Heldigrad tied up in a corner, but that could be seen as a prop, by the faire-goers, so I didn't concern myself with it. Willy Nilly knew what he was doing.

I needed to get to the privies soon, but I couldn't help watching for just a moment as Brinlynn wielded an enormous broadsword and cut through Mylmar, one of the Wild Hunt. He screamed and flew apart but then reformed right after she'd laughed with triumph. The crowd went wild, and that was enough for me.

A glimmer of something caught my eye out on the field, a green bump on the brown dirt. It shouldn't have been there. It flashed once, twice, and on the third time it burst out of the ground and showered sparks of yellow and blue not ten feet from Seawaddle the kelpie.

And no one flinched, not even the kelpie. Not a single person, being, or ghost in the field seemed to see it, either. I'd been working with Mavis, my retirement village crone, on not only what I could do myself but also what the seventeen ley lines could do and how to maintain them.

This looked like a ley line thing, so I focused inward and blinked my eyes to see those very same ley lines and if there was a disruption in the system. I thought it had only been at the tavern, but this was proving me wrong.

I realized at that instant I really should have done that earlier. I took a breath in through my nose and let it out as I opened my eyes.

I couldn't see them all the time—and didn't want to, as it was extremely distracting to know how many connections there were in the ground, and how powerful they could be if activated.

The bump and burst was definitely one of the ley lines, though. A ripple of energy ran along the ground, arrowing straight for the privies. I turned, and so did Fig, though I didn't know if he had seen it or not. The two of us followed it as it traveled along the crooked line in a slow fashion but gaining speed with every second. By the time we reached our destination it was speeding along, and we were trying hard to catch up without alerting anyone that anything was wrong.

But maybe nothing really was wrong, and I was just looking for trouble that didn't exist.

I sighed when it finally came to rest outside the entrance of the privies. I didn't know why I was so afraid of it going into the building, except that maybe I'd have more to deal with than a burst of water in an unused toilet, if it got out of hand.

I waved to a bunch of ladies exiting the building in full costume. "Stay here, Fig. In case anything happens, I'm going to need a man on the outside to deal with any trouble."

Thankfully, he listened to me and plunked down with his blue tongue hanging out. The sigil of protection on his tongue did not glow, so that was a good thing, at least. And he was also still my small little pup instead of the hulking form he could take on when danger was approaching.

My heart stuttered as I remembered seeing that blue tongue go dark and the magic seep out of him into the ground after he'd been hit by magic lightning.

Shaking off that thought mentally, I also shook my head physically. I was not going to dwell on that. He was better, and he would remain that way forever if I could do anything about it. Worrying about him dying again or somehow leaving me was not something I allowed myself to do because it was debilitating, to say the least.

The ghost. I needed to see about this Irene and then try to get her to cross. Yes, I had hoped to only be focused on the faire and Halloween today, but Patrice's and Gargy's warning was way more important than what I had *thought* I was going to do.

Stepping in through the entrance, I made my way down the concrete aisle that separated the two long rows of stalls. We liked to stay true to the time period here at the faire, but I was not about to have a bunch of garderobes hanging off the outside wall of a castle, or make holes in the ground for people to go to the bathroom. So we had a nice little building, all decked out with solid stall doors and modern toilets. Honestly, it looked like a horse barn from the outside, but who cared?

And one of those modern toilets was geysering up over the top of the stall door. Not to the point where water was leaking out on the floor, but more like a contained fountain. What on earth was Irene doing?

I looked at Griselda, the attendant for today, and nodded at her. We put up an out-of-order sign with directions to the other privy on the front door, just in case this took longer than I thought it should.

Once I shooed Griselda out, I got ready to reckon with this ghost for the very last time.

I was set. I was ready. I was going to convince her that her time had come to go.

Or at least that was my intention until Althea, my dog trainer, showed up with Dorsey, one of our tarot card readers.

"Hey there, just have something to do for a moment, and then I'll be right with you," I said.

Dorsey laughed this really deep, low laugh that sent shivers up my spine, and Althea's eyes lit up with the fires of hell. For real.

Uh-oh.

"Ladies, how can I help you?" I was never so thankful and scared at the same time. Thankful, because I'd left Fig outside where he'd be safe, but scared because something was very off with both of the women facing me.

Dorsey was my tarot card reader, a woman who made flower crowns in her spare time and always had a kind word for anyone who passed by her. I had no idea what she should have been as a paranormal, only that she had no real powers to speak of as a misfit.

I was reminded of Finn and his demand when he'd first come back here that we get papers from everyone to know who they were and where they'd come from. The faire owner, Morty, had never wanted to do that because of protecting people's privacy. I'd gone right along with him. Why did I get the feeling that might bite me in the rear end right now?

I stared at Althea, though, because I did know what she was supposed to have been, and that could be a serious problem. Althea was capable of being rigid and commanding with the dogs. She was an excellent trainer and a good friend. I'd seen the fires flicker for her before and knew she should have been a sin eater. But she wasn't actually capable of performing that task because of something that happened at her birth.

These thoughts whizzed through my head as the fountain continued to geyser in the toilet, and Irene keened for release.

"There's a sin eater here, Verla." She popped up over the top of the stall and hung over the door with her arms dangling and her head at a strange angle. Being able to see through her didn't make her appearance any less frightening. "A sin eater! Just like I asked for. Is it my birthday? Did you bring me a present?" She laughed and twirled around, to then land next to me on her feet.

"I..." Had no idea what to say...

"I can eat your sin, woman." Althea stepped forward on jerky legs. It reminded me of the time I'd tried to play with a marionette. I'd never been able to get the timing and the hand gestures right with the strings, and instead of smooth movement, it was like trying to maneuver Frankenstein.

"I don't think you should do that, Althea." I stood my ground as she stumped her way closer, but it was getting really hard not to turn and run. I had my phone in my pocket, so I thumbed up the screen and hoped I hit the right button to emergency-call Finn.

"It's my destiny, Verla. Don't make me fight my destiny." Her smile was nothing short of malicious, and it made my skin crawl.

"Destiny," Dorsey said in a mimicking voice. "And I have my part to play as the necromancer. I can raise all the dead that Althea needs to feed on, and we can make this faire what it should have been all along." That wicked laugh again, and I got goosebumps on top of my shivers. What in the world was going on?

Irene floated toward Althea as if drawn by an invisible cord. The door opened behind me, and I debated whipping around to see who it was, but I didn't want to take my eyes off what was happening in front of me.

Then it got to be too much, because the presence behind me had something wrong with it. I did a quick-turn and found myself face to face with Irene's body. Where the hell had that come from? As far as I knew, she was buried in the small cemetery the Weatherby clan had allowed the local church to keep in operation when they'd bought the land.

My heart nearly stopped. Had this body walked through the whole faire? Were the people outside being overrun by freaking zombies? Why wasn't I hearing screaming, or running, if that was the case?

I sent a quick shout-out mentally to Fig, not sure if he'd hear me but asking for him to get Finn and stay safe.

"Althea and Dorsey, please stop this now," I said in the calmest voice I could muster, which wasn't very calm, but at least I was trying. "We'll sit and talk about your abilities in a minute, but I really need you to stop right now. We have people outside, ones that need to be safe at the faire. And they can't be safe if you have corpses wandering into the bathroom."

Althea laughed, and I so wished it was the carefree laughter that we often shared over a glass of wine while we complained about our love lives and how we didn't know what the right move was.

But this was far more sinister. Out of the corner of my eye I saw another green bump in the ley line and then a burst again of the blue and yellow. Althea shivered, Dorsey's hair stood straight up from her head, and they both converged on the ghost and the corpse.

Where the hell were Finn and Fig when I needed them? This was seriously out of hand, and I might just have to throw away the Days Without Incident board altogether, because I had no idea how I was going to stop this from happening.

I tried to pause time, but my mind was split in so many different directions, and hounded with so many worries, it didn't work.

And they just kept coming.

Another toilet geysered, and another ghost peeked over the top of the stall, and another corpse wandered into the privy. I couldn't even. Like seriously, my brain just started short-circuiting, and

I wasn't sure where to look first, or what to take care of before anything else.

Then Fig, bless his little furry behind, started corralling the corpses into the various stalls before blocking the exit. Someone pushed on the door behind the dog, who had grown several sizes in the process of trying to get things in order, and he turned to growl horribly…more horribly than I'd ever heard.

I threw caution to the wind and pulled out my phone. Finn was saying hello over and over again, and I almost cried at the sound of his voice.

"Come quick, like right this second. We have more trouble than just Irene in the women's bathroom."

"Don't you mean privy?" he asked, cheekily.

I stabbed the Off button on the screen and prepared to face whatever the hell was about to happen.

Chapter Six

SINCE I HAD NO weapons at my waist, peace-tied or not, I grabbed the nearest thing to hand and started brandishing it to prevent the women from getting to the corpses and the ghosts.

Unfortunately, it was a toilet-cleaning brush. Of course it was.

But I'd do what damage I could with it, come hell or high water. The hell I felt like I could probably deal better with than the water, right now, though. The water that was no longer just geysering into the air but was starting to pour out across the floor. Little pops of blue and yellow sparked across the surface of the rising liquid that was coming close to going over the tips of my shoes.

I glanced around to find Fig standing on the counter with the sinks and snapping and snarling to keep anyone else from entering the building. But for how long? I needed help.

It came in the form of a man I still didn't quite know what to do with. I heard scraping and thudding on the roof above me and wondered if I was going to have a crush of zombie corpses fall through the ceiling. But no, it was Finn, slipping through the opaque skylight in the ceiling.

I was never so happy to see him. Though I still didn't know what exactly I expected him to do. He was a wraith who would only live as long as I did. That didn't make him the best of cohorts when it came to eradicating ghosts or corpses, but again, beggars couldn't be choosers at this point.

"See if you can help Fig keep anything else from coming into the bathroom. I don't know what we're going to do with all these dead bodies, but I need it to stop before I can think my way through that. And protect the faire-goers."

He was off and manning the door with a broom and a mop before I finished my sentence. I appreciated that more than I would probably ever be able to express.

But my stomach was churning acid. Did I call security? Cordon this area off and make them go around while I handled whatever this new craziness was?

I heard a shout go up outside. For a second, I was very afraid that someone had gotten hurt. But the shout turned into words, and I debated between rolling my eyes and sighing in relief.

"Dude, it's the zombie apocalypse! I wonder if they're allowed to touch us or if it's a total hands-off kind of thing like that haunted hayride we went on last week."

"This is awesome! Seriously, they look so real. Should we chase them? Anybody have a pitchfork or a broomstick? Where's my Twinkies?"

I decided both eye-rolling and sighing were in order. As I did them simultaneously, Finn looked over at me and shrugged.

"Yeah, I guess we just go with how excited everyone is to be in the middle of what they think is part of the show and hope none of these zombies are actually after brains, just sin-eating."

"Sins are to be eaten."

While I'd been eye-rolling and sighing, Althea had snuck up on me and stood less than five feet away.

"Totally understandable, and I get what you're going through, but I can't let you do this, Althea. You're my friend, and I'm afraid that once this thing —whatever it is—passes, that you'll be changed forever and upset that I didn't stop you."

"You cannot stop us, Verla. Stand aside or be taken with the rest of them." This was Dorsey talking, my favorite tarot card reader and gentlest soul in the world. She was everyone's mother, everyone's shoulder, and now she was turning into something else that I couldn't watch.

However, I saw the flash of cards in her pocket, and my fingers literally itched like a mosquito bite to touch them, to use them.

"Fig." I said it in my mind because I didn't want to yell it over the hubbub outside and the moaning that had just started inside. "I need the cards from her pocket. Can you sneak them away, or are you going to have to tackle her?"

"I do not tackle people, thank you very much." Ever since his death and resuscitation, he'd been so much better and faster at responding. I appreciated that, but I did not need his commentary, just his maneuvering.

"Sure, okay, got it. Just…can you please get the cards out of her pocket? I might be able to use them."

"Are you sure?"

"No, but I keep getting these flashes, and you were very fiercely protecting Finn. Everyone seems to be able to do the one thing they were supposed to be when they were born but weren't, and so they ended up as misfits here. I was supposed to be able to tell the future and use the tarot cards to do that. If I'm right, then maybe I can do more than just get a flash or two about whatever the universe wants without me having to ask all the questions to direct the answer."

He nudged my hand on that last sentence. When I glanced down, he had the cards in his mouth, and Finn had managed to use Figiggly's leash to tie both Alethea and Dorsey to a purse hook on the back of a bathroom stall door. Well, then...

I felt a little useless, but when I took the cards out of Fig's mouth, they got the same glow that was still lighting up my legs and torso. My hands were warm, my mind on fire, and my heart racing like Seawaddle galloping.

Would I know what to do with these? Would I be able to tell anything or guide the visions with these?

Since I had not had the talent when I was growing up, no one had taken the time to actually teach me anything. I'd been learning this new talent of crossing the dead as I went along, with the wonderful help of Mavis from the nursing home down the road, but I was still very unsure of what all I could do. Now, even that was not certain, and I wasn't sure where to go from here.

I'd been left at an orphanage at a young age because I hadn't manifested the powers that were expected from me. And now I was faced with a big, huge issue, no guidance, and just a hope and a prayer to whoever was listening that I wouldn't make things worse.

Please don't let me make things worse.

I shuffled the cards as I'd seen Dorsey do a thousand times. She growled at me and tried to grab them out of my hands, but she was a little tied up at the moment. I shuffled them faster, and they began to emanate a light all their own in an amazing blue that bordered on purple. I thought for a second that my hands should be cramping from how fast I was shuffling. I stopped to shake out my hand preemptively, but the cards hovered in front of me and kept shuffling on their own. Even Dorsey stopped her growling to stare in awe at the display.

Three cards popped out of the deck simultaneously. I had no guide to the tarot on me and very little retained knowledge of what each card meant, but it was like the knowledge was right there in the front of my brain just as I started to panic. The anxiety settled down and the meaning came to me without much more than a thought that I'd like to know. It was both wonderful and a little sad, to be honest.

The three cards were Judgment, the Knight of Coins, and Strength. And they told a story that seemed to whisper in my ears.

"*Listen to the call, Verla. It is possible that this is bigger than you understand, but it has power that you must protect. Stick close to home, shore up your foundation, choose practical things to manifest, and know they are waiting for you with that protection. We remind you that you have so much within you to keep moving forward when you trust your ability. You will get the sense of power and harmony. You walk with the big cats and tell the big stories.*"

I shook my head because with each sentence another voice chimed in, and it sounded like I was in a cathedral with an entire men's chorus singing in my head. It was distracting and yet so incredibly beautiful. My mind blanked as I concentrated on the noise and let my sight turn inward.

"No!" That one word echoed through the chambers of my mind. It jerked me back, and I looked up to find Grandma Jean hanging in the rafters. She floated down, then bent her knees when she hit the ground. She looked far more solid than she ever had before.

"What's—"

"Do not ask me what is going on, or what I'm doing here, or anything else. Just listen. You are in desperate danger. This is worse than anything you have ever faced before. I should have considered that this was going to happen. Damn it!"

I stood with my mouth open but didn't say anything for a few seconds while she grumbled. She was taking too long, though, and the chaos was still rising. "You haven't told me what's going on yet, Grandma. I need to know. I have to save everyone in this faire. There are hundreds, if not thousands, of faire-goers, and my population is doubling as we speak, with corpses coming from the graveyard down the lane."

"Yes, yes, yes, I know. Okay, let me think of how to say this…"

"No thinking, just freaking blurt it out already. What the *HELL* is going on?" I restrained myself from using the interrobang but that was a close thing, in case you were wondering.

"The ley lines are fully activated. Everyone is what they were supposed to be when born."

"Yes, I figured that out already and have checked in with as many as I could. Zane is a danger, and so is Buford. Buford is fighting it as best he can, but I'm afraid he's going to lose. I get that there's danger here. Why is it more than before?"

She shook her head. "Something is coming through the lines. Something that is far darker and older than anything I've heard about in centuries."

"What the hell is it?"

"Funny you should say it like that because it's not hell, it's worse."

"Worse than hell?"

"It's a band of Strigoi, and they've been waiting for this very moment for centuries. They not only drink blood, but the more they drink the more they materialize, and we can't kill them once they reach full stature."

Well, crap.

Strigoi. The name and an image of a ghoul from beyond the grave flashed into my mind. In myth, it was closest to a vampire. However, instead of the person being turned and dying to live again and need blood, it was a person who died with a witch's curse and came back from the grave to be reborn and live the curse of the witch over and over again.

A band of them was certainly worse than hell. They were particularly fond of children, and we had hundreds here. Hundreds. And I had to figure out how to save them all, along with getting rid of a bunch of corpses and ghosts who wanted the sin eater, as well as a demon who was fighting himself, and a few others that I hadn't been able to find, like our resident werewolf, who as of yesterday could only turn his nose and tail, and tonight could be on the hunt to rip anyone apart.

I was going to be sick. Maybe I could lock myself in one of the stalls and just heave out the delicious mac and cheese triangles I'd downed earlier when I was happy and myself.

Now, I was a future seer who had dancing cards and great chemistry with the universe to tell me what could be coming up next, but no way to use any of the skills I'd been so sure of until a few hours ago.

"What can I do?" I asked instead of being sick.

"I'm not sure." My grandmother shrugged.

But a thought had popped into my head along with a vision so real that it felt like a memory instead of the future.

"Open the door, Finn!" I yelled. "Let all the corpses in, and then go get the Wild Hunt. We need their services."

Chapter Seven

FINN WAS QUICK TO do as I asked, but along with corpses came one of my worst nightmares... Morty was here. The man who owned the faire, who paid my salary, who let me run things as I saw fit, was standing in the doorway of the privy looking like he was about to rain down hellfire on not only yours truly but probably everything within a ten-mile radius.

Why on earth was he here, and why today when things were as bad as they'd ever been?

There was nothing I could do but return his nod, quickly but gently move him away from the door, and then put the rest of my plan into action, what little of it there was.

No one stopped to acknowledge Morty except me. Finn shoved a few more corpses in through the door and then slammed it shut. Through the screen windows I could hear his boots thudding on the paved road and his shouts of, "Excuse me," and, "Pardon me," and one last, "Please move now," before his voice faded.

"Quite the scenario you have here, my dear," Morty said. As always, he had a pipe in his hand, and he wore a waistcoat with a stylized cravat. Today's clothing choice leaned toward the hunter green and beige, set with a flash of orange in the breast pocket, in the form of a handkerchief.

"I—"

"No need to explain at the moment. We have far more important things to do right here and now that don't involve convoluted explanations and you trying to explain them away." He gazed over the group of animated corpses—I hesitated to call them zombies because I really did not want anyone to start yelling for my brains—the spirits who belonged to them perched above their heads, and the two women who had completely stopped struggling against the bindings holding them hostage.

Althea may have been quiet, but that didn't stop her from sneering at me when I glanced her way too. I knew it wasn't real and that my best friend Althea would never hate me as much as the disgusted curl of her mouth showed, but it still hurt.

I mouthed *I'm sorry* as she turned her head away from me.

I had not asked Finn to close the skylight because I wasn't sure how the Wild Hunt was going to get in here. I half expected them to show up any moment, so I wasn't completely surprised when something came through the portal into my own personal little hell. But I *was* surprised it was Gargy in full gargoyle form. Everything about him was gray and grim, particularly his face. I was so used to seeing him happy with his new family that I'd forgotten how menacing he could appear, especially with his eyes glowing red.

A shriek went up throughout the facility as he landed on the cement flooring with a thud. Every soul immediately zipped into the bodies they had been hovering above, and Althea's sneer went directly into a smile usually held in reserve for her time with Grayden, the man she loved—though she wouldn't admit to it.

Yeah, I wasn't alone in not knowing what to do with an ex who showed up unexpectedly. I valued all the talks we'd had over the last few months, and I just couldn't fathom that I wouldn't be able to share stories with her anymore if her sin-eating kept her looking like a fiend instead of the woman I cared so much for.

"A gargoyle, how apropos," Althea purred. I did not like the sound of that.

"You looking for me to keep the evil spirits away, Sin Eater?" he ground out in that voice that sounded like two rocks shifting against each other.

"Possibly." She looked him up and down in a way that made my skin crawl.

"We're not doing this!" I yelled into the deafening silence. "We. Are. Not. Doing. This!" I could make my voice lower and gravelly too, and I was having none of these shenanigans.

"We might have to," Morty said, placing a hand on my shoulder and pointing at the green energy that looked like a rope flowing between Finn and me. It was fading, writhing, and fluctuating from bright green to dull dying-grass green. "There's more here than you can possibly know, even with the help of Melva from the nursing home. I've seen this magic before, and if we don't get things under control, then it's not just the faire itself that's going to be in danger. It will be every single person within about a hundred-mile radius, everyone in the faire, every misfit paranormal, human and animal."

I gulped because I really wanted to shove someone out of the stall across from me and get down on my knees to bow to the porcelain god. But the look on Morty's face told me not only that this was very serious but also that we didn't have time for me to fall apart right now. I could do that later.

"So what do we do?" I squeaked those words out. I cleared my throat and went to try again, but Morty put his hand up.

"Let Althea do what she was meant to do from the beginning. I know her mother and father, who are both sin eaters. She'll be okay, and she'll still be the woman you adore. But we can't move forward with any kind of plan until this is taken care of."

I gulped again and nodded my head, though I stared at the floor as I did it. I felt a shriek of wind on the back of my neck and looked up to find the Wild Hunt hovering at the ceiling. It was getting a little crowded in this privy.

"There's nothing you can do here, guys. Sorry for bothering you."

"Let Finn in," said Willy Nilly, the leader of the Hunt. "He'll be able to help, and he needs to be near you right now."

I didn't want to let him in, because I wanted him to be safe and not in the thick of this, but Morty reached for the door and turned the knob. Finn burst through the door like a wild man and immediately stood as close to me as he possibly could without wrapping himself around me. His arm went around my back, and he held onto my thick waist like an anchor. I immediately felt better. I wasn't surprised by that, but I was surprised when the green tether between us faded even more. Soon it would be gone, and then what? I'd deal with the aftermath and the plethora of emotions, from relief to devastation, another time.

"Untie Althea and Dorsey, please, Finn. Your uncle says this has to happen."

He balked, but I placed my hand on his forearm and begged him with my eyes to listen to me.

And he did. After untying the two women, he was quick to step back and grab a hold of me again. I wasn't going to complain.

"Althea," Morty said in a commanding tone. "Help these people, and then let's remove ourselves to the river, where Verla can cross them into the underworld."

My heart stopped in my chest. What if I couldn't still do that because I was now a seer and so no longer a dead-crosser? I didn't bring it up, though, because all my attention immediately turned to Althea and the way she stood before each of the corpses, placing her palm on their hearts, one by one, and dropping her head to look at the floor. A whisper of smoke came out of the person's chest and curled around and around Althea's forearm and then up to her chest. It worked its way up and down at the same time. Curling around her bicep and also her thighs, taking a pathway to her toes as well as her head. And then she absorbed the cloud of darkness into her skin with a gasp and immediately looked ashen.

The first corpse stood to the side and smiled very cheerfully as it made room for the next and then the next and the next. I wasn't sure how many she could take on before it became too much.

Dorsey was actually the one to help with that. "I'm so sorry, Verla. I don't know what came over us with that evil cackling and wicked smiles. I have never acted like that a day in my life."

I watched as another cloud of black seeped into Althea's pores. She shuddered this time, her color remaining not good but not worse. Another and another. It became like an assembly line, but she never had the same reaction as with the first one.

But being me, I still couldn't keep myself from stepping forward after the thirteenth one, when she shuddered again, and her knees buckled a little. Morty placed his hand on my shoulder once more and quietly asked me to just watch and be here to support but not interfere.

The corpses were congregated over by the sinks, where Fig had shrunken back to his normal size and was letting the people who were long dead pet him. His blue tongue with its sigil of protection hung out, and his tail was wagging enough to create a slight breeze.

Finn remained behind me with his arm around my waist as Althea finished the job she should have had since she was born. She breathed out a sigh that sounded a lot like relief and turned to me.

"I'm ready to go to the river, Verla, if you'd be so kind as to help me get there. I'm weary and heavy at the moment, but all will be right as soon as I can step into the flow of the water." And her face wore this almost blissful look, like she was happy. To be carrying everyone's sin within her? How was that possible?

I opened my mouth to ask, and Morty clamped his hand down. "Save it. Let her do her thing, and then we'll have plenty of time for questions once the park is closed."

Since he was my boss, there wasn't much I could do to contradict him and still keep the job that meant the world to me, even more than being a dead-crosser or a seer.

When we opened the door again, Grayden was standing outside, looking like he might be losing his ever-loving mind.

Chapter Eight

"WHERE IS ALTHEA?" IT came out as a question, sort of. If I were being honest, though, it came out more as a demand, and from a man who was not going to take anything but the absolute truth as an answer.

"She's behind me. She's also very full of sin from the many corpse-type people you see wandering around also behind me."

His face went ghost white and he gulped hard. Then he stiffened up and stood far taller than I thought I had ever seen him stand. "Hand her over to me. You cannot make her do this. Whatever is going on at the faire is not her business if it will ruin her."

"Grayden, I get it. And please believe me when I say I don't want to have to do this, but she chose to eat the sin, and now I have to take her to the river to cleanse her."

"How could you let this happen?" He clenched his teeth and his fists.

My heart, which was already having some issues with beating regularly, skipped a beat. Was this all my fault? Had I unknowingly brought this all down on the very people I loved more than my own life? Maybe I had. Maybe decisions I'd made, things I'd decided to pursue in my education had made this all happen. Maybe in playing with the powers I hadn't known about, or the ones that had come to me recently, I'd inadvertently set off this horrendous chain of events.

But there was nothing I could do now except clean up the mess and figure out where that left me later.

"I'm going to ask you to step aside and let me finish this. I do understand that you're not happy. I also know there is every possibility this is my fault. But that also makes it my responsibility to clean it up, and I can't do that with you blocking my way." I stared into his eyes and waited for whatever would come next.

Surprisingly enough, he stepped aside. Yeah, he growled when he did it, and yes, there was definitely a serious promise of retribution in his glare, but there was nothing I could do but walk past him with my parade of zombies, flying ghosts from the Wild Hunt, the owner of the faire, my ex-that-wasn't-actually-an-ex, a necromancer, a sin-eater, and a dog that might have started all this.

We were quite the spectacle as we made our way along the paved roads of the faire and traveled to the river. There was no way I could stop faire-goers from following me, and I wasn't going to try. If they wanted a show, they were going to get one with no extra cost as I tried to figure out if my previous powers had been replaced by these new ones.

It wasn't far to the river, but it felt like forever. I couldn't ignore the sounds of shuffling and shambling behind me as the previously buried people followed along. And the excited chatter of the crowd didn't make it any easier to ignore the occasional moan or groan from my merry band of dead people.

"We should close the faire and do this after," I said quietly to Morty, who walked beside me.

"No, this has to be done right now, and we don't have the time or the manpower to get everyone out of here right now. Plus, I don't think we could completely count on everyone leaving. There are too many people involved to get the right ones out and keep the right ones in."

At least that wasn't my decision. So, if it all went to hell, I wouldn't be the only one to blame.

A warm hand enveloped mine. I glanced up to find Finn at my side. Still slightly green, still dealing with a case of indigestion that probably burned like he'd swallowed coals.

"I'm so sorry about all this." I squeezed his hand, and he squeezed back. The thread between us faded to a smoky gray trail of almost nothing.

"You have nothing to apologize for. I'm the one who brought Figiggly here. I can't help wondering if that's what stirred the pot of all the magic in the first place." He traced a small circle on the back of my hand.

"I was thinking the same thing, but I don't regret having him here." Or Finn, but I wasn't sure how to say that in the middle of this crisis without sounding like an idiot.

We both stopped for a moment when a huge pumpkin came bouncing over a hill and rolled down to cross our paths. It flashed fire and a trail of bluish smoke as it and about ten smaller pumpkins bounced through the grass and then rolled into the river and extinguished themselves.

A cheer went through the crowd. I shrugged and so did Finn.

"Stop with the morose crap," Morty said, inserting himself between us and hooking an arm around each of our waists. "This is going to go down in history as the most magnificent Halloween ever at the faire. Imagine the ticket sales for next year!"

Finn and I looked at each other over his uncle's head. And something clicked for me. Some small thing that I had been running around and from and into for the past several months. This man was everything I had ever wanted. I'd been devastated when he left, but I'd made a new life for myself. I had lived well, done the things that made me happy, gone on with life without him by my side. But there had been something missing, some small thing that would have made the journey that much better. And that thing was being able to communicate without words, to be so understood by someone so well that you didn't need the words. And maybe that wasn't such a small thing after all.

"I love you." I said the words before I could think better of it or stop myself.

"Finally!" Morty said and Fig howled. The two seemed to skip in front of us, leaving Finn and me in a sea of people as we stopped and stared at each other.

"You think this is the right place to do this?" I asked him.

He'd sunk to one knee in front of me, and in his faire clothes he looked like some noble knight finally laying claim to his fair lady's hand. Or faire lady, as the case may be.

"Oh, yeah. This is totally the right place." He dipped his hand into his shirt and came out with a ring on a chain from around his neck. My engagement ring. The really cheap one that had been the only thing we could afford when he asked—over French fries at a fast-food restaurant—if I'd marry him.

"You still have that?"

"I've always had it in safekeeping for when you might need it again. Do you want it, Verla? Do you want me?"

I hesitated for a split second. The thoughts of doing this over the winter, of taking my time and making a good decision, of considering what I wanted and how I wanted to go about it, all flew through my head. And then something furry bumped into my leg, and Finn caught me and kept me from falling. As he always would, tether between us or not.

"Yep. Put that baby on the right finger and let's go kick some ass."

The ephemeral energy rope between us disintegrated before my eyes, but I couldn't find it in myself to be sad, because we had a bond that had nothing to do with an outside magic. It was only the kind of bond that we made ourselves.

And now I was more than ready to get this show on the road and make it everything everyone and anyone could have ever wished it to be.

"Hear ye! Hear ye!" I cried into the lowering dusk. "The valiant knight Sir Finn has agreed to see our marriage in the making after we fell this horde of the undead and possibly others that are meant to keep us from our merriment of the most wonderful of Eves! Come, let us make haste and decimate the foe, so that we may have a celebration that befits a faire of our stature!"

This time the crowd roared. Then again, that could have also been the werewolf, who had not only changed his nose and tail this time but all of him, and he was standing at almost seven feet tall with a whole lot of fur. "Lars, nice to see you."

"Yeah, well, get this done because I am itchy as hell. I might have thought I was missing out by not being able to change all the way, but this is totally not the experience I'd wish on anyone." He lifted his back leg to scratch at his belly and nearly fell over.

I was very proud of myself for not laughing even though I felt giddy inside. And now I just had to take care of everything else before I could have my happily ever after. Easy Peasy. Right? Abso-freaking-lutely.

"Where's Barnaby?" I called out. My lovely faire folk started moving toward me, edging out the crowd but still letting them see everything that was going on. "I need him to make a path. And, Elyssa, if you could be at the ready to turn some very hostile beings into stone at a moment's notice, I would totally appreciate that. I wish I had Zane."

"You do."

Some serious anxiety pumped through me when I heard his voice, but it was different from before.

"I talked with Buford, and he was able to help me fight whatever this is. I'm here for you. I can control it. What do you need?"

"I need you to shield us. Grandma Jean says there are Strigoi waiting to jump, and I can't have that when I'm crossing people at the river."

He leaned in close. "Can you still do that?" he asked.

"I sure hope so, but if not, then we'll move on to Plan Z."

"We're here for whatever you need."

And they were, as they had been for years and years.

Tyler helped Lars keep people from stepping into the river. Elyssa was on the lookout for any Strigoi that might come in to play when they most definitely weren't wanted, and Grayden kept a protective hand on Althea through everything.

Finally, we arrived at the place in the river where I hoped to cross this many people, and I directed Althea to my side as I worked out how I wanted this to go.

"Just let it come to you," Fig said in my mind. "Don't worry about pleasing anyone or making sure that everything is done exactly as it should be. Lead with your heart, and everything will work out."

So I did. "All zombie-esque people get in the water." Some jumped, others tiptoed like they weren't sure if the water was going to be cold, and still others tried to slip off into the woods, but Fig was having none of that and used Tyler to help him corral them back where they belonged.

Once everyone was in the water, I stepped in too. "Cross now, and hold your peace. May the life you lived give you the eternity you seek."

I led the way across the shallow waters to the other bank and then turned to watch each and every person disappear in a poof of sparkle that rained down into the flowing creek. The crowd cheered uproariously.

That had never happened before, but I was not going to question anything right now when it was actually going well.

And now Althea. I had no idea what to do with her and no idea how to cleanse her. I only hoped something would come to me.

I took her hand and motioned Grayden back. "I think we have to do this together," I said as Finn landed a hand on the other man's shoulder and pulled him back from the edge of the creek.

"Will you help me?" Althea looked so gray I was afraid I might never be able to get her fully back to herself.

"Of course. This is why we're here. I'm going to help you." I took her hand and drew her into the water with me.

And we got hit with a wave of energy so intense I was surprised it wasn't accompanied by a wave the size of a ten-story building.

Chapter Nine

"HOLD ON," I TOLD Althea. "Do not let go under any circumstances." I braced myself against the current that was trying with everything in its power to sweep me off my feet, and not like Finn could do but more like an undertow on steroids. I focused the glow from my body and made a bubble for us, with the water swirling around us like a cyclone but not touching us.

"Please, help me," she answered with tears in her eyes. It might have been water droplets from the initial crush of water. I doubted it, though. She looked distraught and ragged and not a little exhausted.

"I've got you, and we've got this. Together."

"Together." She closed her eyes and drew in a deep breath. "You can release the water."

My hands were shaking—hell, my whole body was shaking with the effort it was taking to keep us dry. But on her command, I let the energy go and instead planted my feet firmly on the ground, let my hands firmly grip Althea, and my mind firmly grip Finn and all the things we'd do with this new future, this second chance, if only I could hold on.

Since I didn't want to drown, I kept my mouth shut even though there were so many words I wanted to say to her. How proud I was of her, how much I loved having her as a friend and in my life. And how much I wished she would think about giving Grayden another chance. How much I wanted her to give herself another chance.

But that would have to wait while we braced against the water.

She, on the other hand, opened her mouth wide as a swirl of black came streaming out of her mouth. Sin after sin was whisked away by the force of the water, each one being whipped up past our heads and then washing away just as quickly. Under water like this I couldn't tell if her coloring was getting better, but I did know that her grip was getting stronger and her presence here more stable.

"Oh, now, I'm not sure it's going to be that easy, Verla my darling."

Helena, the woman who did not want to be a bride in the Underworld. Well, that wasn't awesome.

"What do you want?" I mouthed in the water but then started choking as water poured down my throat.

Helena snapped her fingers, and the water rose higher but left us dry, like we were in a cave in an air pocket.

Althea collapsed at my feet in a heap.

"What. Did. You. Just. DO?" If you ever wanted to talk about low growls, that was probably the lowest and growliest anyone in the history of the world had ever talked.

She flicked her hand, as if waving away a pesky fly. "She's fine. Actually, she'll be better than fine, since I took the rest of the sin from her, the pieces that were trying to worm into her heart and her mind and not let go. You should have known better than to put her in this situation without knowing what to do. Or your dog should have at least been here to help you. This ley-line thing is all because of him being here anyway."

"Look, I so do not need a lecture right now, and if you're here to mess things up even more, you can just show yourself right on out the wall of water. I need you like I need another hole in my head." I bent down and cradled Althea's hand in mine.

Helena checked her nails, then buffed them on the crimson velvet of her ball gown. A crown of bones rested on her mass of dark curls. "I've moved up a few steps in the world of down under. I'm actually here to help you."

"And I'm supposed to believe any of that why?" The thought of Fig being the reason all of this was happening and the other thought on the heels of that was almost too much to bear. I would not lose him or give him away to make the ley lines stop.

She groaned and slapped her hand over her eyes. "We don't have time to fight about this right now. Those days are over, and I'm better for it. Your dog might have started it, but we have to finish it. Are you ready to do your thing?"

I bit my lip because I had so many questions but didn't know if I should trust her. I was going with my gut, though. "Can I still do this?"

A circle opened in the wall of water, and there was my lovely Figiggly. "Yes, you most certainly can," he said in a way that everyone could hear him for the first time.

"He's not wrong. You *can* do this and you *will* do this. The rest was never yours to have." Helena drew a star in the river bottom and stepped into it. "Let go of Althea and let her stand on her own."

Althea raised bruised and bloodshot eyes to me.

"No. I'll take any help you want to give me, but we're doing it my way and my way is that I don't let go if I promised I wouldn't." I gripped Althea's hands and pulled her closer to me. "Together."

A cloud of the darkest black puffed out of Althea's whole body, seeming to come from every pore and hair follicle. I nodded at Helena, and she whisked the sin energy out into the water surrounding us. Fig stood by my side as each body that had poofed out of existence only a little while ago lined up to create a circle around the four of us.

"You may pass," I said to each person, and then Helena gave them a nod as they touched Fig and disappeared, for good this time. I could feel the energy of their presence move on as I had before, and this time it was far less in the way of fireworks and far more in the way of a gentle crossing to the other side where they'd be whole again and hopefully happy.

Once the last person had been moved to the hereafter, Helena magicked a bucket out of the water and used it to pour water over Althea's head. My friend stood, shivering in the deluge of bucket after bucket, the color finally returning to her face. And with each bucket, she lifted her head just a little more until she was staring me straight in the eyes, and I could see that my friend was back.

"Hi, there." I pushed her hair out of her face, and she smiled, completely dry.

"Thank you, Verla." She hugged me, and I hugged her back. Hard. Then we both turned to Helena.

"No need to thank me," she said, tossing her hair over her shoulder.

But I knew better, and I knew that, especially in the paranormal world, acknowledging a good deed went a lot further than expecting things to just happen because they should.

"Thank you, Helena. We all appreciate your helping with this."

"You'll owe me," she shot back, and I figured that was what had prompted her in the first place. But I'd take it.

"Let me know when you want to collect." I petted Fig and, still holding Althea's hand, backed out of the bubble into the very shallow riverbed where everyone on the shore was yelling and laughing. Well, everyone who was a normal human being. Because everyone else was throwing magic around like we were in the end battle scene of some epic fantasy saga.

Taking account of what was going on took less than a second when I saw a trio of shadowy figures also throwing magic in the form of lightning bolts and clouds filled with what looked like hail.

And then there was Elyssa, my resident gorgon, who couldn't change anything into stone, ever. Except for today. She took off her sunglasses, aimed her gaze at the trio, and her hair began writhing on her head like a nest of snakes.

Everything went completely silent as we all stared at the three figures being turned into very solid stone statues.

The applause when the three stopped moving in mid-run and froze into stone sculptures seemingly made by an expert hand was thunderous! It sounded more like a huge stadium instead of a tiny piece of land turned Ren Faire in Central Pennsylvania.

But Morty was clapping right along with everyone, and that was something, at least.

"And that ends our most joyous and phenomenal day of Halloween, gentle people of the faire," he said in a booming voice. "If you'll please exit out the gate on your left, we'll make sure you get to your cars and send you on your merry way. Until next season…"

I took a deep breath as my fellow misfits came streaming in around me, not unlike the current of the river. But this didn't feel like I was suffocating or drowning. This felt like I was breathing for the first time in a long time, and it was wonderful.

"Wow, Verla, that was wicked awesome."

"I can't believe you did that!"

"It was like things were crashing in the water, and all we could see was a green glow that put you and everything else in shadow."

I took in the comments and praise from everyone, glancing at Morty every few seconds. Was he going to have to get rid of me and my dog?

Had he heard what Helena had said?

Finally, he was done clapping and ushering and stood in front of all of us misfits that were no longer misfits. He gestured one hand in the air, and a book flew out of the sky to land in his flattened palm.

After opening the book, he licked a finger and turned the page. He made a check with his same finger and then closed the book and rocked back on his heels.

"What is that?" Perhaps not the first, best, or most important question, but something inside me told me I had to know.

"This?" He waved the book around, and the air seemed to coalesce around the thing like a magnetic field.

"Yes, that." I put one hand on my dog's head and the other around Finn's waist.

"Oh, just a list of prophecies that I've been waiting for you to start and finish. There's a reason you're here, Verla. There's a reason you're all here, and yet another reason why all these things are coming to pass now. Figiggly—and I love that name by the way—has a purpose and a reason, and I had to set things in motion to get you moving in the right direction. And now we've accomplished six of the nine things you're supposed to do. I'd say it's moving along rather nicely. The ley lines will calm themselves in a few hours, so anyone who is excited to mess with their talent should go romp now, because when the clock strikes midnight it will go away. I did help the ones who were suffering already, so you don't have to worry about that. I miscalculated a little when I was planning this. I hope you understand that I had to do it to make sure we're in the right place when the big battle comes..." That last word trailed off as Morty disappeared in the blink of an eye.

"What the hell just happened?" I asked Finn.

"I'd say Morty has quite a lot to answer for, and we'll get to him soon enough. For right now I want to talk about those words you threw in my direction before you disappeared into a wall of water, which I have to admit I'd like you to never ever do again. Not the words part but the disappearing part."

I laughed and reached up to give him a kiss. The glow that had surrounded me pulled him in too. The rope between us was gone, but we'd replaced it with a commitment that was far stronger and more deliberate. I could use magic in my life in a lot of ways, but the magic of loving Finn was a whole other type of magic that I was willing to work at this time.

"I'd like to do the disappearing part," Figiggly piped up. "Especially if you're going to keep kissing like that. Sheesh. I don't need to see that."

"Then you might want to close your eyes, because I'm about to do it again," Finn said.

And he did, delivering on his promise yet again. And this time I wasn't taking any chances. The man was mine. The dog was mine. The faire was mine. These people were mine. Now I just had to figure out how to get that book from Morty and see what other feats of prophecy he thought I was supposed to do.

But that was a task for another day.

Grabbing Destiny

A Bonus Short Story

Chapter One

MARILYN FREYA SAT ON top of her suitcase on the side of the road somewhere in the middle of Central Pennsylvania and tried to figure out what came next. She'd been dumped here about forty minutes ago and left in the dark about what she was supposed to do and how she was supposed to do it. Not to mention it was almost midnight. So, the literal dark on top of not having any information about her assignment. Wonderful.

While this was normally the way things worked for her, something felt different about this particular trip, and she wasn't sure she liked it. But when you were part of the Protection Against Mayhem team you did not question why they were sending you out, and certainly not how they managed to get you there. And if you were a Gorgon that couldn't turn a man into a stone with your gaze, no matter how hard you stared—and therefore were useless according to your family—then you definitely did not look a gift horse in the eye if you didn't want to be completely cut off from anyone and everyone.

Although sometimes not asking where you were going got you nowhere, as the case may be.

Looking around, Marilyn saw not a single familiar landmark. The full moon hung high in the sky and stars twinkled against the velvet darkness, but there wasn't much else out here at the moment.

"Moo!"

Except the cow standing about ten feet from her and giving her the best side-eye she'd ever seen. "Good evening, Jazzy. Do you have any idea where we are?"

"Moo!"

"Come on, Jazzy, don't play games. As my familiar you're supposed to help me, not mock me."

"Moo!"

Perhaps the side-eye wasn't exactly what she thought, and this really was just a normal cow. Fortunately, one that was behind a fence, so Marilyn took a moment to say hello back, then elongated the handle on her suitcase and started walking along the desolate road.

The cow hung back for a few seconds but eventually started following behind her. Eventually, it caught up to her and kept pace no matter how fast or slow she walked.

"Seriously, I do not need an escort, and there's no way the PAM would be so ridiculous as to send a cow to do the escorting." Even if they had once left her at the mercy of a camel in the Sahara Desert, she felt they would have remembered her warning from last time and not done that to her again.

Finally, they reached the end of the cow's fenced-in yard, and Marilyn was able to escape to a solitary journey, even with the mooing cow continuing to moo.

"Marilyn, I was kidding. Sorry!"

For her part, Marilyn rolled her eyes. Of course, Jazzy would think it was funny to moo at her in the middle of the night on a side road in the middle of nowhere. She turned around to address the cow, who had stuck its head through the railing of a gate and smiled at her.

"Why do you think this is the right way of helping me?" Marilyn asked as she walked back to the fence.

"Why don't you ever think I'm doing things right?"

"Fair enough." It was weird to see a cow's mouth move around the words, but it wasn't the weirdest thing ever. That would have been the time Jazzy had decided to take over a baby octopus at the beach and shot out of the water to plaster herself across Marilyn's face. Once Marilyn had been able to peel the little shit off, she'd had suction marks on her cheeks for days after. The worst Jazzy could do as a cow might be to spray her with milk, and that wouldn't be the end of the world. Though, of course, Marilyn wasn't going to mention that and give her familiar ideas. "So, what am I supposed to do?"

"There has been some activity around this area that we haven't seen for years."

"Yes, and?" Marilyn said after a long pause that did nothing for either of them. She wanted to get on her way. Now, preferably.

"And this activity is at that Ren Faire of misfits thing around here somewhere. Efferton? Efferhon? Crap, what was the town name? Effington!"

"That's an important piece of information," Marilyn said with exasperation.

"I was getting there. Don't judge me. Back to the matter at hand. Ahem! We don't want them using this ancient energy as they see fit, since they tend to walk a little close to the line of acceptable behavior. The manager called to let us know there might be something weird there, but it might be more than she's letting on. The higher-ups think you might have to convince the lady to cede her control, and if you can't convince her then you might have to just take it."

Marilyn's heart seized in her chest. Fortunately, that was not something anyone could see, and it was certainly not something she was going to share. But horror filled her at the mere suggestion. She'd never do that again if she didn't have to. There was often a way that the higher-ups hadn't considered. She'd find it before she took anything from anyone.

Keep it contained, she told herself. "I'll see what the situation is and get back to the management about my recommendation."

"I don't know..."

"You don't have to know, Jazzy. You did your part, and now I get to walk all night to this Ren Faire. I didn't bring the right shoes."

The cow raised herself to cross her forelegs on the top railing and rest as if she were human and they were having a nice little chat over the backyard fence. Jazzy was neither human nor animal as far as Marilyn could tell. The spirit of her familiar could overtake anything it needed to, but what form it took when it wasn't invading was something Marilyn still didn't know. Even after almost a hundred years and thousands of interactions.

"You'd better get down before you leave that poor cow. It won't know what to do with itself if you leave it standing up like that."

Jazzy laughed an echoing laugh, but the cow had all four legs back on the ground as Marilyn watched the spirit race away as a cloud of just slightly darker mist than the sky. Of course, she had to be one of the few people in the entire world without a familiar that was corporeal.

Okay, so she had a few instructions other than to assess a power source somewhere in Effington and that the situation had to do with a woman that would consider herself a misfit and therefore not be very willing to give up her status.

Marilyn was also considered a misfit in some quarters, but few actually knew what she was supposed to be able to do and what she couldn't do. It was no one's business but her own. However, this could work in her favor, so she understood why management chose her to complete this task.

Easy-peasy. Right? No, definitely not.

But she hadn't signed on for easy-peasy jobs. She always asked for the hard jobs, the ones no one else wanted, the ones that were going to be complex, because it was what she did best. Not to mention, it was a way for her to immerse herself in someone else's reality and forget about hers, if only for a little while.

She passed a mailbox and stopped to check her position with her phone. Maybe if she could pinpoint where she was, she could figure out how to get to the place where she needed to be. Why the GPS department at the PAM institute hadn't yet figured out how to put someone down right where they belonged was beyond her, but at least she wasn't sitting behind a desk. She wasn't going to complain. Too much, anyway. And definitely not out loud where anyone could hear her.

"Okay, so if I'm at 413 and I need to be at 2290 Faire Way then I'm thinking I should have definitely worn different shoes." She sighed and another cow mooed. There was country and then there was *country,* and she had a feeling she was not in the former but most definitely in the latter. Any moment now she'd start craving biscuits and gravy, or chicken and waffles. Perhaps be open to what some people called S.O.S. or shit on a shingle, a coarse name for creamed chipped beef. At least it wasn't grits this time.

Using her phone, she hit the maps section again and then plugged in the address. She almost dropped the phone when it told her that the trip would take another fifteen minutes driving at high speeds. With that information, she probably wouldn't show up until first thing in the morning on foot. Confirming it by toggling to the on-foot part of maps would only make her feel worse.

Since she wasn't aware of a deadline on this assignment, she wasn't worried about the timing so much as how not-in-the-best-shape she was, and why on earth they'd make her walk so freaking far!

But there was nothing she could do about it, so she just kept trundling along. Granted she also mumbled swear words to herself and wished that things were different but, in the end, the only thing that was going to work was to work.

∞

"I don't think it's a good idea to allow these people here, Verla. What if something happens and they're not able to tell us anything? Or what if something is wrong with the area and they want to bring in surveyors or mages to infiltrate our wonderful home?" Everest Youngsten pulled at the bottom of his beard and wished Verla had thought this through before involving anyone. She was a wonderful person as the manager of the Ren Faire where he and those like him worked and lived, but maybe this was more than she could handle.

"It's going to be okay. I promise. Wes just called and saw a woman approaching through the parking lot. I'll go greet her and then we'll go from there."

"No, it'll be better if I go meet her. You stay here and I'll be back. I need the air anyway." He grabbed his walking stick and headed for the front door. When he got to Verla, he made every effort to smile at her, and she smiled back as she patted his arm. Thankfully, her dog Figiggly was not around. The little beast tried to pee on him all the time, no matter how often he explained to the dog that he was a Greenman, not an actual tree.

"I'm sure we'll be able to sort this all out. Don't worry about meeting the woman. I'm sure it'll be fine." She hesitated and squinted her eyes at him. "On second thought, if you need to be the one to make first contact, I'll stay here."

"Thank you," he said. "I just need..."

"You don't have to explain anything to me, Everest. Go do what you need to do."

He left after one last glance over his shoulder. He did not want this woman from the PAM Agency to come to them with her mind set in stone on anything that might change his world. He'd lived for centuries now, readjusting everything around him and about him to be able to fit in. He'd lost one of his gifts in the process for no reason other than he'd trusted the wrong person.

Now that he'd finally found somewhere that not only tolerated him but welcomed him, he would fight hard to keep it. If this PAM agent wasn't prepared for that fight, then she was seriously going to be in for a surprise, and a nasty one at that.

He yanked his fedora lower on his brow and gently closed the door behind him. No matter what happened, he would keep his fears to himself and do what he'd always done, fix things behind the scenes. Whatever it took.

The village of misfit paranormals was situated at the back of the best Ren faire in the world as far as he was concerned. He'd arrived here about ten years ago and had been through several managers, but none as good as Verla. He knew she was only trying to do the right thing by allowing this stranger into the faire to assess the situation, but he'd see that the situation was assessed in a way that kept his world intact.

He waved briefly to Wes at the guard station as the ogre-sized dwarf let him out into the parking lot.

At first, he didn't see anyone approaching and was afraid Wes had been wrong when he'd called Verla. Then again perhaps *afraid* was the wrong word. Everest was honest enough with himself to admit he would be more than fine with this outsider not showing up at all. He'd considered waylaying her and making sure she never got close enough to Verla to ask anything, but had quickly discarded that idea.

If the Protection Against Mayhem agency was determined to have a say in this particular case, they would do anything to get their hands into the situation. He knew from years of dealing with them how narrow-minded they could be. So, if it wasn't this woman, then it would always be someone else.

And at least with this woman he would be prepared and ready to tell his own version of things. Whether that was the truth or not would depend entirely on his initial impression of her, and whether or not he felt she was someone who could at least be marginally trusted.

He would save that decision for when she finally made it to the gate. Tapping his foot, he looked back and forth through the partially lit parking lot, wondering where on the green earth and stone-filled parking lot she was. He saw nothing and no one at first. But then a cow mooed to his left, and he turned to find not only a bovine, who should not have been in the parking lot, but also a silver-haired beauty, riding sidesaddle without a saddle at all, on its back. There were no reins, nothing to hold her aloft on the big brute, and yet she smiled as she slid down the animal's side and extended a hand encased in a glove.

"Marilyn Freya," she said, introducing herself as if they had not known each other over a decade ago. Right about the time his world had sunken into a quagmire of lies and innuendos, deceit, and half-truths. He'd been almost completely destroyed on the day she'd brought him to his knees literally and tried to take him down into the quicksand of her betrayal with her.

"Well, then, this ought to be easy enough," he said and folded his arms across his chest. Her gasp was enough to satisfy at least a small part of his ego. Now to satisfy the rest by getting rid of her. No matter what it took, he looked forward to having not one single regret for whatever he'd have to do to make sure she never set foot into not only the faire but into his life, in any way, ever again.

Chapter Two

THERE WAS NO WAY on this round globe of hell on earth she could have stopped herself from gasping. But heaven above and Hades below she wished she could take back that one breath.

Everest Youngsten.

Everest.

Youngsten.

The one being she'd been able to touch without her gloves. The one man who had made her brittle heart pound in her chest and yet never break. The one being who had made her feel like a blessing instead of a curse...

Holy Zeus, she was going to start spiraling any second, and she might never be able to stop the spin.

With great difficulty, she stiffened her knees and her spine and looked him in his sneering eyes. With everything inside her on high alert, she gave him the best possible smile she could muster. She could fall apart later. Melt into a puddle of remorse and guilt and stuttering hearts at a different time. Not now. And most definitely not in front of him.

Now... the question was, did she play it off as if she didn't remember him? Or just acknowledge she did and move forward as if that was not in any way significant, when in fact it was the most significant thing in her mind over the centuries she'd been alive?

Right, she was made of sterner stuff and had been broken many times since they'd been together. She could do this, and she'd leave just as soon as she could. Intact. Happy. After fulfilling her duty, as was expected.

Shit.

Stiff upper lip!

"Everest, I had no idea you'd be here." She waved her hand around as if shocked to find him in such humble surroundings, when in fact, her very essence felt peace here, a kind of acceptance and grace that would weave its way into your soul and make you feel like maybe, just maybe, you were enough.

She shook her head at herself and then turned the gesture into shaking her platinum hair back off her shoulders. Stiff upper lip.

"I figured as much." His sneer didn't lessen at all, especially when he glanced over at her transport and then raised an eyebrow at her.

Smoothing down her skirt, she made sure her heels did not fail her in the rock-filled parking lot and gave him a second smile. This one far more playful than the first had been. Then she turned to the cow. "Thank you so much, Bessie, for granting me the privilege of riding you. I know it's not your usual job, and I can't thank you enough." She patted the bovine on the back before sending her on her way with a flick of her covered wrist. The cow transported from one field to another, going about half a mile at a time until she was out of sight.

"A new trick?" the infernal man asked.

Should she deign to answer him? It wasn't new to look down her nose with disdain and make the other person feel as if their question was not only beneath her but also inappropriate and unworthy of her attention. In fact, it was something she'd used over the years multiple times with good results. However, it was the one thing she hadn't had to demonstrate when she'd been with him. She had many parts of herself she'd never shown him. Perhaps it was best to keep it that way, even now.

"No, nothing new. A quaint little thing I'm equipped with to use as the situation dictates."

"So many facets of the Marvelous Marilyn Freya. Who knew? Certainly not me..."

He let his sentence trail off, and so did she. They had a brief staring match and then thankfully her phone rang in her purse. She didn't glance away so much as deliberately break eye contact with him when *she* wanted to.

"Yes, Heather?" She didn't turn her back on him, as she wasn't that confident in her stance. But she did give him the cold shoulder and a side view that he used to drool over. Before she'd ruined it all.

That thought had her missing what Heather said, but Marilyn was unwilling to ask her boss to repeat herself and let on that she wasn't quite as comfortable as she'd like both her boss and her former lover to think.

"I've just arrived. I'll handle things as quickly as possible."

"Babe, why do you sound like you've seen a ghost? You know they can't hurt you. We've talked about this before."

"Thank you. I'll handle it from here. I'll get back to you as soon as I've looked over the situation and made a decision." She nodded for emphasis and kept an eye on Everest in her peripheral vision. He remained with his arms crossed over that impressive chest that hadn't diminished in the last decade. She might be the one drooling.

"Do not think for a second that you're going to get out of telling me what the heck is going on with you right now. But I'll leave it for the moment. I'm glad you got there okay, and I hope it's something that can be handled in your very special brand of mediation."

"I'm sure that will happen. Thanks for checking in. I'll report to you as soon as I can."

"Oh, you'll do more than just report. And I'm thinking this might demand a bottle of the good wine and perhaps some mozzarella sticks. I'll cheat on my diet for you. But only for you."

That nearly made Marilyn laugh, but the situation was much too serious for mirth. She signed off with a terse goodbye and then faced Everest again. How could one man look like so much divine goodness and yet be such a complete journey straight through hell?

Fortunately, she would not be here long enough to have to answer that question. Once her duties were done, she'd simply chalk this up to one more rough job and move on. Like she always did.

"Since we've said our hellos and you know who I am, can you please take me to the manager of the faire so I can determine what's to be done? I'd like to complete this in time to get back to the office for a meeting."

"The one with the wine and the mozzarella sticks with someone who calls you babe and will cheat on their diet for you?" Everest said with less of a sneer and more of a smirk. The damn man had way too many facial expressions that called into question her sanity and her dignity.

"You know, when you eavesdrop, it's rarely good news for the eavesdropper?"

"Yes, I'm fully aware of that, but I didn't find any reason to be offended or slighted in there. And at least I'm not the only one who can tell that you're on edge, even if you don't want to admit it."

She been trying very hard not to scoff at him, or show in any way that she was affected by him, and therefore could not possibly care less what he thought, but that all went out the door when she didn't just scoff, she snorted.

Dammit.

"I've dreamed of that sound," he said with a real smile this time.

Now she did scoff and blush. But thankfully it was dark outside, and he wouldn't be able to see the way she was surely red from her chest all the way to her hairline.

"Can we just get a move on and get this done?" she asked in the most professional voice she could muster.

"Of course, of course. Would you like assistance over the gravel?" he asked, sticking his elbow out to the side for her to place her hand in the crook.

A wave of longing so intense it almost buckled her knees washed over her. She hadn't felt any flesh but her own in over ten years. Ten years, three months, twenty-two days, and four hours to be exact. She could probably work it out to the minute if she could see the time, but she was not going to take her phone out and look. Just then, a clock chimed midnight somewhere behind her in the park. Ten years, three months, twenty-two days, four hours, and nine minutes.

Shit.

"I'll be fine. Thank you for offering, but I don't need you—I mean, I don't need your help."

He gave her a look that told her he was fully aware of what was zinging back and forth in her brain, and then he shrugged. "Suit yourself. If you'll follow me, I'll take you right to Verla so you can be on your way. You're good at that, aren't you?"

"If you mean my job, then yes, I am." She stared him down, knowing that giving in at this moment would be the worst possible thing to do. No glancing away this time.

"Touché."

Great, touché. Shit.

∞

There were so many things running through Everest's mind right now that he was incredibly thankful he didn't have to think about how to breathe. His body did it automatically for him as it did for everyone. And even that was iffy when he'd first caught the scent of her on the light breeze winging through the parking lot on this late autumn night.

Why? Why did it have to be her, and why did he have to care? He'd been fine for ten years without her. Well, ten years, three months, twenty-two days, four hours, and twelve minutes.

And every time he'd wanted to think about her, every time a stray thought would pop into his head because he saw the color red, or smelled a lilac, or felt the soft crush of velvet, he'd forcefully re-engage himself in whatever he was doing. Like working with his hands to create walking sticks and umbrellas and canes. No softness there. No smells other than the tang of burning wood as the saw chewed through a plank and started the process of his creations. He used to be able to create walking sticks and umbrellas with nothing more than his mind, but that skill was lost to him—and the reason was taking wobbly steps in the gravel. Marylin—the woman he never thought he'd see again.

He walked a slight distance ahead of her because he just couldn't make himself walk beside her. Some part of him feared he'd brush fingers with her and not be able to stop himself from grabbing her hand. And letting her walk in front of him, forcing him to watch the sway of those hips, would be a different kind of torture that he just didn't think he was up to tonight. Or any night really.

There was a slight scrabble of slipping gravel behind him and a quick release of breath. He turned to find her more than wobbling on those ridiculously high heels that made him think of her long legs that then made his brain move up her body to...

"Are you sure you don't want any help?" he asked as he reached out a hand.

She batted it away and straightened that pencil-thin skirt again. "I'm fine. Just a quick misstep."

Ah, missteps. There had been so many of those between them he didn't know who had first flubbed the dance they'd been doing, but he knew for certain who had suffered more for it. And it wasn't her.

"Follow me then, and we'll get you to your destination."

Not that he had any intention of actually taking her to his manager. He'd decided after watching her try not to blush, but failing miserably at it, that perhaps there was a way he could get her to leave before she made it to the house. He wasn't proud of his thought pattern, and he wasn't even certain he could pull it off, but he wasn't going to skip at least trying to distract her.

And part of that distraction was taking her the long way around.

He started up the path to the ticket booth then waved to Wes as he went through the turnstile and held it for her. She sidled past him. And he wasn't stupid enough to pass up the chance to let their bodies brush. A soft gust of air escaped her mouth and drew his eyes to her lips.

He'd spent hours kissing her and being kissed by her. Huge swaths of time with a soft peck there and a deeper, more involved embrace here. Teasing and playing and enticing each other to new heights. And then the whole thing had crashed to the ground, and he still didn't know completely why.

Maybe that was what had kept her on his mind for all these years. Yet, even now, he wasn't going to be the one to ask questions. He had a mission—to keep her away from Verla—and he wasn't going to fail this time.

"I hope the trip here wasn't too difficult." He glanced back to find her trying hard to keep up with him. Slowing his step, he waited for her to catch up as they wound their way through the darkened concession stands at the front of the faire. A brief smile flashed across her face, but then she seemed to think better of it and quickly flattened those lips.

He found himself cutting his gaze to the side and caught sight of the games section of the faire. Elyssa, who ran the games during the day, was also a gorgon, and perhaps he could get Marilyn to forget about what she was here for by talking instead of giving her longing looks that would never amount to anything.

"We have archery at the faire, but it's in a different section. Here though, we let all our guests throw daggers and axes and the children like to climb the ladder and ride the gauntlet." Damn, he sounded like a car salesman. "Elyssa is also a gorgon and likes to be a part of the faire because she's unable to use her gift of stoning at all. She, instead, is very good at getting people to play the games and works with Verla to make sure the games are as real as possible without being able to hurt anyone."

"Interesting."

Everest waited for her to maybe ask about Elyssa's family, or how she felt about not being able to turn things into stone, but that one word was Marilyn's only answer. And then she bypassed him on the path as he stood next to the balloon-popping stall.

He quickened his step to catch up with her.

"This section here is where we have fake funerals. The mound of dirt is the same every day, but we make it look like it's a new grave to keep people involved."

"Fascinating."

A very flat delivery of a word that should have meant she really was listening to what he had to say. Instead, she seemed to be honed in on getting to the houses in the distance. He was going to have to redirect her, or they'd be there way before he'd had a chance to talk her out of seeing Verla and get her back out of the park without turning his life upside down. Again.

"I can take you by my umbrella stand."

She stopped in her tracks and stared at him straight on. The moss green of her eyes shone even in the dim light of the moon. He was entranced even though he knew better. He couldn't look away no matter how much he told himself to do just that.

"Everest, I don't think this is the correct time of night for a tour. I'm assuming the houses are over that way and that's where I would find the manager I'm here to see. If you could please lead me to them in a straight line, I'd appreciate it far more than being shown a faire that I'm sure is wonderful, and perhaps I'll come back some day, but not at midnight when I have an assignment. I'd like to complete the task the Protection Against Mayhem gave me and get back to my own bed."

Bed...

No, he could not think about that.

"I'd really like to show you the umbrella shop. Or perhaps you'd like to see the dish-throwing shack? The steam pipe organ?" He sounded desperate and didn't know how to stop himself.

She peered at him, stepping closer to lay a hand on his arm. He wanted nothing more at that moment than to take off her glove and have her fingertips touch him, but he couldn't do that to her without her consent.

And especially if she didn't want to touch him anyway.

But maybe that was what would send her running.

He took her hand from his arm and brought it to a mere inch from his lips. "May I?" he asked.

The slightest nod, but still a nod.

He slipped the glove off and kissed the back of her hand. A gong sounded somewhere overhead, and a snap of green fire ran from her flesh to his mouth.

Chapter Three

SHE SHOULDN'T BE DOING this. She should never do this again. This was a mistake of epic proportions, and she knew better. Why was she...Oh!

The flash of green fire caught Marilyn completely off guard as it arced from the back of her hand to Everest's tempting mouth. Those lips were ones she had kissed any chance she got when they had been together. His arms around her, his fingers caressing the back of her neck, the length of him pressed up against her. So, it wasn't just the kissing, but the whole experience. She'd never thought about it that way in all these years...

And yet nothing like this had ever happened.

She jumped back without thinking the action through and stumbled in the damned high heels.

And then it was the whole experience, not just him touching her hand. He caught her mid-fall, his arms sliding around her waist and his hand cradling the back of her head. As he brought her upright, she slid along the length of his chest and tingled in places she hadn't tingled in years.

The sizzle of green had turned into more of a ropey vine and slid down to his heart from his mouth. It connected them from body to body. Or maybe soul to soul.

That thought was way too whimsical for her taste. This could be a serious issue and something to take back to the Protection Against Mayhem offices. What was it, and what did it mean? Was this the ancient magic Jazzy had been talking about?

She tried to take a more measured and deliberate step back, but the vine went taut, and she couldn't move beyond three feet from his chest. She was torn between horror at the restraint and being entranced with their proximity, even as it was the weirdest feeling in her chest. Ever.

Glancing down at the vine, she reached her hand out to see if it was as solid as it looked. But her fingers passed through the green connection like it was water. So, not solid, but still very much there, and it didn't waver at all.

She looked up to find Everest staring at her.

"Do you see it?" she asked, not sure what exactly what was going through his mind.

"I do. Have you seen something like this before?"

Even though she worked for the department that specifically looked for anomalies to protect paranormals, she certainly had not seen it "all", but never this. What was it, and what did it mean?

And what was she supposed to do about it?

The extensive training she'd done, and the years she'd spent in PAM, told her to immediately call it in and start documenting what it was and how it worked. The part of her that was attached to Everest really wanted to just stand very still for a few moments more and bask in the connection she'd lost so many years ago for reasons she couldn't currently think of.

"It's beautiful," Everest said in a reverent tone he'd used the first time they'd kissed. He'd told her she was beautiful, and because she'd rarely heard that before, because she was not up to snuff with her powers, it had hit her hard in the chest and then softened as it had gone straight to her heart.

"It is." Her voice was way too dreamy for her liking, so she cleared her throat. "It's also an anomaly and must be taken care of. I'm assuming this has not happened around here before?"

"Oh man! I was really hoping that wasn't what I thought I had heard." A redhead in a pair of pajama pants, that had as many colors as the rainbow on them, and a top to match, came up next to them, stomping her fuzzy unicorn slipper on the paved path. "Everest, are you okay? Did anything hurt you?"

His eyes softened, his posture softened, and he looked at this new woman with a smile reminiscent of how he used to look at Marilyn. The brief clench of jealousy rammed into her stomach and made the vine tethering them to each other quiver.

"Verla, it's fine and no, no one was hurt." His gaze moved to Marilyn, and she watched as his eyebrow quirked. "I'm sorry. I guess I shouldn't have answered for both of us. Are you hurt?"

"I'm not." She straightened her shoulders and tried to take another step back without thinking. The tether didn't just grow taut this time, it actually strained and then snapped her into his arms.

He caught her without even the slightest of hesitations. But then he also released her without a glance in her direction.

"I'm not sure what this is, Verla," he said, shaking his head. "Marilyn is here to see you, and I was bringing her to the house. But then there was a snap of green fire between us, and we appear to not be able to move away from each other more than three feet."

He was missing some very important details in that statement, and Marilyn was pretty sure this Verla didn't miss the fact that he wasn't giving her all the information.

"Interesting. Nice to meet you, Marilyn. It seems you strayed a little farther afield than I would have thought since the village is in that direction." She hooked a thumb over her shoulder. Marilyn was not surprised to see her point to where she had originally thought they'd be going, until Everest decided to take her on a mini-tour of the faire at midnight.

"It seems we did," Marilyn answered, not taking her eyes off Everest as she replaced her glove.

His face maintained its smile, but his eyes went dark.

And even darker when Verla said, "I think you should both come back to the house. We need to talk, and Marilyn should be able to do her job without any more...detours."

⁂

His plan had failed. There was no way he could avoid going to the house with Marilyn and Verla. He would not cross the woman he owed his life and his salvation to. And he couldn't keep the woman who'd changed his heart away any longer.

He couldn't walk more than three feet from the latter, but he tried to stay to her side and a step behind. It was awkward and uncomfortable to be this close to her after their interaction earlier, yet there was nothing more he could do than keep up as best he could.

Before he was ready—and he didn't think he would have ever been ready, so there was that—they arrived at Verla's small cottage on the fringes of the faire.

He had one last chance, and he took it. Mounting the steps two at a time wouldn't work well, since he'd only drag Marilyn behind him, so he blocked the staircase to the porch instead.

Verla shook her head at him and put her hands on her hips. Marilyn kept as much distance as was possible, which still put her within arm's reach.

"Please, Marilyn. Can you let this go, just this once? We'll figure out how to cut the tie and then you can go on your way. There's no need to bring the faire to anyone's attention, especially the Protection Against Mayhem people. I can't go through this again. I haven't had family in years. I just got my sister back. I haven't had anyone but my faire friends since..." He gulped to swallow the words that rested on his tongue but couldn't make them go away. "Since you left me. I...I can't let you take that away from me again." He spread his arms out, opening up the path to his chest and not being able to care that it left him vulnerable and without any shield. "Is there anything I can do to make you go away?"

Verla placed a hand on his arm and shook her head. "Everest, it's going to be okay. I hadn't realized the two of you were acquainted, or I wouldn't have let you go out and meet Marilyn. She's here to gather information for a statistic report, not to take anyone anywhere. Isn't that correct?"

Marilyn, for her part, glanced at him then glanced at the ground. "I do have the ability to make a report and not mention the particulars."

"There's magic here," Verla said. "But it's not the bad kind. It's part of a ley-line system that PAM already has a ton of information on. If there are any questions, I can give you whatever data you need."

"No, looking around, I'm satisfied that you have the ability to handle things and will obviously call us if you need assistance. I can tell them that and convince them it's handled presently."

"And will you?" Everest asked. "If Verla can cut the cord between us, will you only make your report and then leave us alone? Or are you going to change your mind as soon as you walk away" Everest wasn't budging, and she'd be better off knowing that from the outset.

"I have a job to do. I do not answer to you."

Just then his sister opened the door with a tiny, blanket-wrapped baby in her arms. He'd hoped he would have at least a few more minutes to think through how to continue to stall everyone, but his time was up.

"I can hear you all the way in the back bedroom, and Isabella is trying to sleep. Not to mention there's a talking coffee maker in the house now? Something of yours, Marilyn?"

His gaze zeroed in on the woman being questioned. What was this?

"Little bit of a foul mouth, a whole lot of sass?" Marilyn asked.

"Yep, although the words are at least being checked before the whole thing comes gurgling out of its mouth, I guess you'd call it."

"Yes, that would be Jazzy. Sorry about the intrusion. Sometimes she doesn't wait for me to actually show up and will assess without me here. We've talked about her behavior before, but that's never stopped her from doing whatever she wants."

"Sounds like someone I know," Everest murmured, then wanted to kick himself for not keeping his mouth shut.

He got a side-eye from his sister and another from Verla. The only one who didn't look at him had her eyes completely set on the baby in his sister's arms.

"May I?" she asked.

"Of course." And Danielle handed over Isabella before he could stop her.

"Such a beautiful child and with so many wonderful things in her future." Marilyn cooed at the little bundle of joy even as Everest wanted to snatch that bundle from her and make a run for it.

But he'd probably just have dragged Marilyn along behind him and made her decision that much easier to destroy him for a second time.

With one more coo, she handed Isabella back to his sister. "You have all the facilities you need to contact us if you're ever in need of assistance? I'll definitely put in the report that you are prepared for whatever this green energy is. Do you have any ideas?"

"Yep, it's ley lines," Verla said. "I'm told I can manage them, and I've been working on it. The one between you seems to be pretty strong, but there might be a way to get rid of it if you'll give me a second."

"I'm sure Jazzy can take care of it. I'm sorry she took over your coffee maker. Sometimes she doesn't think before acting." Marilyn glanced at him and then glanced at the ground.

"No problem. Do you need anything to make her come out? I've got a lot of things here that might help. Plus, Everest is quite the man with the tools."

"I remember." Marilyn straightened her skirt and then shook her hair behind her again. "Jazzy, can you cut this?" she called out.

A spirit zipped in and out of the front window and then the irritating dog came trotting out the door.

Everest wanted to like him, really he did, but it didn't help that the little thing constantly thought he was something to mark as territory as opposed to respect as a living human being.

"I've talked with the dog, Everest, and he won't try to pee on you anymore," Jazzy said through the dog's mouth. "He thought the two of you were just playing, but I explained you are suck at not understanding situations. He agreed to stay away from you. You're welcome."

Everest didn't mean to, but he looked at Marilyn for confirmation.

"Thank you, Jazzy," she said.

"I didn't do it for you," the dog said. "I did it for him, just like I did last time, and Everest didn't understand that situation any better than he does this one. I don't know what you see in him, although I do like the beard. Nice touch there, Everest. Very manly." The dog turned to the path and trotted over to a tree to mark his territory.

"What?" Everest was lost.

"Never mind," Marilyn said quickly. "Who knows what familiars are talking about half the time." She cleared her throat. "I'll let the head office know that you have this under control, Verla, and that you don't need any interference from us."

"I told her you'd say that!" Danielle rocked the baby in her arms and seemed extremely pleased with herself. "When we worked together, I always thought you were one of the most efficient and fair people in the whole damn place and I can't thank you enough for pointing me toward Everest or I never would have found him. Now it seems I owe you two favors."

Two favors? Marilyn had sent Danielle to him? But she'd ruined his life before. She'd taken away his ability to talk to the trees because she'd been told to neutralize him or she'd lose her job. Was this just her guilt eating her up so she made up for it by doing little things?

"This is not one of those things you repay, Danielle. It's actually a part of my job to make compromises, if at all possible. This is definitely something I can defend in my report without taking too much heat, and I'm happy to do it."

Compromise? Take heat? Why wasn't that an option before she'd stolen his power and then pranced off into the night, taking everything important to him with her?

Verla smiled and smacked him on the arm. "See? Nothing to worry about. I don't know why you were so worried about this. I told you it was going to be fine, but you just had to run out and get yourself tangled in things. You're impossible sometimes."

He nodded because it was the only right thing to do. "That's me. Impossible. I was just...worried." He looked to find Marilyn still at his side but looking at Verla.

"So, it's not just me? I really thought he was this amazing individual who could get along with nearly anyone as long as it wasn't me."

"Oh my word, no." Verla laughed. "He doesn't even always get along with my little, floofy dog. And that baby is the sweetest ever. Everest is just like the trees he favors, often unbending without a stiff wind like a hurricane and sometimes willing to break before he bends. It's one of the things I value most about him, while at the same time being frustrated out of my mind. I'm sure you understand."

"Maybe a little better than I thought I did…" Marilyn trailed off and both she and Verla laughed.

At him.

"If you'd like to continue this conversation about what a pain I am, I'd like to be cut loose if you can, Verla, please. I might be a trial, but I don't have to stand here and listen to all the things I do wrong."

"Oh, Everest, you know we're not doing that. Everyone loves you, even Fig, but I don't have to tell you that." She turned toward the path that led to the river she loved, and then turned back. "If you want to have that cut, you just have to let her go, and it won't stick. As I said, there's magic here, but it's not the bad kind, Marilyn. I've seen these ropes before and they're part of a ley-line system that PAM already has a ton of information on. Sometimes it picks up connections between people and won't let them go until the connection has been worked out. There are cookies in the kitchen and coffee if you need it."

She stepped onto the path and waved a hand behind her as she walked away. Which left him and Marilyn together with no reason for her to still be here.

"I've heard of these ties before. I've been told they stay if there are unresolved issues." Marilyn passed a hand through the line again and took off her glove.

"But I don't think we've left anything unresolved. You still despise me as much as you did when we parted. I'm sure Jazzy could sever the tie."

The dog—with the spirit of Jazzy inside him—moved to sit between Everest and Marilyn with his tongue hanging out. Marilyn petted him and then he rose up on his hindquarters and positioned his powerful jaw over the vine of green fire.

Chapter Four

"NO! WAIT!" EVEREST WAS shocked to find those words had come out of his mouth. What the hell was he doing?

"Wait?" Fig/Jazzy said, sitting back down. "Why? You want out. It's physically hurting Marilyn to be this close to you because she can feel your angst even with those gloves on. I might be a familiar, but that doesn't make me stupid. I know what happened before and how you didn't listen—"

"Jazzy, that's enough." Marilyn snapped the words out at the dog, who bowed his head. "If you can cut the tie, do it. We can still get home in time to get some sleep before sunrise. I'd like to leave."

Marilyn glanced away from Everest, and he felt a shift in the vine as well as his heart.

Looking down at the tether between them, he watched it waver and get lighter and lighter in color. It was swirling as if the color was being diluted with water and draining down the sink.

"What's happening?" he asked.

"I'm letting you go, Everest. I didn't realize how much I've carried with me all these years. I can't give you your powers back, and I can't give you an answer that would satisfy you. I did the best I could with the information I had, and I've worried about it every day of my life. But that cockatrice you were hiding in the woods was not as benign as you thought it was. It had killed fourteen people in the village."

"You never told me that. You simply said to let you handle it with no information."

"And I thought that would have been enough to get you to stop. At the end, it all went too fast for me to explain before you left. It told lies to the trees, and I had to do something because it had a child in its grasp. But you wouldn't listen, and I wasn't going to be able to find it until you couldn't thwart me at every turn by talking the trees into hiding it."

"I—" His mind had been awhirl earlier when he saw her and smelled her, but now it was a stew of true chaos.

"I asked you to stop. I asked you to let me do my job, and you ignored me. I couldn't risk that child because that child was your sister, and she came to live with me after you left. You might think everyone left you, but really it was the other way around."

She had tears standing in her eyes, and he wanted nothing more than to wipe them away. But he had no right.

"Cut the tie, Jazzy. I can't do this."

And the tie was cut as the dog rose back up and clamped his powerful jaw over the connection, severing it in one fell swoop. Everest stumbled back and landed on his front porch steps.

Marilyn walked away with the fluffy dog at her side and not a single glance back. He couldn't, and wouldn't, blame her.

Resting his head in his hands, he let the chaos crowding his brain have its reign. Why stop it now? Why want anything when he had so much to consider and no leg to stand on if everything Jazzy and Marilyn had said was true?

"Isabella finally went to bed without that coffee maker talking up a storm." Danielle sat on the steps next to Everest and laid her head on his shoulder. "I know eavesdropping is usually horrible for the person doing it, but this time I think I'm just going to be grateful I was within hearing distance."

"Funny you should say that, since I said the same thing to Marilyn earlier." Even her name felt like jagged shards of glass in his mouth. What had he done?

"Don't be so hard on yourself, brother. She was a good guardian and gave me everything I needed, including a relationship with you. I know you were trying to do the best with what you had, too. We were younger. We all made mistakes. Now it's up to us if we can move past them and into a future together."

"I don't think I can forgive myself."

"You're going to have to. You and Marilyn are Isabella's godparents and that was a decision I made as soon as I got pregnant. It's my fault that you lost your powers and the love of your life. I can't go back and fix it, so I'd like to make it better now." She squeezed his hand.

"This was not your fault at all."

"But it was. I sought that creature out and wanted it to take me away. Marilyn forgave me for my immaturity and my missteps, now I think you need to work on that yourself." Releasing him, she stood up. "If I know the Protection Against Mayhem

Agency, they've probably left her in a field somewhere waiting for someone to bring her back to the office. If you hurry, I bet you could still find her."

He jolted as he felt a pull in his chest. Looking down, he saw a faint shadow of green spiraling out from his chest. This was his chance. He'd take it, and if he lost then at least he'd tried. That was better than the alternative.

∞

"Dammit, Jazzy. I can't believe you knew he was here this whole time and told the agency to send me instead of anyone else." Marilyn tromped through the tall grass on the side of the road. She could have grabbed a cow again, but she had so much turmoil and anger inside her that it helped to walk it off.

"I've heard you talking in your sleep at night. He comes up all the time. All. The. Time. Not to mention that every time you snort, you look like someone kicked your dog. What does that sound signify? I saw Everest's real smile when you did it earlier and then you blushed."

"Wait a minute, were you spying on me the whole time?" That really was more than Marilyn could handle, but it would make sense in a convoluted sort of way.

"Yep, I usually do. I've been offered a body several times by the Agency, but to be honest I like being able to jump from thing to thing." Just the spirit whipped along on the wind, transparent and nebulous but very much there. "I mean, who doesn't want to be a coffee maker? Or a cow, for that matter. That was fun. And if I can transport to anything, then I never have to leave you alone to handle stuff by yourself."

"Oh." She was never alone, but she'd always be without someone corporeal to hold her.

"Yeah, so I just keep jumping from thing to thing so I can follow you around and not be intrusive. It works for us, and us is a good thing. Right?"

"Right." And she meant it. She just wished she hadn't seen that stark grief in Everest's eyes when she'd told the spirit to cut the tie. She had a feeling that memory was going to replace the one where he stomped away and told her he never wanted to see her again.

They both were painful, but the small moment before the tie was cut had flooded her with all the could-have-beens. It was not going to be easy to put those feelings in a box and stash it in the back of her mind.

"Right," she said again. "And now we have mozzarella sticks and wine to look forward to. We'll get another assignment and be off and running again. It's good."

"Could it be better?"

Marilyn stopped in her tracks, wobbling on the horrendous shoes once more. A hand cupped her elbow to steady her, and it did physically, yet set off all kinds of signals emotionally.

Taking a deep breath, she let it out slowly through her nose before facing Everest. She should have known he wouldn't be able to let this go.

Meeting his gaze, she waited for whatever he needed to say so she could get on her way again.

"Could it?" he asked again. "Could it be better? I know I'm not exactly a match for mozzarella sticks, but if I tried really hard, I might be able to find you wine or at least give you a head massage when you come home a little further into the cups than you meant to be."

She would not laugh and give him hope.

"I could use that lotion that always smelled of lilacs to take the ache out of your feet after a long day of walking around in those spiky things." He pointed at her shoes. "I could make sure you were always stocked with peanut butter ripple ice cream, the really good stuff from Rakestraw's."

Under no circumstances would she cry, either.

"I could make sure that every day was officially Marilyn Freya Day. I have this great coupon for one of those websites that makes calendars. I bet they'd be happy to print that in tiny letters like a holiday." He took his fedora off and placed it over his chest. "I could do all that, but what I'm going to do is tell you that I'm so sorry for not listening before. I'm so sorry for not trusting you or us. I'm so sorry that I let my own ideals get in the way of knowing you would never hurt me without thinking things all the way through. And I'm sorry you had to save my sister from my own clouded vision. I'm so incredibly grateful that you did save her, that you did the right thing even though it tore you apart, that you were so much braver and smarter than me. I'm grateful you're you, but me? Well, I could be better."

She did not laugh, and she did not cry, but Hades below she snorted and took off her gloves to touch the man she loved for the first time in a long time. He kissed her there on the side of the road with the spirit looking on and a stray cow or two lowing in the moonlight.

And that's what began again a romance that would last through the ages. They had years and years to figure out how to make it work, but for now it was perfect, and that just couldn't get any better.

The next Magically Suspicious story will be available in June 2022. Keep an eye on social media or via my newsletter to stay up to date for when it goes on pre-order!

Don't miss out on other books by Misty Simon

www.mistysimon.com

THE IVY MORRIS MYSTERIES
Poison Ivy
The Wrong Drawers
Something Old, Something Dead
Frame and Fortune
For Love and Cheesecake
Hoedown Showdown

TALLIE GRAVER MYSTERIES
Cremains of the Day
Grounds for Remorse
Deceased and Desist
Carpet Diem
Varnished Without A Trace
INK
Wicked Ink
Protective Ink

ADVENTURES IN GHOSTSITTING
Desperately Seeking Salvage
Don't Dream It's Rover
Every Death You Take
All Died Out

I Wear My Ghost Goggles at Night
Ghosts Just Want to Have Fun

KISSINGER KISSES
What's Life Without the Sprinkles
Making Room at the Inn
Go Ahead, Make My Bouquet
Christmas in Kissinger
Liv and Breathe

Also writing as Gabby Allan:
Much Ado About Nauticaling - A Whit and Whiskers Mystery

About Misty Simon

MISTY SIMON ALWAYS WANTED to be a storyteller... preferably behind a Muppet. Animal was number one, followed closely by Sherlock Hemlock... Since that dream didn't come true, she began writing stories to share her world with readers, one laugh at a time. She knows how to hula, was classically trained to sing opera, co-wrote her high school *Alma Mater,* and can't touch raw wood. Never hand her a Dixie cup with that wooden spoon/paddle thing. It's not pretty.

Touching people's hearts and funny bones are two of her favorite things, and she hopes everyone at least snickers in the right places when reading her books. She lives with her husband, daughter, and two insane dogs in Central Pennsylvania where she is hard at work on her next novel or three. She loves to hear from readers so drop her a line at misty@mistysimon.com.

Printed in Great Britain
by Amazon